# RAVES FOR
# JAMES PATTERSON

"Patterson knows where our deepest fears are buried.... There's no stopping his imagination." —*New York Times Book Review*

"James Patterson writes his thrillers as if he were building roller coasters." —Associated Press

"No one gets this big without natural storytelling talent— which is what James Patterson has, in spades."
—Lee Child, #1 *New York Times* bestselling author of the Jack Reacher series

"James Patterson knows how to sell thrills and suspense in clear, unwavering prose." —*People*

"Patterson boils a scene down to a single, telling detail, the element that defines a character or moves a plot along. It's what fires off the movie projector in the reader's mind."
—Michael Connelly

"James Patterson is the boss. End of."
—Ian Rankin, *New York Times* bestselling author of the Inspector Rebus series

# THE
# PERFECT
# ASSASSIN

A Doc Savage Thriller

*James Patterson*
*and*
*Brian Sitts*

For a complete list of books, visit JamesPatterson.com.

# THE PERFECT ASSASSIN

A Doc Savage Thriller

# JAMES PATTERSON
## AND BRIAN SITTS

GRAND
CENTRAL

NEW YORK  BOSTON

Copyright © 2022 by James Patterson

In association with Condé Nast and Neil McGinness

Hachette Book Group supports the right to free expression and the value of copyright. The purpose of copyright is to encourage writers and artists to produce the creative works that enrich our culture.

The scanning, uploading, and distribution of this book without permission is a theft of the author's intellectual property. If you would like permission to use material from the book (other than for review purposes), please contact permissions@hbgusa.com. Thank you for your support of the author's rights.

Grand Central Publishing
Hachette Book Group
1290 Avenue of the Americas, New York, NY 10104

grandcentralpublishing.com
twitter.com/grandcentralpub

First Edition: November 2022

Grand Central Publishing is a division of Hachette Book Group, Inc. The Grand Central Publishing name and logo are trademarks of Hachette Book Group, Inc.

The publisher is not responsible for websites (or their content) that are not owned by the publisher.

The Hachette Speakers Bureau provides a wide range of authors for speaking events. To find out more, go to hachettespeakersbureau.com or call (866) 376-6591.

ISBN 9781538721841 (trade paperback) / 9781538726617 (large-print paperback) / 9781538721872 (ebook)

Library of Congress Control Number is available at the Library of Congress.

Printed in the United States of America

LSC-H

Printing 1, 2022

# ONE

*Eastern Russia*
*30 Years Ago*

A MOTHER CAN sense a disturbance in her world, even in her sleep.

Marisha did.

The late-night snowfall made the small village on the Kamchatka Peninsula look like a cozy Christmas painting, but the wind was harsh. It whistled around the cottage and seeped through the walls of the tiny nursery where the six-month-old twins slept in a single crib, spooned together for warmth. Like tiny dolls. They were just five minutes apart in age, with matching features and the same delicate, pale skin. But the similarities stopped at the top of their heads. One girl had her father's dark, straight hair. The other had lush copper-colored curls, like nobody else in the family.

Marisha was a physicist. Her husband, Mikhail, was a mathematician. In their courting days at the university, they had long talks about what extraordinary children they would have together. And that's exactly what happened. Two in one day. The babies were remarkable—so beautiful and loving. And now, at just half a year old, already advanced for their age. They were everything a parent could wish for, and more.

Mikhail had put the girls down just after seven. At 2 a.m., Marisha woke suddenly. Something was off. She could feel it. She pushed back the covers and slipped out of bed, not bothering to nudge her husband or find her slippers. She grabbed her robe from the wall hook and wrapped it hastily over her nightgown as she hurried down the short hallway, feeling the cold tile against her bare feet.

When she opened the door to the nursery, a waft of frosty air crossed her face. In the next second, she felt a matching chill in her gut. She took a step toward the center of the dark room and inhaled sharply. Snow dusted the floor under the half-open window. Marisha grabbed the side rail of the crib with both hands, then dropped to her knees and screamed for her husband. Mikhail stumbled into the doorway seconds later, his eyes bleary and half closed. He saw his wife on the floor and then—the empty crib. His eyes opened wide.

"They're gone!" Marisha wailed. "Both of them! *Gone!*"

# TWO

A MILE AWAY, two thickset men in heavy wool coats were making their way up a rugged slope. The village lights were already fading behind the scrim of windblown snow. The footing was treacherous, and they were not familiar with the terrain.

Bortsov, the taller of the pair, used a heavy hiking pole to probe the path ahead. Gusev, the shorter partner, carried a high-powered hunting rifle. In their opposite arms, each man carried a tightly wrapped bundle. The men were killers by trade, and this was their first kidnapping. In fact, it was the first time either of them had held an infant. They clutched the sixteen-pound babies like rugby balls.

After twenty minutes of steady hiking, they were out of sight of the village. Still, Gusev kept looking over his shoulder.

"Stop worrying," said Bortsov gruffly, pointing at the trail behind them. "We were never here." He was right. Just a few yards back, the snow was already filling their tracks. The search would begin at dawn. By then, it would be no use.

Bortsov had scouted the campsite the day before. It was

a natural shelter beneath a rock overhang. He'd even taken the time to gather wood for a fire. By the time the kidnappers reached the spot, it was nearly 4 a.m. They were both exhausted from the climb and their arms were cramped from gripping the babies. Bortsov walked to a snowdrift about ten yards from the shelter. He bent forward and set the bundle he'd been carrying down in the snow. Gusev did the same with his.

They stepped back. The twins were about four feet apart, separated by a snow-covered log. They were both squirming under their tight wraps, their cries muffled by wool scarves around their heads. Bortsov pulled a handful of coins from his pocket and placed them on a rock in front of the baby on the left. Gusev placed a bunch of coins in front of the baby on the right. Then they shuffled back toward the shelter and started a fire.

When the wood caught, flames and sparks illuminated the small recess. The kidnappers tucked themselves under the rock and pulled their thick coats up around their necks. Gusev fished a flask of vodka out of his coat pocket, took a deep gulp, and passed it to his partner. A little extra warmth. Before long, their eyes were glazed. Soon after that, their stupor faded into sleep.

The babies, left in the open, were no longer crying.

# THREE

MORNING. GUSEV WOKE first, stirred by an acrid waft of smoke from the smoldering fire. He brushed the snow off his coat and shook his flask. It was empty. Gusev's head throbbed and the inside of his mouth felt thick and pasty. He glanced across the small clearing to where the two babies lay silent in the snow. He elbowed Bortsov in the ribs. Bortsov stirred and rolled over. Gusev nodded toward the twins.

Both men rose slowly to their feet and walked on unsteady legs to the snowdrift. Over the past few hours, the wind had blown a fresh coating of white over both babies. Bortsov pulled the stiff scarves away from their faces. In the dawn light, their skin was bluish, their lips and nostrils coated with frost. Obviously dead. A total waste of a trip.

"Weak! *Both* of them!" said Gusev, spitting into the snow.

Bortsov turned away, snarling in frustration. "Food for the bears," he muttered.

As Gusev retrieved his rifle, he heard a small mewing sound. He turned. The baby on the left was stirring slightly.

Gusev hurried back and knelt down. He pushed the frozen scarf back off the baby's head, revealing coils of copper hair.

"We have one!" Gusev shouted. "She's alive!"

Bortsov tromped over. "Mine!" he called out with a victorious sneer. He scooped both sets of coins from under the snow and pocketed them. Then he lifted the copper-haired girl from the snowbank and tucked her roughly under his coat. Gusev gave the dark-haired baby one final shake, but there was no response. He kicked fresh snow over the tiny corpse, then followed his partner up the mountain, cursing all the way. He hated to lose a bet.

The walk down the other side of the mountain was even harder than last night's climb. Bortsov's knees ached with every step, and Gusev was coughing in the thin, cold air. But they knew the effort would be worth it. They had conducted the test with the babies, side by side, as they had been instructed. A survivor this strong meant a big payday, maybe even a bonus. An hour later, Bortsov and Gusev pushed through the last of the tree line into a rolling snow-covered valley.

Straight ahead was a campus of sturdy buildings made of thick stone. A few simple balconies protruded from the top floors, and most of the windows were striped with heavy metal grates. In the early morning, a light glowed from a corner room, where they knew the headmaster would be waiting for the new student. Bortsov pulled the copper-haired baby out from under his coat as they approached the imposing school gate. He knew the headmaster would be pleased. This child showed exceptional promise.

# PART 1

# CHAPTER 1

*University of Chicago*
*Present Day*

I'D FORGOTTEN HOW much I hated first-year students.

I'd just finished a solid fifty minutes of a cultural psych lecture, and I might as well have been talking to a roomful of tree stumps. I was already pissed at Barton for asking me to sub for him at the last minute—and a 9 a.m. class, no less. I hadn't taught this early since I was an anthropology TA. That was twelve long years ago.

Barton's lecture notes were good, but since I'd actually written my thesis on South Pacific cultures, I was able to ad lib some interesting insights and twists on tribal gender roles. At least *I* thought they were interesting. Judging by my audience, not nearly as interesting as TikTok.

After class, the students moved toward the door with their eyes still glued to their screens. I felt like I was forgetting something. *Shit. The reading assignment!* I scrolled through Barton's notes. *Jesus. Where is it? Right here. Got it.*

"Sorry!" I called out to the departing crowd. "Listen up, please! Reading for next class!" I held the textbook over my head like a banner. It was as heavy as a brick. "In Muckle and

Gonzalez! Chapters Five and Six, please!" Most of the students just ignored me. I tried to catch their eyes as they walked past, but up-close contact has never been my strength. Lecturing to a class of a hundred, no problem. Just a faceless mass. Close up, I tended to get clammy.

Sometimes I thought I might be on the spectrum. No shame in it. So was Albert Einstein. I definitely met some of the criteria. Preference for being alone? Check. Difficulty in relating to people? Check. Stuck in repetitive patterns? Check. On the other hand, maybe I was just your garden-variety misanthrope.

I plopped the textbook down on the lectern. Two female students were the last to leave. I'd noticed them in the back row—way more interested in each other than in my cogent analysis of the Solomon Islanders.

"Awesome class," said the first student. Right. As if she'd heard a word of it. She was small and pert, with purple-streaked hair and an earful of silver rings. "So interesting," said her blond friend. Were they trying to suck up? Maybe they were hoping I'd be back for good and that I'd grade easier than Barton, who I knew could be a real prick.

"Good, good, thanks," I mumbled. I stuffed Barton's iPad and textbook into my briefcase and snapped it shut. Enough higher education for one day. Out of the corner of my eye, I saw Purple Hair nudge her partner. They looked over their shoulders at the whiteboard, where I'd written my name in big capital letters at the start of class.

DR. BRANDT SAVAGE

Purple Hair leaned in close to the blonde and whispered in a low, seductive voice, "I'll *bet* he's a savage!" She gave her friend a suggestive little hip bump. Nothing like freshman sarcasm. Make a little fun of the gawky PhD. Got it. And not the first time somebody had made the point: I was about as far from a savage as a man could possibly get.

I headed down the hall to the department office to pick up my mail. As I pushed through the heavy oak door, I could hear Natalie, our department admin, helping a student sort out a snafu in his schedule. When she saw me, she held up her index finger, signifying "I need to talk to you."

I liked Natalie. She was all business, no drama. Quiet and efficient. Herding cats was a cinch compared to keeping a bunch of eccentric academics in line, and she did it well. The student jammed his new schedule into his backpack and headed out the door. Natalie leaned over the counter in my direction.

"So where will you be going?" she asked, flashing a knowing smile.

"What do you mean?" I asked. My only travel plans involved heading home and heating up some soup. Natalie leaned closer and looked both ways, as if she were revealing a state secret. She gave me an insider's wink and held up a slip of paper.

"Your sabbatical," she whispered. "It's been approved!"

# CHAPTER 2

HOW THE HELL did *that* happen, I wondered? I headed down the corridor with the slip in my pocket, dodging students as I went. I'd put in the sabbatical request eight months ago and hadn't heard a thing. The university system was definitely not built for speed. Ulrich, my department head, was unearthing a crypt somewhere in the Middle East. I'd given up on an approval until he got back. Had somebody gotten to him? I guess miracles do happen.

My only problem was that I hadn't really given any thought to a destination. All I knew was I'd earned six months of peace and quiet. Now I just had to figure out where to spend it.

I pushed open the main door and stepped out through the Gothic stone front of Cobb Hall. My glasses were immediately speckled with falling snow, and the cold cut right through my overcoat. That Chicago wind everybody talked about was no joke. I put my head down and almost banged into two students rushing up the steps.

"Sorry," I said. "My bad."

Even on sub-zero days, I looked forward to the

twenty-minute walk to my apartment. Time to clear my head. A break from crowded classrooms and talky colleagues. As I headed toward East 59th, my shoes lost traction on the sidewalk and I had one of those real-life cartoon moments, where your arms flail in the air while you try to keep from falling on your ass and you hope to hell nobody is watching. Once I got my footing again, I walked the rest of the way across campus with short, careful steps. Like an old man with an invisible walker.

I dipped my head into the wind and headed up the city sidewalk, squinting to keep the snow out of my eyes. Most people who passed me from the opposite direction gave me a wide berth, probably because I looked half blind. The next time I looked up, I saw a young woman in a puffy parka headed toward me through the snow.

She was walking at a quick pace, staring straight ahead. As she passed, our elbows bumped.

"Sorry, sorry," I mumbled. I was a real menace to humanity today.

The woman stopped and turned abruptly. "Don't apologize!" she shouted.

The shock froze me in place. Before I could open my mouth again, she grabbed my upper arms and turned me to face the curb, like a cop getting ready to frisk a suspect.

Adrenaline shot through me. "Hey!" was all I could get out. I saw a green van with an open cargo door right in front of me. She shoved me forward, and I sprawled into the van head first. My face slapped hard against the rubber floor liner. When I flipped myself right side up, the door was sliding shut.

My heart was beating so hard I could hear my pulse in my ears. This had to be a prank, or some terrible mistake. I kicked against the inside of the door, but my rubber soles didn't even make a mark. A second later, I heard the passenger door open. There was a thick divider between the cargo section and the front seats. It was black metal at the bottom with thick, clear plastic across the top. I saw the woman slide into the driver's seat. I pounded on the plastic with my fists. She ignored me and turned the key in the ignition. She cranked the wheel and pulled out onto the street. Then she floored the accelerator. I fell backward against the rear door. I didn't bother trying to stand up. I crawled forward on my hands and knees.

"Hey! What are you doing??" I shouted. "Where are you taking me??"

My face was jammed right up against the plastic. The woman stared ahead, arms straight out on the steering wheel, weaving through the morning traffic like an Indy racer. We were heading north, out of Hyde Park. I turned to the side and started pounding on the sliding door. I twisted the door handle back and forth. It wasn't just locked. It was unscrewed. Totally useless. I tried the rear door. Same thing. I put my face against the cold metal of the truck wall. "Help!" I shouted. "I need *help!*"

"No whining!"

It was her. She was shouting at me from the front seat. Her voice cut right through the divider.

I kept on yelling. Every true-crime show I'd ever watched flashed through my brain. Rule Number One: Never get into a stranger's vehicle. Once you're taken, your chances of survival go way down. Why hadn't I put up a fight? Because it happened so fast, that's why. In real life, you don't get time to think about it. All I could do now was keep making noise and hope that we'd pull up next to a police car. *Any* car. But when

I looked out through the plastic, I could see that we were now on a deserted street, or maybe in an alley. There was nobody around.

I kept pounding and shouting for dear life anyway. Suddenly I felt the van pull over and skid to a stop. I flew forward and my shoulder banged hard against the partition. I was frantic, confused, terrified. My knuckles were bruised and bloody. As I got up from the floor, the cargo door slid open. The woman was outside, leaning in.

She had a no-bullshit look on her face. Her voice was low and even.

"I said, no whining."

The punch came so fast I barely saw it. There was a sharp pain in my jaw and I felt my head snap back. I was out cold before I hit the floor.

# CHAPTER 3

WHEN I CAME back to life, I was lying on my back inside some kind of bag. I could feel thick rubber against my glasses and forehead. It was hard to breathe. I was on top of a narrow cushion, and I was rolling forward. I could feel the vibration of wheels on a hard surface. My jaw ached and my head throbbed.

Everything was hazy, like coming out of anesthesia. The rolling stopped, then started again. I heard a door slide closed and felt a thump. I was in an elevator, going up. I heard the rattle of chains in the shaft. The elevator stopped with a lurch. I started to thrash around inside the bag, but I realized my hands and ankles were wrapped tight. I felt a hard slap on the side of my head.

"Quit moving." It was her.

I was rolling forward again. A couple of turns. Then another stop. A series of beeps. The sound of a heavy door swinging open. Wheels rolling again. Different surface now. Stopped again. Boots on wood. I felt hands rustling the top of the bag. The sound of a zipper. Then a wide gap opened over my face.

The sudden light made me blink. I was looking up at an industrial ceiling—raw aluminum ductwork and beige pipes. The woman's face appeared in the opening, leaning over me. She yanked the zipper down to my knees. I saw the flash of a blade. I felt tugs at my hands and feet and then I realized that I was loose.

"End of the line, Doctor," the woman said. "Up you go."

She crooked her arm under my neck and lifted me to a sitting position. I pulled my feet out of the bottom of the bag. There was gray duct tape clinging to my ankles and wrists. I sat on the edge of the cushion and then slid off and stood up, dizzy and disoriented. I rubbed my jaw where she'd clocked me. She reached out, tilted my chin up, and appraised the damage.

"First lesson," she said. "When I tell you to stop doing something—stop doing it."

"Who the hell *are* you?" I asked. My brain was foggy and my jaw hurt when I talked.

"Wrong question," she said. She rezipped the body bag and folded it on the cushion, which I could now see was the top of a hospital gurney. I swiveled my head to look around, looking for accomplices. I didn't see anybody.

"It's just us," she said. "Go ahead. Take in the atmosphere."

You're a trained observer, I told myself. So *observe*. Like they say on a dig, everything is evidence. We were on a high floor. Brick walls. The wood planks had dark outlines and metal plates where heavy machinery had been bolted down. This was no modern high-rise. It was a high-priced renovation. I was pretty good at estimating spaces, and this place was big—over a thousand square feet, not counting whatever was behind the doors at the far end. My apartment would fit in here twice.

The space was wide open, with one area flowing into the other. Trendy. And expensive. There was an industrial-sized kitchen at one end. At the other end, I saw a classy seating area with a cushy leather sofa, a glass table, and a baby grand piano. In the middle of the space, on a black rubber surface, there was a bunch of high-tech workout machines with names like Precor and Cybex. Luxury loft meets CrossFit gym.

"This is yours?" I asked. "You live here?" Make a human connection, I was thinking. And maybe she won't kill you.

"Yes," she said, matter-of-factly. "And as of now, so do you."

My gut turned. She sounded like a psycho. She unbuttoned her parka, took off her cap and scarf, and tossed everything onto a bench. Underneath, she was wearing black tights and a long-sleeved athletic jersey. I tried not to be obvious, but I studied every inch of her. I wanted to be able to give a good description to the cops, if I ever got the chance. Late twenties or early thirties. Tall. Probably five foot ten. Athletic build. Blue eyes. Pale skin. No visible piercings. And one really distinctive feature: long curly hair, the color of a bright copper penny.

I suddenly felt woozy, like I was about to pass out. I leaned back against the gurney.

"Hold still," she said. "You need water."

She turned and walked toward the kitchen, her boot heels clicking on the hardwood. I glanced toward the elevator. It was about six feet away. I took a small side step in that direction. The woman took a glass from a cabinet and turned on the faucet. Her back was to me. I took a deep breath and lunged for the elevator button. I pounded it hard with my closed fist. Nothing happened. No light. No ding. No hum. I heard footsteps behind me. Shit! I whipped around. My glasses flew off and skittered across the floor. Everything went blurry. I panicked. I dropped to my hands and knees and reached for my frames. Her boot heel came down and smashed them to pieces.

"You don't need those anymore," she said. "I mean, you *won't*."

# CHAPTER 4

*Eastern Russia*
*26 Years Ago*

IT WAS MIDNIGHT. Headmaster Alexei Kamenev was still in his office at the school. The curriculum he had inherited was excellent, but he often worked on small tweaks late into the night, refining a technique or devising a new challenge. The wall facing his desk was covered with 5"x7" black-and-white photographs of his students, hundreds of them. So many that the faces practically filled the space from floor to ceiling. Kamenev felt a deep interest in every single one. Affection, even. He understood all their strengths and weaknesses—but most of all, their potential for greatness. After all, he had chosen each of them personally. By now, he knew them better than their parents ever had.

Kamenev looked up as a thin shadow passed across the frosted glass panel of his office door. He usually left bed check to his staff, but tonight he felt like stretching his legs. He closed his leather notebook and put down his pen.

When he reached the doorway to the preschool girls' dormitory, Matron Lyudmila Garin was already walking the room like a wraith. Maybe sixty years old, she looked ten years older, pale and sickly. She looked up at Kamenev with hollow eyes and gave him a respectful nod.

The narrow beds were arranged in neat rows a few feet apart. Garin glided easily between them, but Kamenev, with his extra bulk, had to be careful not to knock against the bedframes. The light from the full moon passed through the window bars and cast shadows across the room. It was a chilly night, and most of the girls were tucked under their wool blankets, but there was one, at the far end of the room, who was not. Curious, Kamenev walked over.

It was the copper-haired girl. She was lying on top of her blanket, curled around a ragged stuffed bear. Kamenev looked up as Garin approached. In the dim light, the matron looked even more frail and wasted. Kamenev tapped the bear lightly.

"What's this?" he asked, keeping his voice low.

Garin looked down at the skinny four-year-old, already tall for her age. She was holding the bear tight, spoon fashion, her arms around its soft belly.

"It's the only way she can sleep," said Garin softly. She stifled a cough.

"An indulgence," said Kamenev curtly. "Remove it." He turned and walked back down the row toward the door. Garin hesitated, then leaned over and pulled the bear gently from the girl's grasp. The girl's eyes popped open. Startled, she blinked and looked up. Seeing the bear in Garin's arms, she reached up with a whimper, tears pooling in her eyes. "No! *Please!*" she said softly. Garin leaned back down and brushed the copper curls away from the girl's forehead.

"You have only yourself," she whispered softly. "Nothing else."

Garin held the scruffy stuffed animal tight to her chest and walked toward the doorway, where Kamenev stood in silhouette. She glanced back and saw the copper-haired girl trembling as she curled herself around her thin white pillow.

# CHAPTER 5

*Chicago*

I DON'T UNDERSTAND how I managed to sleep, but I guess I did. For all I know, the water she gave me was drugged. When I opened my eyes, I instinctively felt around for my glasses. Then I remembered. Right. Crushed. The whole world was fuzzy, which made it even more terrifying.

It took me a few seconds to realize where I was, which was in some kind of cell in a rear corner of the loft. Cot up against one side. Metal stool bolted to the middle of the floor. Metal toilet against the back wall. Clear shower stall. And transparent Plexiglass all around. Maximum security. Zero privacy.

My suit and shoes were gone. I was wearing gym shorts and a Nike T-shirt. Had she actually undressed me while I was unconscious?? Jesus! I didn't see or hear her anywhere. Was she gone? Did she leave me here to starve to death? Was she watching me right now on a camera? I squinted to make things a little sharper, but I couldn't make out any movement.

I slipped out from under the blanket. My bladder felt like a water balloon. I stared at the toilet. Normally, there's no way I could pee right out there in the open. But my body wasn't giving me a choice. It was either that or wet my pants. I walked the two steps to the toilet and tugged the leg hole of my shorts aside. As the stream hit the bowl, I heard footsteps.

"Morning, Doctor."

*Shit!* Her voice put a crimp in my flow. I hunched forward, doing my best to shelter my privates. I saw her shape pass by on the way to the kitchen.

"Don't mind me," she said. "Do what you need to do."

I did my best to finish up, then tucked myself back in and flushed. She was heating a kettle, putting a teabag into a cup. "Sorry about the Hannibal Lecter setup," she said. "Probably overkill. At least in your case."

I pounded on the clear wall facing her and shouted. No words, just a guttural scream—at the top of my lungs.

"Speak normally, Doctor," she said. "The cell is wired. I can hear you perfectly."

This was insane! Sociopathic. She was going about her business like she was talking with a house guest. On the other hand, if she really wanted me dead, she'd had plenty of chances. Or maybe she was just drawing it out. Making me suffer. A sociopath *and* a sadist. What had I done to deserve this?? Why *me*??

She poured her tea and carried her mug over to the front of my enclosure. She pulled up a rolling stool and sat down. She took a sip of her tea and tilted her head. Her face was blurry from where I stood, but I felt that she was looking at me like I was some kind of rare zoo specimen. She set her mug down on the floor and crossed her legs. She cleared her throat.

"Okay," she said calmly. "A few things you should know."

I stood with my hands pressed against the Plexiglass, my heart racing. I was all ears. I wanted any information I could get.

"The loft is totally sealed, soundproofed, and lead-lined,"

she said. "The elevator is locked, as you discovered. There are two staircase exits, also locked. Against fire codes, I know. But my house, my rules. In terms of the university, you've decided to take your sabbatical, effective immediately, on an island with no cell service. Your colleagues are annoyed by your sudden departure, but they'll get over it. For now, Professor Racine will be taking over your classes."

"Racine??" I said. "That moron wouldn't know an Aborigine from an Inuit."

"Not your first choice for a fill-in, I realize, but under the circumstances, he was the best option. He had some holes in his schedule."

I pounded on the Plexiglass. I was confused and furious. How had this woman managed to get control of my life??

"Who the hell *are* you??" I shouted.

"Wrong question," she said, and then pushed right on. "Your colleagues will be receiving occasional emails from you through a VPN. The IP address will be untraceable. Your snail mail is being forwarded to a post office box. Your rent has been paid in advance. Your landlord has a note from you that you'll be abroad and unreachable. Obviously, since you have no friends, nobody else will be looking for you."

That stung. But she wasn't wrong. I guessed that she knew that I also had no family, no girlfriends, no pets, no Facebook account. I realized that if you were looking for someone who could disappear without a trace, I was a great choice.

"In case you're holding out hope," she continued, "nobody witnessed your abduction. The street was clear and the surveillance camera at the intersection was disabled. The van will never be found. And according to the building plans, this floor does not exist."

*"Tell me who you are!"* I shouted.

"Wrong question," she said again.

"What do you want??" I asked. "Is it *money*?" I was getting frantic.

"Do you mean the five thousand, three hundred and sixty-two dollars in your PNC savings account?" she asked.

She stood up and walked right up to my enclosure. We were just two or three inches apart. I could see her face clearly, even without glasses. She was very attractive. Stunning, in fact. It felt weird to even be noticing that.

"What do you mean, 'wrong question'?" I asked.

She leaned in even closer, almost touching her side of the clear cell wall.

"I don't need money, Doctor," she said. "All I need is you. This may be hard to believe, but I'm actually going to turn you into somebody worth kidnapping."

# CHAPTER 6

SHE TAPPED A combination on a keypad and let me out of my cage. Then she nodded toward a shoebox on a chair. "Put those on," she said, walking back to the kitchen.

I picked up the box and pulled off the lid. Inside was a pair of orange and turquoise running shoes with the Nike swoosh on the side and *ZoomX* stamped on the heel. I slid them on over my socks and laced them up. Perfect fit. Light as air.

"Nice, right?" she called out from the kitchen. "Carbon fiber sole plates."

I had no idea what that meant, but they were the most comfortable shoes I'd ever worn. I walked over to the kitchen counter and pulled up a metal stool. Morning light was streaming through the massive windows. It felt like a cozy little domestic scene, except for the fact that I'd recently been snatched off the street, punched in the jaw, and stuffed in a body bag—and the perp was fixing breakfast. I figured I had no choice but to play along until I found a way to escape. Unless she decided to kill me first.

I watched as she pulled ingredients off the shelves and out of the fridge. Fruit. Powder. Seeds. Olive oil. She started dumping everything into a huge industrial blender. She gave the blender a couple of quick pulses and then dumped in a load of plain yogurt and a bunch of spinach leaves. She put the machine on high until the ingredients turned into a thick green fluid.

I waited for the blender noise to stop, and then I spoke up. I was sure she would say "wrong question," but I had to give it a shot.

"Do you have a name?" I asked. "Or should I just call you Dear Leader?"

She gave the concoction a few more pulses and lifted the top to check the consistency. She looked up. "Call me Meed," she said.

"Is that your real name?" I asked.

"Not even close," she said.

She lifted the pitcher off its base and poured two glasses of the gross-looking drink. She slid one glass across to me and raised the other in front of her chin.

"Bottoms up," she said, and started gulping.

I stuck my nose into the top of the glass. It smelled like compost.

"*Now*, Doctor," she said. Her glass was already empty.

I could feel grit and chunks in my throat as the slime went down. I could see Meed—or whatever her name was—staring at me, hands on her hips. In a few seconds, it was over. I shoved the glass back across the counter.

"That's vile," I said, wiping my mouth with the back of my hand. I could feel the mess churning in my stomach, threatening to come back up.

"Get used to it," said Meed. She slapped her hands together. "Anyway, time to get started!"

"Started with what?" I asked. I was feeling weak and queasy. And her enthusiasm made me nervous.

"Training, Doctor," she said. She walked around to my side of the counter and poked me hard in the belly. "In case you hadn't noticed, you're not exactly in Wheaties-box shape."

That poke was all it took. I hunched over and vomited my entire green smoothie into the sink.

# CHAPTER 7

*Eastern Russia*
*25 Years Ago*

FIVE A.M. A line of groggy, sullen five-year-old girls shuffled down the stone corridor from the dormitory toward the dining hall. Teenage hall monitors in blue uniforms were stationed along the way. At the back of the line, the copper-haired girl followed along, eyes down. Her mind was dull, but not from sleep. She had simply found a way to turn herself off. Every day, she ate her meals, learned her lessons, did her chores. But she wasn't really there. At least not in her head.

Suddenly, there was a new sound in the hall. Piano music. Complex and dramatic. It echoed off the stone walls and filled the corridor. The copper-haired girl looked up. It was like nothing she had ever heard. Something in her brain woke up. There were speakers everywhere in the school buildings, but the music was coming from somewhere else, close by. It didn't sound like a recording. Someone was playing it live, right now.

The girl turned her head from side to side, trying to figure out where the music was coming from. As she passed a doorway, she paused and stood on tiptoe to look through the thick glass pane. Inside the small room, a woman was hunched over an upright piano. It was Miss Garin, the matron. She looked lost in her own world, rocking slowly, her fingers flying back and forth across the keys. The girl stood, transfixed, as the line moved ahead without her. A moment later, she felt a knee in her back.

"Move it!" the monitor growled.

The girl doubled her pace to catch up to the others. Suddenly, a dark-haired girl darted away from the front of the line. She ran to the wall and pulled herself up onto a stone window ledge. The copper-haired girl recognized her right away. Her name was Irina. She slept in the next cot but never spoke to anybody. She had dark, flashing eyes and a face that looked angry even when she was sleeping.

One of the male monitors lunged for her. Irina already had one leg out of the window bars, and she looked skinny enough to slide the rest of her body through. The boy grabbed her trailing leg and wrapped his thick arm around her waist. He pulled her down and slammed her onto the floor like a slab of meat. The other girls winced at the sound of it. Irina stood up slowly, rubbing her side. The monitor slapped her on the cheek, sending her back down to her knees. Irina didn't cry. She barely flinched. She just stared back at him and slowly stood up again.

"To the back!" the monitor shouted into Irina's face, spittle flying.

Irina wiped his saliva off her chin and walked slowly past the long row of stunned, silent girls until she was next to the copper-haired girl, the last in line. Instinctively, without thinking, the girl reached out to hold Irina's hand. She squeezed it tight. Irina squeezed back—so hard it hurt.

# CHAPTER 8

*Chicago*

I WAS BEGINNING to feel like a science experiment. Meed had me standing in the workout area in just my shorts and new training shoes, with electrodes connected to my bare chest and a blood-pressure cuff around my left biceps. She reached into a metal instrument drawer and pulled out a pair of creepy-looking black pincers. My heart started speeding until I realized that they were skin calipers. She pinched the loose folds on my chest, belly, and right thigh. She checked the gauge and shook her head.

"Twenty-two percent," she said. "I need you under ten."

Besides exercise equipment, the workout area was filled with high-tech medical gear. The university clinic would have been jealous. After my body-fat shaming, Meed did a pulmonary function test and a flexibility assessment. Both results were disappointing. She wasn't surprised.

"That's what happens when you spend ninety percent of your existence sitting on your ass," she said. "That's about to change. Big time."

She sat me down on the weight bench, then tied an elastic band around my biceps. She reached into a drawer and pulled out a plastic packet with a small syringe inside. I twisted away. She yanked me back.

"Quit moving," she said, in that low, even voice. I didn't want to get punched again, but I really hated needles.

"What are you *doing*?" I asked. I was squirming. She tightened her grip and tore open the packet with her teeth. She curled my fingers into a fist.

"What do you *think* I'm doing?" she said. "I'm turning you into a heroin addict."

I tried to jerk my arm loose. She held it tight.

"Kidding, Doctor," she said. "I just need a blood sample."

She tapped the inner hollow of my elbow and jabbed the needle into a vein.

"Don't faint on me," she said.

I watched my blood trickle through a narrow tube into a small glass vial. When the vial was full, Meed pulled out the needle and swiped a small Band-Aid over the hole it had left. She set the sample on a chrome tray next to a machine. "We'll run a CBC later," she said, "and then we'll tune up your supplement mix."

"Are you licensed for this??" I asked.

"This—and bartending," she replied. "Stand up."

The wires from the electrodes dangled from my chest. She connected them one by one to a white plastic machine with an LED screen and a bunch of colored buttons.

She wheeled the device, with me attached, over to a serious-looking treadmill.

"Hop on, Doctor," she said.

I was still weak from tossing up my breakfast. My arm was sore from the needle stick. And I was tired of being led around like a lab monkey. Enough.

"No way," I said, planting my feet. "These things make me dizzy."

She reached back into the instrument drawer and pulled out a slim black metal rod. "Okay," she said. "Let's try this." She poked the tip of the rod under the bottom edge of my shorts. I felt a hot shock on my ass cheek.

"Fuck!" I shouted at the top of my lungs.

"That's the spirit," she said, shoving me onto the machine. She punched the touchscreen, and I felt the belt start to move under my feet. I took a couple of quick steps to get up to walking speed. She started cranking the control higher—and higher. I was jogging. Then running. Then sprinting. I grabbed for the handrail. The wires on my chest were bouncing up and down. I had no idea how to stop the damned thing, and if I tried to jump off at this speed, I'd probably break an ankle. I felt sweat seeping from my scalp and armpits. I was already panting so hard it hurt.

"Are you trying to kill me?" I gasped.

"What fun would that be?" Meed replied.

She tapped another button. Music started blasting from speakers hidden in the ceiling. I heard Eminem's voice. The song was Dr. Dre's "I Need a Doctor."

"Not funny," I wheezed. My legs ached. My lungs ached. And my butt was still tingling. Meed dialed the incline up to twenty degrees.

"While we're at it," she said, "we also need to work on your sense of humor."

# CHAPTER 9

*Eastern Russia*
*20 Years Ago*

THE TEN-YEAR-OLD STUDENTS were high on a snowy mountain far above the school. The air temperature was below freezing, and the wind took it down another fifteen degrees. The atmosphere was thin, and the students were struggling to breathe. They had been hiking for five hours.

Annika, the blond sixteen-year-old instructor, was at the front of the line, with the students linked behind her by lengths of climbing rope. She had led this hike three times since first completing it herself. It never got any easier. As the students pressed forward, thigh-deep in snow, Annika peppered them with questions. The exercise was designed as an intellectual challenge, not just a physical one. Annika had started with simple questions. Now it was time to push. Her trainees needed to be able to think under stress.

"Square root of ninety-eight!" she shouted over her shoulder.

"Nine point eight nine nine," the class called back in near unison, their voices weak and almost lost in the wind. Irina and Meed were near the end of the line, separated by a five-foot length of rope. Meed stared ahead at the tips of Irina's dark hair, almost frozen solid.

Annika called out the next question. "Six major tributaries of the Amazon!"

One by one, from various students in the line, the names came back. "Japurá!" "Juruá!" "Negro!" "Madeira!" Then, a pause.

"Purus!" shouted Irina.

Annika waited, then stopped. That was only five. She turned and stared down the line. "Meed!" she shouted. "What's missing?"

Meed was so cold she could hardly feel her fingers. Every breath burned her lungs. She closed her eyes and let her mind flow. She imagined herself as a bird over the rainforest. She was being carried on a warm breeze. The geography appeared below her like a map on a table. And the answer came. "Xingu!" she called back.

Annika turned forward and led on, her long braids stiff from the cold. She had been in charge of this group since she was just thirteen. Kamenev had chosen her personally. At first, it was hard for her to keep her charges straight, so she had given the students Russian nicknames, based on their attributes. She called the speedy Asian girl Bystro. The kid who bulged out of his uniform was Zhir. The dark-skinned boy was Chernit. *"Fast." "Chubby." "Black."*

As for the girl with the unforgettable hair, nobody had ever called her anything but Meed, a nickname derived from the word for copper. Annika had tried out a few nicknames for the sullen dark-haired girl. But she only received glares in return. Irina would only respond to "Irina."

"Zhir!" Annika called out over the sound of the wind.

"Name the most celebrated Roman legions!" Silence. Meed looked back. The boy with short legs at the rear of the line was sunk into the snow almost to his waist. His eyes were glazed. Meed knew the signs. The boy's brain had stopped working on higher-level problems. It was in triage mode, redirecting resources, calculating how to survive another minute.

"Zhir!" Annika shouted again. "Answer!"

Zhir did not reply. He didn't even hear the question. His lips were blue, and his breath was coming out in short bursts. His head tipped forward like a deadweight. His knees buckled. He groaned once and fell facedown into the snow.

Meed was just a few steps ahead of him. She turned around and tugged on the rope attached to the boy's waist, struggling to turn him over.

"Zhir!" she shouted. The boy was heavy and half buried in the snow. Meed leaned back with all her strength, but he wouldn't budge.

"Stop!" Annika's voice. She was walking back down the ridge, her pale cheeks reddened by the cold. She pulled a hunting knife from her belt and sliced through the green rope connecting Meed to the unconscious boy.

"Leave him," said Annika. Then she turned and headed back to the front of the group. Meed stood still for a moment, looking back.

Irina grabbed her arm and pulled her forward.

"Stop being weak," she whispered.

Meed stared straight ahead, cold and numb. The class moved on. They had another five hours to go. On Annika's orders, they all smiled the whole way.

# CHAPTER 10

THAT NIGHT, IN Kamenev's fire-lit office, Garin and the headmaster stood in front of the wall of photographs. Garin was bent forward, her right palm pressed against her abdomen. Her pain was worse at night. Kamenev reached up and pulled down the photo of a round-faced boy. Garin had heard about the incident during the mountain exercise. Now the victim had a face.

"Zhir?" asked Garin. "He was the one?" She had been fond of the boy. Not as fit as the others, but a hard worker.

Kamenev nodded. The death had been regrettable, but not totally unexpected. The training was demanding, and not every child lived up to expectations. He slid the photo into a folder and placed the folder inside an open safe. He closed the heavy steel door with a thud. Outside the office, music filled the hallway. Rachmaninoff. The Piano Concerto no. 3 in D Minor. Garin knew it well. A very challenging piece. Kamenev tilted his head to listen.

"She's advancing," he said.

"The best student I've ever had," Garin replied.

In the small practice room down the corridor, Meed sat at the piano, head down.

The feeling had finally returned to her fingers, and she played her lesson with fierce intensity, blocking out everything else.

Even the body on the mountain.

# CHAPTER 11

*Chicago*

"STICK THIS IN your mouth."

I was moving from the Pilates reformer to the mini-trampoline when Meed shoved a small round plastic device between my lips.

"Bite down," she said.

I was drained and panting after a ninety-minute workout. And I knew I still had another thirty minutes to go. Just like every morning. "Whasthis??" I mumbled through clenched teeth. It felt like a mouthguard attached to a whistle, and it tasted like melted plastic.

"It's an exhalation resister," said Meed. "Stimulates deep diaphragmatic breathing. Which you need. Because your respiration stats suck."

In the two weeks since I'd been taken, I'd pretty much stopped arguing. Every time I even made a sour face, Meed waved her little shock wand at me and I'd fall right into line. I'd gotten used to my see-through cell and my daily smoothie. I'd even gotten used to needles. I had no choice. Every day started out with an injection of Cerebrolysin, taurine, glycine, and B6. At least, those were the ingredients Meed was willing to tell me about. For all I knew, I might have been getting steroids and hallucinogens, too. It was obvious that I was being biohacked. I just couldn't figure out why. Every time I asked, I got the same answer: "Wrong question."

After twenty minutes on the trampoline, the exhalation resister had me feeling light-headed. I spit it out onto the floor. Meed glared at me.

"Time for some capillary stimulation," she said.

I had no idea what she was talking about. But I got a twinge in my gut. When she brought up something new, it usually involved pain.

"This way," she said.

All I knew about the layout of the loft was what I could see from my cell or from the kitchen and workout area. And without my glasses, I couldn't see much. We never went into the living room on the far side of the space. Every night, Meed disappeared behind a door next to the kitchen. Now she was leading me to an alcove I'd never seen, tucked on the far side of the elevator shaft. As we rounded the corner, I saw a semicircular ribbed wooden door. She pulled it open.

"Step into my chamber, Doctor," she said.

I didn't like the sound of that. I got nervous in tight spaces. A dim light behind the door showed a small room, no bigger than a closet. The sweat was cooling on my back and shoulders. I felt clammy and sick to my stomach. It was getting to be a familiar feeling.

Meed nudged me inside the tiny space and stepped in beside me. She closed the door and pressed a button on the wall. A motor hummed. Two large panels in the floor moved apart, revealing a tank of water below, lit from underneath. I could feel freezing cold wafting against my ankles. It was ice water.

"Hop in, Doctor," she said. "Does wonders for the circulation."

I tried to back away. She raised her shock wand. The message was clear. I could either jump in on my own, or get prodded like a cow in a slaughterhouse. I inhaled once and jumped in, feetfirst. The instant the water covered my head, I felt my blood vessels constrict. My brain felt like it was about to explode. I could see the blur of an eerie blue light illuminating the tank from underneath. When the ringing in my ears stopped, I heard another sound, so loud it actually pulsed the water against my body. Underwater speakers were playing Kanye West. The song was "Stronger."

# CHAPTER 12

AFTER I'D SPENT ten minutes in the ice bath, my lips were turning blue. Meed was sitting in a lotus position a couple feet back from the edge of the tank. She didn't take her eyes off me the whole time.

"How much longer?" I asked. My teeth were chattering.

"I'll let you know," she said.

I knew this was some kind of endurance test. I just didn't know how much more I could endure. But she did. She knew *exactly* how much. At the point where I stopped feeling my limbs, she stood up.

"Out you go," she said. I put one numb foot on a narrow ledge inside the tank and pushed myself out and onto the small deck. I was trembling all over. Meed reached into a wooden bin and tossed me a towel.

I was still shaking as I shuffled across the floor to my cell. I dropped my wet clothes on the floor and stepped into the shower. The hot water felt like it was searing my skin, and my numbed hands and feet ached as blood and oxygen flowed back into them. I closed my eyes, breathed in the steam, and eventually began to feel human again.

Then I heard tapping on the shower wall. I reached over and wiped a small patch of condensation off the enclosure. Meed's face was peering through from the other side. Jesus! This woman had absolutely no sense of personal space.

"Enough," she called out. "I don't want you pruning up on me."

I turned off the tap. When I opened the shower door, she was gone. I reached for a towel and patted myself dry. I got dressed. My cell door was open. I stepped outside and immediately smelled something wonderful.

Meed reappeared. She was holding two bowls of freshly made popcorn. Was this a reward for good behavior, or some kind of trick? Popcorn did not seem like something Meed would allow on a strict training diet. She handed me a bowl.

"Organic, gluten-free, and non-GMO," she said. "Also excellent roughage." She headed across the loft toward the living room area. "Follow me, Doctor," she said. "We're going to the movies."

I followed and sat down next to her on the thick leather sofa across from a massive flat-screen TV. I started to relax a little. I took a handful of popcorn. It tasted amazing. I thought maybe she was actually giving me a break. I thought maybe, for once, we were actually about to do something normal.

"What are we watching?" I asked.

"You," she said.

Meed clicked Play on the remote, and the screen lit up. Sure enough, there I was. The footage was a little shaky, like it was taken with an iPhone. The first scene zoomed in on me walking across campus in the middle of winter. I looked gawky and awkward. I could tell I was trying not to slip on the sidewalk. The first scene dissolved into a shot of me in the aisle of Shop & Save. I was wheeling a mini-cart down the cereal aisle, picking out oatmeal.

Next came a long scene of me sitting at Starbucks before class. Then a shot of me buying a magazine and a pack of gum at a newsstand. There was a hard cut and then I was sitting at a long table in the university library. I had a thick comparative cultures text in front of me. The shot was so close I could read the title on the spine of the book. She must have been shooting from the next table. About ten feet away.

"You were following me?" I asked.

"*Surveilling* you," she said. "Every minute. For months."

"What the hell . . . ?"

"Keep watching, it gets better," she said. "Actually, it gets worse."

I put down my popcorn. I'd suddenly lost my appetite. The next few scenes came in quick succession: A long shot of me buying an umbrella during a rain shower. Me walking through Lincoln Park Zoo. Then a grainy scene of me sitting in my recliner in my living room. *My living room!* I looked over at Meed.

"Needed my extra-long lens for that one," she said, tossing a handful of popcorn into her mouth. By now, I was used to feeling violated. But this was something else. And it made me mad.

"What was the fucking *point*?" I asked. "Tell me! You obviously knew who I was. Why didn't you just grab me the first day you saw me? Why all this Peeping-Tom bullshit??"

Meed nodded toward the screen. "Pay attention. I don't want you to miss the theme here."

I looked back to see myself opening my door for a pizza delivery guy. Then riding a rental bike on the Lakefront Trail. Then tossing bread to a family of ducks in a pond.

"See what I mean?" said Meed. "Boring, boring, boring. Also repetitive, dull, and monotonous. That's what your life was. Same Caffè Americano every morning. Same tuna sandwich for lunch. Same miso dressing on your salad. Your favorite cable channel is Nat Geo. You subscribe to *Scientific American* and *Anthropology Today*. You watch YouTube videos of Margaret Mead, for God's sake! In four months, you went to three museums and not a single rock concert."

Yep. There I was, walking into the Chicago History Museum. Then the Museum of Science and Industry. Then a night shot of me walking out of the Adler Planetarium. I felt my face getting red. I was starting to feel embarrassed and defensive.

"I live a quiet life, so what? We can't all be spies and kidnappers."

Meed leaned in close. I could smell the popcorn on her breath. "Correction," she said. "You don't live a quiet life. You live a *nothing* life. But don't worry, that's all about to change. Believe me, you'll *want* it to change." She turned back to the screen. "After you watch this a few hundred more times."

# CHAPTER 13

*Eastern Russia*
*18 Years Ago*

MEED, AGE TWELVE, stood on a frozen lake wearing a blue one-piece swimsuit and rubber sandals. Nothing else. She hunched and trembled along with her classmates as they stood in a ragged line about a hundred yards from shore. In front of them were two large circular holes in the ice, exactly thirty yards apart. The holes had been cut before dawn by supervisors with chainsaws. Meed had heard the sound from her bed. The shivering had started then. For weeks, she'd known this test was coming.

Annika was wearing a fur jacket over black leggings and boots. She walked to the edge of the closer hole. Bluish-green water lapped against the opening. The ice that rimmed the hole was three inches thick. Annika turned to the class.

"Keep your wits," she said. "Swim in a straight line. Block out the fear. Block out the cold. Block out failure." She looked over the class. "Who's first?"

Meed glanced sideways as Irina stepped forward.

"Good, Irina," said Annika. "Show them the way."

Irina stepped up to the hole. She kicked off her sandals.

She knelt on the ice, her knees at the edge of the opening. She raised her arms over her head, leaned forward, and tipped herself into the water. The soles of her feet flashed for a second at the surface, and then she was gone, leaving a swirl of bubbles behind. Annika pressed the Start button on a stopwatch. Desperate and scared, some of the students began to huddle together for warmth, pressing their bodies against one another. Until Annika noticed.

"No clusters!" she shouted. "This is a solitary exercise. You have only yourself." The girls stepped back, restoring the gaps between them. Annika looked toward the distant hole and checked her stopwatch. Fifteen seconds. Then twenty.

Meed stamped her feet on the ice and stared through the mist. From where she stood, the far hole looked like a small, dark wafer. Suddenly the water in the hole frothed. Two arms shot out. Irina! Wriggling like a fish, she worked her way onto the surface and jumped to her feet. She trotted with small steps toward the class, doing her best to stay balanced. When she got close to the group, Annika reached into a plastic tub and tossed her a thin blanket. Then she turned toward the rest of the line.

"Next!"

One by one, the students made the dive. One by one, they emerged shaking and stunned, grateful to be alive. Meed was second to last, just before Bystro, the Asian girl. When it was her turn, Meed did not hesitate. She jumped in feetfirst.

The freezing water hit her like a hammer, forcing the breath out of her. She surfaced again for a second to take a fresh gulp of air, then started scissor-kicking her way under the ice. Below her, the water was pitch-black. She stayed close to the surface, letting her shoulders and heels bump against the ice roof as she swam. Her lungs burned. Her heart pounded. White bubbles trickled from her nose and mouth.

Just as her air was about to give out, she sensed a slight shift in the light above her. She stretched one arm up and felt cold air. As soon as her head cleared the water, she looked back to see Bystro plunging into the first hole. The terrified girl had waited until she had no choice.

Meed walked quickly back toward the rest of the class. Annika tossed her a blanket as she checked her stopwatch for Bystro's time. Twenty seconds. Then thirty. She began to walk toward the distant hole. Forty seconds. The students walked forward, too, a few steps at a time, staring down at the ice.

Meed spotted her first. "Bystro!" she shouted.

The slender girl was just a faint shape beneath the ice, yards off course, flailing and twisting. Meed dropped to her knees, pounding on the hard surface. But there was no way to break through. The ice was too thick. Annika was standing over her now. The white of Bystro's palms showed through the ice, pressing desperately from the other side. Then, one at a time, her hands pulled away. Her pale figure faded. A few seconds later, she dropped completely out of sight. Meed screamed with rage.

Annika stopped her watch.

# CHAPTER 14

*Chicago*

*DAMN!* I WAS impressed. She never missed.

The target was a male silhouette made of plywood. Meed's knife hit the upper left chest, right where the heart would be. It was my job to retrieve the knife after every throw. When I handed the knife back, Meed threw again. And again. Overhand. Underhand. Over the shoulder. A kill shot every time.

The next time I returned the blade, she wrapped my fingers around the grip. "Your turn," she said.

I looked across the room at the target. I squinted. From a distance, it was nothing but a dark blur to me. I felt the weight of the blade in my hand. I did my best to imitate Meed's stance. I whipped my hand forward and heard the blade clink off the brick wall.

"Can you hit the side of a barn?" said Meed.

Now I was pissed. I was tired of being a joke. I lost it.

"You're the one who stomped on my glasses!" I yelled. "How the hell do you expect me to see anything??"

Meed pulled herself up next to me and waved a finger in

front of my eyes. She lifted my eyelids one at a time and peered into my irises.

"You have convergence insufficiency," she said.

"No," I corrected her. "I have congenital corneal astigmatism."

She took another look, deeper this time, waving her finger back and forth.

"That, too," she said. "Your adjustment might take a little more time."

She flipped the blade over her shoulder. Another kill shot. I could tell without looking.

"Visual training starts tomorrow," she said. "I need you to be able to hit a target."

I knew better than to ask why.

By then, it was almost time for lights out. She was very strict about that. I needed my REM sleep, she kept saying. Good for tissue repair and muscle growth. I knew the drill. I walked over to my cell and let myself in, like a trained dog. I pulled the door shut and heard the click of the electronic lock.

I sat down on my cot and watched Meed walk up the two steps to the door of her bedroom. At least, I assumed it was her bedroom. For all I knew, it could have been a passage to another apartment or another whole building. Maybe there were other rooms with other prisoners. Maybe she was assembling an army of mind slaves. Why should I be the only one? Or maybe she had a night job as a dominatrix. I'd gone from a world where everything was predictable to a world where *nothing* was.

From my cot, I could see one of the big flat-screen TVs that hung from brackets all over the loft. Some were tuned to CNN, some to the local news channel. Usually, the volume was down and the caption setting on, but sometimes during my workouts Meed turned up the sound. I always kept my ears open for news about a missing anthropology professor.

But Meed was right. There was nobody looking for me. I was starting to believe what she kept telling me, over and over. "You have only yourself."

# CHAPTER 15

*Eastern Russia*
*17 Years Ago*

MEED, NOW THIRTEEN, felt the blood rushing to her head and with it, the sickening feeling of defeat. She was upside down, bound with thick rope, hanging from a long wooden beam ten feet off the ground. She was wriggling and red in the face, trying her best to get free. But nothing was working. The situation was even more humiliating because she was the last to finish. All the other students had already completed the assignment. She could see their inverted faces below her in the school courtyard. They were looking up at her with eerie smiles.

She saw Annika's face most clearly, just inches away. Annika reached up and tapped Meed's forehead with her index finger.

"Time's up, Meed," she said. "Do what you need to do."

Meed sucked in a breath and clenched her teeth. Of course, she knew the last-resort procedure, but her brain was telling her not to do it. Would not allow it. So she simply overruled the warning, pushing past logic and fear and reason, as she'd been trained to do. There was no other way.

She hung limp and then, with a violent twist and flex of her torso, she wrenched the ball of her humerus from its socket. The pain was like an electric shock, stunning her into semi-consciousness. The muscles in her arm spasmed and tingled. Her vision dimmed. But through it all, Meed focused on the next step. As her upper arm dislocated forward, the ropes slackened around her chest—just by millimeters. But enough.

She pushed through the agony and flexed her body upward. She grabbed the middle coil of rope in her teeth and jerked her head back, pulling the rope with it. The other coils loosened. More wriggling and struggle. More excruciating pain. A second later, Meed felt herself slipping down. Then, suddenly, she dropped from the beam, landing on her back on the hard dirt. She was writhing and grimacing, but refused to scream. Her classmates crowded around her. Through a haze, she saw Annika nod to Irina.

Meed felt Irina grab her limp arm and extend it out to ninety degrees. It felt like the limb was being torn from her body. She felt Irina's foot against her upper rib cage and then a steady, strong pull on her wrist. There was another blast of stunning pain and then a loud click as the joint reassembled. Meed felt her head spin as she fought to stay conscious. A sheen of cold sweat coated her face. She rolled to her opposite side and struggled to her knees, and then to her feet. She set her legs to keep from dropping again and clutched her relocated shoulder.

She heard the sound of distant clapping—but not from a crowd. Just from one person. As she looked up, she saw the headmaster observing from the stone balcony outside his office. Standing next to him was a guest, a tall man in a well-cut suit, with blindingly white teeth. Meed could tell that the guest was impressed. He was the one applauding.

# CHAPTER 16

KAMENEV PLACED HIS hand on his guest's elbow and guided him back into the oak-paneled office. The visitor had a thick mane of black hair to go with his impressive teeth. He spoke in an accent that could have been Middle Eastern or Central European or a blend of both. Or it could have all been an act. Kamenev knew the type well. The guest gave his name as Mazen. But, of course, that could have been made up, too.

"My contacts did not exaggerate," Mazen said. "Your students are highly..." He searched for the right compliment, then found it: "motivated."

"They do what is necessary to succeed," said Kamenev. "As do you, I'm told."

Mazen shrugged off the transparent flattery. "I sell weapons of mass destruction to self-destructive people. It's a lucrative business. I never run out of customers." He cocked his head at his host.

"And what, exactly, is *your* business, Headmaster Kamenev? Help me understand. What degree does your institution confer?" There was a touch of playful sarcasm in his voice. He knew the school had never handed out an actual diploma.

Kamenev pressed his hands together. In conversations like these, he always picked his words carefully. His guest had been fully vetted, but no need to reveal more than necessary. Just enough to make the sale.

"Thousands of our graduates are already at work in every country," he said. "Every government. Every agency. Every organization. Every multinational company. We handle intelligence, operational assistance, special assignments." He was sure that Mazen could translate the euphemisms. "For fair compensation," Kamenev continued, "we support the right people, and they support us." Kamenev smiled. "As you say, it's lucrative."

"And the price?" asked the guest, with his brows raised.

"Numbers are not the point," said Kamenev. "Whatever we charge, you can afford."

The guest leaned back in his chair. He knew it was true.

"As you've seen," Kamenev continued, "our students are highly skilled, with no messy political or religious preconceptions. Raw clay, to be molded to the needs of the assignment. They have been raised here since infancy. They are infinitely adaptable. They live only for the mission."

The guest appeared to be thinking something over, then revealed the full glory of his brilliant smile. He stood to shake Kamenev's hand.

"Very well," he said. "Arrangements will be made." He rebuttoned his suit jacket and picked up his slim attaché case. "To start with," he said, "I will require an attractive female."

As it turned out, he already had one in mind.

# CHAPTER 17

*Chicago*

THE RACKET WAS so loud I could hear it through my cell walls. The treadmill was whining at top speed, and Meed's feet were pounding hard on the belt. She'd unlocked my cell door and left it open a crack so I could get out on my own. It was one of the few tiny ways she'd eased up on security recently, but I knew cameras were on me the whole time. I still couldn't even use the toilet in private.

She'd installed a small TV hanging from a bracket near the ceiling of my cell. She ran the movie of my solitary life on a loop, 24/7. Her idea of motivation, I guess. At night, I tossed a towel over the screen.

When I walked out into the kitchen, my smoothie was waiting on the counter. I picked up the glass and guzzled the slime like always, then walked over to a bench near the workout area. I glanced up at the flat screen overhead, where a CNN correspondent was reporting on a mudslide in Ecuador. Out of the corner of my eye, I watched Meed. In her black workout outfit, she looked like an Olympic athlete or some kind of superhero.

Her hair was pulled into a bun on top of her head. After a minute, she reached up and pulled out a hairpin and let her curls fly. She was wearing a short-sleeved top, which was a different style for her. I'd never seen her in anything but long sleeves. As her arms pumped, I could see marks on both of her forearms—small red welts, like cigarette burns.

For a split second, I considered asking about them. But I knew better. Wrong question, no doubt. Since she seemed to be a stickler for physical perfection, it felt strange to discover that she was a little less than perfect—which somehow made her even more of a mystery.

It was all very confusing. I still hated her for keeping me a prisoner and not telling me why. And for working me to exhaustion every single day in her private boot camp. But that didn't change the fact that she was the most gorgeous woman I'd ever seen, scars and all.

I saw her punch a button on the console. The treadmill slowed down. She grabbed the handrails and vaulted off to the side like a gymnast. Sweat was dripping from her nose and chin. Her hair was soaked and matted around her neck.

She grabbed a towel from a cabinet and pressed it against her face. Then she tossed the towel aside and took a step toward me. She set herself on the balls of her feet and bounced from side to side. She shook her head, sending sweat drop-lets flying from her hair. The adrenaline started to shoot through me.

"Front!" she shouted.

I knew the drill. By this time, I was like one of Pavlov's pups. I jumped up and lowered my head. I set my feet, then charged full out across the room. I launched myself toward her waist, already thinking through the move, just like I'd practiced—how my shoulder would slam into her gut, bringing her down hard onto her back. But that's not what happened. That's not what *ever* happened. This time, she whipped her right leg around and caught me in midair. Her foot hit my ribs like a baseball bat. I landed on the mat so hard I saw sparks. I hadn't laid a finger on her. Not once. But I'd swear this time I got close.

When I rolled over, I felt her heel in my diaphragm. With one hard shove, she could have turned my liver to mush. I knew, because she'd drawn me a diagram.

Then I felt the pressure ease off. I crunched myself up to a sitting position as she walked away with her copper curls bouncing. She turned to look at me over her shoulder.

"Better, Doctor." she said, as she headed toward the door to her room. "Not great. But better."

I thought it was the nicest compliment I'd ever heard.

# CHAPTER 18

*Eastern Russia*
*16 Years Ago*

SOME SCHOOL DAYS, like this one, stretched long into the night. The classroom on the top floor was totally dark, windows blocked with heavy shades. Meed and her classmates stood on one side of the room wearing night-vision goggles. Gunich, the owlish instructor, walked to the opposite side of the room, which was shrouded by a black curtain. He tugged a cord. The curtain dropped, revealing a row of iron safes—all types and sizes, from compact office models to bank-sized vaults, sealed with the most ingenious locks the industry had ever devised.

Meed had studied hard for this drill. Her mind was a maze of mechanical diagrams, electronic circuits, and metallurgy formulas. It was a maze she needed to solve, under challenging conditions and extreme time pressure. But that was her specialty.

"Execute!" said Gunich. He stepped to the side and put on his own goggles to observe.

The students rushed to the safes, reaching for the lock dials and electronic keypads. Working alone or in teams, they fished in their pockets for listening devices and electronic readers—all permitted during the exam. One team produced a compact acetylene torch. Gunich was impressed. Points for ingenuity.

Meed ran to the largest safe in the row, claiming it for her own. Through her goggles, the whole scene had a bizarre glow. In the greenish image, her classmates looked like bug-eyed reptiles. Gunich, in his long lab coat, looked like some kind of spectacled Druid.

Meed pressed her ear against the safe door and rested her fingers lightly on the dial of the combination lock. She rotated the dial with the lightest touch, letting the sensation flow through her fingertips. She pictured the tumblers, the wheel pack, the lever nose, the whole internal mechanism concealed behind four inches of tempered steel. But it wasn't the image that mattered. It was the sound. She had trained for months using a physician's stethoscope, but now she had sharpened her senses even further.

She pressed her ear tight against the metal and slowly turned the dial. There were three metal wheels buried inside. Meed was listening for the distinctive clicks the wheels made as they lined up. Her first try, at the start of the semester, had taken her five hours. But that was then. This was now. She heard the first click.

She turned the dial again and sensed another. She heard the beeping of a digital code reader from two stations down. She could tell that Irina was getting close to solving her challenge on one of the electronic locks. Meed concentrated on the safe in front of her. No distractions. One more twitch of her fingers. She felt something give inside the door, almost imperceptible—the feel of a small metal arm dropping. She leaned on the heavy handle. The massive door swung open. Twenty-five seconds.

Gunich's eyes opened wide behind his goggles. The lock-whisperer had done it again.

Meed moved on to the next safe and nudged a classmate aside. In twelve seconds, that safe was open, too. One station away, Irina gave Meed a small nod and fussed with her own quirky lock. She wanted to succeed on her own. Meed stepped past her, working her way down the rest of the row. Five minutes later, Irina yanked open the door to her safe. She looked up. Meed had opened all the rest.

The other students set their tools down on the floor. They were stunned and embarrassed. And they knew the consequences. Gunich stepped out of his corner.

"Meed and Irina pass," he said. "The rest of you will repeat the class."

The students yanked the goggles off their heads. A few of them glared at Meed. She glared right back.

"Dismissed," said Gunich. He opened the classroom door, letting the dim light from the hallway spill in. "I suggest you review your manuals. Section 5 in particular."

The students shuffled out the door past him, handing him their goggles as they went. Meed hung back until she was the only student left. Gunich walked over and plucked the night-vision goggles from her head.

"Time to go," he said. "You did well."

Meed leaned back against one of the open safes and brushed her fingertips against her shirt, as if honing them.

"I think I'll do some extra practice," she said. "Please. Just a few minutes more."

Gunich had never seen a student like her. A savant. Who

was he to interfere with genius? He shrugged and headed out the door. Meed called after him.

"I'll lock up when I leave," she said.

She knew Gunich would not appreciate the joke, much less her true plans, and the real reason she needed to be alone. Safe-cracking (technically, "Barriers & Intrusions") was the only class held on the administrative floor. Meed knew this was where the school's deepest secrets were kept. And there was one secret in particular she intended to uncover. It was her own personal extra-credit project.

For Meed, passing the exam had been the simplest part of her night. The real challenge was about to begin.

# CHAPTER 19

THE PLAN HAD taken months of careful preparation. Meed hadn't told anybody about what she was up to. Not even Irina. Walking to class day after day, she had mentally mapped the entire floor and watched the comings and goings of every administrator. Especially Kamenev.

As it turned out, the headmaster's schedule was as predictable as the menu in the dining hall. He paid no attention to the students as he walked back and forth from his office. But Meed had certainly been paying attention to him.

An hour after Gunich left the classroom, all footsteps in the corridor had stopped. The last doors had been closed. The only sound was the rattle and hiss from the metal radiators.

Meed slipped through the classroom door and tiptoed down the paneled hallway. The walls were white plaster with dark oak wainscoting. The floor was covered with lush Persian rugs. The rest of the school buildings were stark and utilitarian, but this was a showpiece, built to impress. The hallway was dark except for the dim security lights along the corridor. There was a large antique clock hanging on the wall at the far end of the hall. Thirty minutes until bed check. More than enough time.

The security camera at the end of the hall was static. An easy target, especially with the low ceiling. Meed pulled a laser from her pocket, stolen during a morning lab. It was a Class 3B model, not strong enough to blind the camera, just enough to cause a little distortion. Two or three seconds was all she needed.

The sensor was right below the lens, similar to a device she'd dissected that morning. Meed gave the sensor a quick blast with the laser, then moved along the edge of its coverage field. If anybody in the security office was paying attention to that specific feed, it would have looked like a minor glitch. Nothing to get alarmed about.

The heavy oak door to Kamenev's office was set into an alcove, out of sight of the camera, but secured with an electronic lock. This part was easy. Meed had watched Kamenev open the door three times and memorized his finger positions on the keypad. One. Zero. Four. Six. Child's play.

Meed turned the knob and pushed the door open. The air inside smelled of stale smoke and wood polish. The office was spacious, lined with heavy bookshelves. With her eyes adjusted to the darkness, Meed could make out the shape of a large sofa, a massive desk, and a wall filled with photographs. She recognized the faces, including her own.

In a corner near the desk sat a huge safe. It was a model she hadn't seen before, but no matter. Her senses were tuned, and her confidence level was high. She rested her fingers lightly on the lock dial and pressed her ear against the cold metal door. She heard a rustle from the darkest corner of the room. Then a voice.

"I can save you the trouble."

# CHAPTER 20

MEED FROZE. SHE let her hand drop slowly from the safe dial, then turned her head to face the corner. A lamp clicked on. Lyudmila Garin sat slumped in a leather chair, her hands clawed tight around the wooden armrests. She was thin and wasted. Almost a ghost. In her lap was a thick manila folder.

"I knew it was just a matter of time," she said. "I thought this might be the night."

Meed thought carefully about what to say. Or not say. Obviously, she'd been caught in the act. No denying it. But if there was anyone she could trust not to turn her in, it was her devoted piano teacher.

Meed stood and stepped forward into the lamplight. "I'm sorry," she said. "All I want..."

"I know what you want," said Garin. "I have it right here."

With a shaking hand, she lifted the folder from her lap and held it out. Meed took it. The spine of the folder was soft from handling, and the edges were frayed. The label tab contained what looked like a random combination of numbers and letters.

"What's this?" Meed asked, pointing at the code.

"It's you," replied Garin.

Meed opened the folder and rifled through the contents. The records went back fourteen years. It was her entire history at the school, starting at the age of six months. In meticulous detail. Height and weight charts. Academic grades and reports. Records and transcripts. Athletic ratings. Intelligence and aptitude tests. At the very back of the folder was a page labeled "Entrance Assessment." Attached to it was a small color photo of a baby in an institutional bassinet. A baby with bright copper curls. Meed felt the breath go out of her. She unclipped the picture and turned it to the light. She stared at it for a long time.

"You were distinctive from the start," said Garin, managing a thin smile.

Clipped to the inside cover of the folder was another photo—a picture of a young man. The image was yellowed, like a picture from a history lecture. The man was posing proudly in front of a building under construction, with stones and lumber all around. Meed recognized the building. It was the one they were in right now. But she had never seen the man before.

"Who is this?" she asked. She held the photo out toward Garin.

"Your great-grandfather," said Garin, her voice thin and hoarse. "A genius, in his own dark way. The school's cofounder."

Meed looked up, stunned and confused. The whole idea of relatives was foreign to her. The subject was never discussed, or even mentioned. None of the students knew anything about their families. And they had learned not to ask. "Wrong question," was the rote response. Meed stared at the picture again, straining to make sense of the connection.

"The founder?" she asked, bewildered. "I don't understand…"

"That's why you're here," said Garin. "That's why you were chosen. Your parents were not considered worthy of his heritage. You are. *You* are the legacy."

"What kind of legacy is that?" Meed asked. She didn't know how much Garin knew. Or how much she would say. But she had years of questions boiling up in her brain, and she realized that she might not get another chance to ask them. Trembling, Meed closed the folder and clutched it tight with both hands.

"*Tell* me!" she said. "What's all this all about? What are we doing here? What are we being trained for? When students leave, where do they go?"

Garin took in a raspy breath. "They go wherever they're needed," she replied. "They go to help others gain power, steal power, stay in power. Eventually, the graduates of this school will control everything, everywhere in the world." She jabbed a thin finger at Meed. "And you could be the best ever. You have the gift. It's in your blood."

Garin straightened herself in the chair. The shift made her wince. Meed reached out, but Garin waved her hand away. "You have only one weakness," she said softly.

"You seek comfort in others." Garin lowered her head to cough, then looked up again. "Always remember—you have only yourself."

Meed heard footsteps from far down the corridor. Maybe the camera glitch hadn't gone unnoticed after all. Garin waved her hand.

"Go," she said. "Disappear. I'll make sure my prints are on everything." A wet rattle rose from her throat. "There's nothing they can do to me now."

As Meed handed the file back to the matron, a small card

fell to the floor. She picked it up. It was a torn sheet with two words printed in pen. Meed stared at the paper and then looked up at Garin. The matron nodded.

"That's your name," she said. "Your true name. That is who you really are."

# CHAPTER 21

AFTER MEED WAS safely away, Garin slipped out of the building through a secret exit, one not even security knew about. She found the well-worn path that led west, away from the school. She had made this same walk many times before over the past five decades—as a student, as a teacher, as a supervisor. But never at 3 a.m. And never alone. She kept her scarf wrapped around her face to muffle the sound of her coughs. Behind her was the glow of lights on the school walls. Ahead, there was only darkness.

The path wound through fir trees until it reached the edge of the lake, flat and frozen. Snowy mountain peaks rose in the distance. Lyudmila took a few tentative steps onto the ice and extended her arms out to her sides for balance, like a tightrope walker. She was so slight that, from a distance, she might have been mistaken for a young girl. But nobody was looking. In a few minutes, she reached the large hole in the ice, its surface lightly crusted over.

Lyudmila looked up at the stars one last time, then closed her eyes. A Rachmaninoff concerto swirled in her head. Her fingers twitched as if touching piano keys. She took one final step forward and dropped through the hole. The dark water closed over her. Compared to the cancer, the brutal cold was a lesser pain—and a much kinder death.

# CHAPTER 22

*Chicago*

MEED CALLED IT a titanium posture brace. I called it a torture device. It went around my waist and pressed into my back like a plate of armor. But I can't deny that it worked. It kept my core firm and tight while I did another dead lift.

"Watch your form," Meed called out from her chair. "Don't get sloppy."

My max was now up to 300 pounds, which I realized would be like lifting my office desk. I wouldn't have thought it was possible. But I never could have imagined I'd be at nine percent body fat either. Or that I could blow through the Marine Corps Physical Fitness Test like it was nothing.

Thanks to Meed's bizarre retinal focus drills, my eyesight was sharp and clear. For the first time since I got my learner's permit, I wouldn't need corrective lenses to drive. Not that Meed ever let me anywhere near a vehicle. Or even a street. I'd been trapped in the loft for four months straight. I did one last lift and dropped the barbell on the mat like a load of cement.

As I shifted to free weights, I decided to quiz Meed again. I'd given up on getting anything meaningful out of her, but we'd made a little game out of personal trivia. I grabbed a twenty-pounder in each hand and squeezed in my questions between reps.

"Ever been to Disneyland?" I asked.

"Twice," she said. "Hated it both times."

"Favorite color?"

"Black."

"Best pizza in Chicago?"

"Dante's."

"Where were you born?"

"Wrong question."

Typical conversation. Three steps forward, one total roadblock.

"Stand up straight," said Meed. I looked over. She was aiming a handheld laser at me.

"I *am* standing up straight," I said, tapping the brace. "How could I not?"

"Good news," she said, checking the readout. "You're now officially six foot two."

Amazing. That was up a quarter-inch in the last month. Plus another three inches around my chest. Another two inches around each biceps. And two inches *less* around my waist. My gym shorts were actually starting to bag a bit. And for the first time in my life, I had something approaching a six-pack. I was being turned into somebody else—somebody I didn't even recognize—and I still didn't know why. I was bigger, stronger, smarter. But for what?

I put the weights back in the rack and wiped my face with a towel. When I looked up again, Meed was tapping a syringe. She definitely had a needle fetish.

"For Christ's sake, what now?" I asked.

"Assume the position," she said. No sense in arguing. I peeled down the waistband of my shorts. She jabbed me in the right upper glute.

"Just a little extra vitamin B," she said. "We've got a training run tonight."

Training run? That was the last thing I wanted to hear. I pulled my shorts back up and slumped against the weight rack. My head sagged. Since my kidnapping, I estimated that I'd run over a thousand miles—going absolutely nowhere.

"I'm so sick of that goddamn treadmill," I muttered.

"Not on the treadmill," said Meed. She nodded toward the window. "Outside."

My heart started fluttering like I'd just gotten a puppy for Christmas.

*"Outside??"* I asked. "You're serious?"

"Why not?" said Meed. "Let's get some fresh Chicago air into those lungs."

I looked out the window. Rain was sheeting against the glass. I wouldn't have cared if it was hot lava. I realized that this was my chance. Outside, I might be able to flag down a cop or jump into a cab. Or lose Meed in a crowd. Or maybe just shove her down an open manhole and run for help. Anything to get away and get my life back again.

Meed picked up the shock wand and waved it back and forth. Sometimes it felt like she could actually read my mind.

"Don't even think about it," she said.

# CHAPTER 23

*Eastern Russia*
*15 Years Ago*

OF ALL THE weapons on the firing range, Meed found the .50 BMG machine gun the hardest to handle. It could vaporize a watermelon at a hundred yards, but the recoil was enough to bruise her collarbone. Her scores on long guns overall were solid, but she preferred pistols. After firing five brain-shaking rounds, she set the big gun back in the rack and picked up a Glock 9mm. Much better.

Irina was standing on the next platform with a Beretta .22, punching hole after hole into the center of a target downrange. Meed slid a clip into the Glock and started firing at the next target over. Compared to the heavy .50, the Glock felt like a popgun.

Meed was matching Irina shot for shot. Within twenty seconds, both target centers were shredded.

All the way down the firing line came the cracks and bangs of every kind of firearm, from MIL-SPEC models to expertly hacked hybrids. Only the instructors wore ear protection. For the students, the noise was an important part of the lesson—how to think with your head pounding and your ears ringing.

In the middle of it all, one student was even more solid and unflappable than the others. His name was Rishi. He was slightly built, with a caramel complexion and thick black hair. He was also younger than everybody else on the range by a couple of years. He'd recently been moved up from a lower class, where he had no real competition.

Between clips, Meed glanced his way. Rishi was lying flat on his belly, cradling a Barrett M82, his sniper rifle of choice. His target was a small circle on a brick wall 150 yards away. Meed could see Rishi's ribs through his T-shirt as he sent another round. There was a small kick of brick dust from the center of the circle. Another direct hit.

Meed glanced at Irina. Neither of them liked being shown up, especially by a runt like Rishi. Irina squinted down the barrel of her pistol and kept firing. But Meed was annoyed enough to take action. She flicked the safety on the Glock and set it down on the shooting stand. Then she walked over to the weapon vault anchored in cement behind the firing line. The vault was the size of a coffin. The heavy steel lid was open. Meed ran her hands over the assortment of armaments inside and found just what she was looking for.

Rishi loaded another round into his rifle. He set the cross-hairs on the target again. His finger moved slowly from the trigger guard to the trigger. Suddenly there was a huge blast downrange. Rishi jerked his head up from his scope. The target was gone. Not just the circle on the bricks. The entire brick wall.

All sound on the firing line stopped. Students and instructors were frozen in place by the violence of the blast. All that was left in the distance was a cloud of dust. Meed lowered the RPG launcher from her shoulder and wiped a streak of soot off her cheek. She leaned down and patted Rishi on the head.

"Don't worry," she said. "They'll give you something new to shoot at."

# CHAPTER 24

*Chicago*

IT WAS 10 p.m. when we stepped into the elevator for our run. Meed pressed the Down button. I heard the chains rattle and felt the car lurch into motion. I thought back to my ride up in that same elevator four months back. The day my life had disappeared.

My new red running suit was a little tight in the crotch, but otherwise it felt pretty sleek. Meed was wearing the female version. In black, of course. We both had our nylon hoodies up, ready for the rain.

The elevator door opened onto a narrow basement corridor with cinderblock walls. Meed led the way up a set of cement stairs with a narrow metal railing. We took a turn on a narrow landing and then up a few more steps to a heavy swinging metal door, the kind you'd find on a loading dock. Meed shouldered her way through, and we stepped out onto the sidewalk. My first taste of freedom. But not really. I was out in the world, but I was still a prisoner. I figured Meed had waited for weather like this so we'd be the only two people on the street. The rain was coming down so hard it sounded like white noise. She looked both ways then headed west, starting off at a quick jog.

In spite of the chilly March rain, I was already starting to sweat inside my tracksuit. I rolled back my hood and let the water roll down my neck. It felt good. For most of the way, I ran behind Meed, just far enough to avoid getting her shoe splatter in my face. I came up next to her while she marked time at a stoplight. My lungs hurt already.

"Where are we headed?" I asked.

"Wrong question," said Meed. She wasn't even breathing hard.

We turned south. After about forty-five minutes, the surroundings started to get sketchy. Most of the streetlights were out and there was a lot of chain-link fencing. I could tell from street signs that we were near Fuller Park. It was a neighborhood I wouldn't even drive through during the day, let alone run through in the dark. On the plus side, the rain had let up. Now it was just a light mist.

Here and there along the street, a few beat-up cars sat at the curb, but this wasn't a place you'd ever want to park overnight. Not if you planned to see your vehicle in the morning.

On the right, a low wooden fence blocked off a site with a half-demolished building. The store next door looked like it was next for the wrecking ball. Meed took a right and turned down the alley just past the store. It took me a few seconds to catch up. When I rounded the corner, I felt a prickle at the back of my neck. The alley was narrow and the far end disappeared into darkness. Meed was nowhere in sight.

I heard a rustle. I picked up my pace. Suddenly, somebody grabbed me hard from behind, lifting my feet off the ground and pinning my hands against my sides. I felt the bristle of stubble against my neck. A raspy voice mumbled into my ear.

"Slow down there, Usain Bolt."

# CHAPTER 25

I BENT FORWARD hard and twisted my shoulders, but it was no use. The guy was a brute. With one hand, he grabbed me by the chin and pulled my head back up again. That's when the other guy stepped out of the shadows.

I could see his pale shaved dome glistening in the light of a streetlight near the alley entrance. He had a ripped T-shirt under a greasy denim vest. A cobra tattoo twisted up his neck. He had a jerky, dangerous energy, jacked up and ready for trouble. My heart was already thumping from the run, but now I could feel my pulse pound even harder in my head. I got a bitter taste in my mouth. I suddenly went cold and clammy all over.

I looked down the alley past the thug in front of me. Where the hell was Meed??

She would have missed me by now. Was she knocked out somewhere back in the dark—or dead? Was I next? I started to shake.

"Whaddaya got for me tonight?" said Cobra Neck. The guy behind me tightened his grip, his forearms locked around my rib cage.

"We *know* you got somethin'," he said, shaking me from side to side.

"I don't!" I said. "I don't have anything!" That was the truth. Meed had my wallet and phone locked up somewhere in the loft. I hadn't touched cash in four months. Cobra Neck flicked the collar of my tracksuit.

"Definitely not bargain bin," he said, leaning in. "C'mon. I know you got somethin' for me."

I felt an arm slide up to my throat. That was the trigger, the second when something kicked in. I rolled hard to the right and reached my leg back. I shoved the guy's elbow up and slipped my head out of his grip. I got my first look at his face—pale, bristled, dead-eyed. I twisted his arm behind his back and kicked him hard behind his knees. He dropped to the wet pavement. I spun back around with my hands up— and froze. There was a gun two inches from my forehead. Cobra Neck waved the barrel. He was pissed off and out of patience. I could hear the guy behind me groaning and cursing under his breath.

"Let's try again, asshole," said Cobra Neck. "Empty your goddamn..."

The shock wand caught him right under the chin. The gun dropped and clattered on the pavement. I saw the flash of Meed's hand as she chopped the guy hard across his carotid artery. He spasmed and crumpled, out cold. I heard feet scrambling behind me and turned around. The other guy was already rounding the corner onto the street. Gone. When I turned back, Meed was in my face, glaring at me.

"I thought I told you to keep up," she said.

The adrenaline was flooding through me, making me dizzy. I'd never felt anything close to this in my life. I bent forward at the waist, trying to catch my breath. I replayed the last minute like a movie in my head. It didn't seem real.

"I broke a choke hold," I said. "I dropped that jerk." I could hear myself trying to sound tough.

"I noticed," said Meed. "Just before you almost got your head shot off. You were too slow on the second target."

She noticed? "You were *watching*??" I asked.

"I was," she said. "Until I saw you failing."

I thought I might get some compliments on my martial arts skills. Instead, I had to eat crow. Nothing new in this relationship. I felt my shoulders slump as I looked up at her. She was tucking the shock wand back into her sleeve.

"Sorry," I said. I couldn't explain it, but letting her down felt even worse than almost dying.

"I won't always be there," she said. "You have only yourself."

# CHAPTER 26

THE NEXT MORNING was brutal. Whatever mission Meed was preparing me for, I clearly wasn't ready, and she let me know it. Again and again, she made me come at her, full out. Front. Back. Side. And every time, she put me on the floor. Over and over, she drilled me on the right way to knock away a gun and leave the guy with a shattered wrist. She showed me the death points on the back of the neck, the belly, the chest.

I learned that the clavicle is an easy bone to break and that it takes about 130 pounds of force to crack somebody's jaw.

What was strange was how normal it was all starting to feel. I'd spent my whole life studying people—their cultures, traditions, religions. Now I was learning how to maim them. And I was okay with it. Meed had done something to change my head, not just my body. I didn't know who I was anymore, or what I was turning into.

After an hour, Meed let me stop to catch my breath. I was aching all over and dripping with sweat. I saw her reach into a plastic bin and pull out a large brown paper sack. It was leaking a watery red fluid. When the bag dropped away, I rocked back. She was holding up a huge severed pig's head, with a long pink snout and its mouth set in a sickly grin. She jammed the head down on top of a metal stand so the pig was looking right at me. Meed shoved me into position in front of the gross, dripping head.

"Set your hands for a punch," she said, "then rip out the left eye."

What the hell?? This was a whole new level of insanity. The smell of the pig head was bad enough—sharp and rancid. The thought of touching it made my stomach turn.

Meed pointed to the outside corner of the pig's eye, which looked disturbingly human. "Right here," she said. "Jam your thumb in hard and hook it."

"You've done this?" I asked, raising my hands to the ready position.

"Wrong question," she replied. "Do it. Hard and fast."

I took a few quick breaths to psych myself up. I re-ran my mental movie of the night before, with a gun barrel pointed at my head. I let out a loud shout. Then I did it. I stabbed my right thumb into the outside edge of the pig's left eye and drove it behind the rear curve of the eyeball. I crooked my thumb and jerked it forward. The eyeball jutted out of its socket like a soft marble, still attached by nerves and small muscles, but now staring wildly to the side.

I gagged and turned away, shaking sticky pink goo off my fingers. I wanted to wash my hands. I wanted to take a shower. I wanted to vomit. I waited for Meed to say something. Like "good job." Or "poke out the other one." But when I looked over, her back was turned. She was suddenly more interested in something on the TV screen overhead.

The TV was tuned to a local Chicago station. A young

female reporter with bobbed hair was doing a remote from a downtown street. At the bottom of the screen was a crawl that read, "AFRICAN PEACEMAKER WILL SPEAK IN CHICAGO TODAY." Behind the reporter was a temporary speaking platform with some of the scaffolding still showing. She was already talking when Meed turned up the volume.

*. . . and if there is any hope of bringing peace to the warring factions in the splinter nation of Gudugwi, it lies with former Ghanaian minister Abrafo Asare. If he succeeds in his mission, a number of African warlords and arms dealers are expected to be brought before the International Court of Justice in The Hague. Which, in some dark quarters, makes Abrafo Asare a very unpopular man. Asare will speak to human rights activists and supporters here in Chicago this afternoon before heading to the United Nations in New York. City Hall will be closed, and expect street closures in that area, because security will be tight. This is Sinola Byne, Channel 7, Eyewitness News, Chicago.*

Without a word, Meed turned and headed for her room behind the kitchen. Apparently, the lesson in eye-gouging was over. It wasn't unusual for Meed to disappear into her private space with no explanation—in the middle of a meal, in the middle of a workout, in the middle of a sentence. I was used to it by now. When she closed the door behind her, I looked back up at the TV. I was staring at a commercial for Jimmy Dean breakfast sausage.

Just me and the dead stinking pig.

# CHAPTER 27

BY THE TIME the commercial break was over, Meed was out of her room and moving with purpose through the kitchen. She had quick-changed out of her workout gear into street clothes—skinny jeans, a sweater, and a burgundy leather jacket. Her hair was tucked under a floppy beret. She looked like she was heading for a brunch date.

"I'll be out for a while," she said.

Out? This was a first. She had never left me alone in the open part of the loft.

Was it possible she trusted me enough to let me roam the whole space on my own?

"Come here," she said. She led me to the weight bench and sat me down. I thought maybe she was about to explain where she was going or what kind of workout she expected me to do while she was gone. Instead, she pulled a length of heavy chain from the floor and wrapped it around my chest in three tight loops, trapping my arms above the elbows. She wrapped the other end around the base of the weight machine. So much for trust.

"What are you *doing*??" I asked. "If you think I'm a flight risk, just stick me back in my cell!"

"Too easy," she said. "I need to expand your horizons."

She reached into the tool drawer and pulled out a padlock with a long shackle. She hooked it through a few links of the chain across my chest and clicked it shut. I was now bound to the Precor trainer, which was loaded with about 400 pounds of weights. My arms were bound tight, with my forearms wriggling out underneath. But she wasn't done yet.

She reached into the drawer again and pulled out a small beige rectangle. Five months ago, I would have thought it was modeling clay. Now I knew better. It was C-4 explosive.

"Jesus!" I said, struggling against the chains.

"Praying won't help," Meed replied.

She jammed a fuse into one side of the rectangle and then dropped it down the back of my gym shorts. I could feel the cool brick against my lower spine. I squirmed and shouted, "Why are you doing this??" She pretended not to hear me. The rest of the fuse was in a thick coil. Meed unwound it quickly as she backed across the living room area to the far wall of the loft.

"What the hell are you *thinking*??" I yelled. She pulled a lighter out of her pocket and touched off the fuse. It lit up like a sparkler as she dropped it onto the hardwood floor. I bounced up and down on the bench, trying to jar the chains loose, but it wasn't working.

"Is this a joke?" I asked. She was heading for the elevator.

"Figure it out," she said, staring at my shorts. "Or there will be consequences."

She pressed the Down button. The door opened.

"Are you *insane*??" I shouted. I really thought she might

be. Or maybe she'd seen some kind of secret code in the TV report? Something that set her off. A reason to get rid of me for good. Maybe I'd washed out as a trainee. Maybe I knew too much. At this point, anything was possible. Including getting blown to pieces, ass first.

As the elevator door slid shut, Meed gave me a little wave.

"Bye-bye, Doctor."

# CHAPTER 28

MEED STEPPED OUT of the cab at the corner of Clark and Madison, near St. Peter's.

It was as close as the driver could get. She handed him the fare and started walking up North LaSalle. Police barriers blocked traffic in every direction, and cops strolled around on both sides of the barricades, scanning the crowd and talking into their shoulder mics. Here and there, state police in camo stood in small clusters with semi-automatic rifles slung across their chests. A K-9 sergeant led an eager German shepherd on a bomb-sniffing patrol from one manhole cover to another.

On paper, the perimeter was tight. To Meed's trained eye, it was a sieve. Loose surveillance. Too many access corridors. Plenty of escape routes. Security seemed to improve as she strolled closer to the speaker's platform, but even there, she saw gaps and lapses. Listening to the radio chatter, she wondered if the local and state police were even using the same frequency.

The platform, now draped in colorful bunting, was placed directly across from City Hall, with its majestic columns.

Police guarded the entrances. Some of the media had set up in front of the iconic facade so the background would lend gravitas to their standups.

There was a controlled space for a small audience directly in front of the platform. Plainclothes agents funneled visitors through a portable metal-detection gate into an area of pavement filled with plastic folding chairs. The metal detector was a solid choke point, which Meed had no intention of testing. Because she was definitely carrying metal.

# CHAPTER 29

ELEVEN STORIES UP on the other side of the street, the sprawling City Hall rooftop garden was already starting to burst into life. The crabapple and hawthorn trees were beginning to bud, and the perennials and thick grasses were getting more lush with each warm spring day. "An urban oasis and an environmental masterpiece," just like the guidebooks said. Also, excellent cover.

At the edge of the roof, just outside the border of the vegetation, a lone sniper took his position overlooking the street, extending the barrel of his rifle over the low parapet. From there, he had a direct line of sight to the speaker's platform and the crowd surrounding it. The distance was around 250 feet. The scope was hardly necessary. He shifted his arms to get comfortable. The bulky CPD uniform was a loose fit on his lean frame, but he hadn't exactly had a choice of sizes. He had taken the first one he could get.

The uniform's original owner was lying just twenty feet away, concealed in a stand of tall grass, his bare limbs turning bluish-gray as his blood oozed into the fertile black garden soil.

# CHAPTER 30

*CHRIST!* THE SPARK on the fuse was snaking its way across the living room. I pulled and strained against the chains, as if that would make a difference. I was a lot stronger than I used to be, but I wasn't the Incredible Hulk. I tried tugging against the weight machine, thinking that if I could rock it, I might be able to flip it over. Then I remembered that it was bolted to the floor through iron plates. Solid as a rock.

I twisted to the side as far as I could and braced my feet against the edge of the treadmill, but I couldn't get any leverage. The treadmill wasn't bolted down, so it skidded when I pressed against it.

I looked back across the room. The spark was just ten feet away and starting to wind around behind me. I stared down at the padlock dangling in front of my chest. I could reach it with my hands, but there was no way I could budge it. Then something flickered in my brain. There must have been a reason Meed hooked the padlock in front instead of in back, out of reach. She wasn't that sloppy. She must have been giving me some kind of hint. Or some kind of hope.

I ran through the endless series of mantras she'd planted in my brain over the past five months. A lot of them sounded like they were translated from a different language. For some reason, the saying that came to me now was, "Become a master or be gone." I could hear the fuse fizzing around the base of the weight machine. I scanned the floor around me. That's when I saw it.

I kicked off my shoes and used my left foot to push down my right sock. When it was halfway down my foot, I shook it off. I stretched out my leg and rolled my bare heel over a tiny black object lying on the side of the treadmill. When it was close enough, I started to work it up between my toes, gripping like a chimpanzee. It was a thin piece of black metal, about two inches long. If I could manage to get it from my feet to my hands in time, I might have a chance.

# CHAPTER 31

MEED MOVED THROUGH the crowd, acting like a curious tourist, watching the cops and soldiers and security people, but trying not to make eye contact. She kept her hands out of her pockets and wore a pleasant expression. When other civilians looked at her, she smiled politely, like a true Midwesterner.

As she passed a thickset CPD officer, she heard his shoulder mic crackle with a two-number code. The officer quickly turned to face south and pounded a few junior officers on their shoulders and pointed.

"One minute!" he said, his voice gruff and tight. "One minute!"

Meed looked in the direction the officer was pointing and saw a stir in the crowd one block down. A CPD motorcycle cop rounded the corner from Washington onto LaSalle. A trio of black Suburbans followed right behind.

As she moved toward the inner perimeter, Meed saw a tall SWAT commander with his walkie-talkie pressed to his mouth. "Station 5, check," he muttered. There was no response. "Station 5, check," he repeated. Still nothing. He looked up to the roof of City Hall and saw his man in position, barrel protruding just as it should be. "Learn to use your radio, asshole," he muttered. Then he gave up and started to move his ground people into position. Meed stopped. She looked up, too. In an instant, she sensed why the sniper hadn't responded. And she knew what she needed to do.

The SWAT squad moved into position as the caravan rolled up. The motorcycle cop pulled to the side and let the three SUVs move slowly into a line alongside the speaker's platform.

In the center compartment of the middle vehicle, behind two inches of bulletproof glass, an assistant handed Abrafo Asare a neatly typed page with the day's remarks. He glanced over the five short paragraphs and slipped the paper into his jacket pocket. He looked through the window at the speaker's stand. Podium in place. Cordon of security. Local officials taking their seats. A Ghanaian flag had been placed to the left of the Stars and Stripes, as requested. A nod to his homeland.

Asare turned to admire City Hall, a solid granite rectangle that looks sturdy enough to withstand a hurricane. The building's massive columns cast deep shadows. It's no wonder Asare didn't notice the flicker of movement along the side of one of those columns. Nobody else did either.

There was a tap on the car window. Asare looked out to see his chief security officer reaching for the door handle. The massive car door swung open and the previously muffled sound of the crowd was suddenly full volume. Asare glanced at his assistant and turned on his full-wattage diplomat's smile.

"Let's do some good," he said. "Showtime."

# CHAPTER 32

MEED WAS OUT of practice. In her prime—maybe age 14—she could have made the free climb up the building in two minutes. Now it was taking her twice as long. She kept to the shadows on the dark side of the column in order to stay hidden from spectators below. Her arms ached. Her legs burned. Her fingers were raw from finding handholds on the stone. But the last stretch was a snap. The elaborate carving on the eleventh-floor corner offered an easy foothold for her final move. As Meed swung herself over the granite top rail, she found herself facing a disorienting maze of plants and grass— a foreign landscape for a city rooftop. She stayed low, skirting around the perimeter of the roof to the west-facing side. From below, she could hear the echo of the PA system from the speaker's platform, where a man was speaking in a smooth, friendly baritone.

"So, thank you, my friends," the man was saying, "for this very warm Chicago welcome, and for the support you've given to the pursuit of peace. . . ."

As she reached the corner, Meed saw the sniper in a crouch

below the wall, his cheek nestled against the stock of his flat-black rifle. He was totally focused—too focused to notice Meed moving quietly behind the vegetation. She saw him tighten his grip and adjust his eye against the scope. She saw his finger slide from the trigger guard to the trigger. *Now!*

Meed covered the short stretch between them in a split second. She kicked the long barrel into the air as the shot rang out, echoing against the opposite building. Shrill screams rose from the street below. Meed dropped hard onto the sniper's back, her elbow in his ribs. He rolled hard to the opposite side and pulled free, then sprang to his feet. When he lifted his head, Meed took a step back, stunned. In an instant, she recognized the sniper's face—still smooth and boyish. It had hardly changed in sixteen years.

*Rishi.*

He stared back at her, his expression quickly morphing from shock to recognition to fury. He unbuttoned the bulky police jacket and stripped down to his black T-shirt.

"Meed! Goddamn you!" he said. "This is not your business!"

Meed stayed cool, watching for his next move, knowing just how dangerous he was. "Does it pay well, Rishi?" she asked. "Is it worth it?"

Rishi moved back from the edge of the wall. "You should know they only pay for a body," he said with a sneer. Suddenly, there was a blade in his hand. "Maybe I can still provide one."

Meed slipped her hand into her jacket pocket and pulled out a knife of her own. The two former classmates circled each other slowly at the edge of a large rectangle of greenery, blocking out the shouts and sirens from below. Rishi lunged. The blade sliced the shoulder of Meed's jacket. She followed his momentum and kicked his right leg out from underneath him. Rishi landed hard on the stone roof as his knife flew into the greenery. In a flash, Meed was on top of him, knife raised, but in the next second, Rishi hooked her legs and flipped her over. His right hand grabbed her wrist, pinning her knife hand against the roof, while his left hand hooked around her throat. Meed gasped as her windpipe was crushed flat. She tried to twist her head and punch with her free hand, but Rishi's grip got tighter. Meed's vision started to cloud. Jagged flares appeared in her periphery. Her chest heaved. Her back arched violently. She could feel herself fading.

Losing. Dying. Rishi leaned forward, applying more force. Feeling Rishi's weight shift, Meed slipped one knee out from under his leg and brought it up hard into his crotch. For a split second, his grip on her throat relaxed. That was enough.

Meed shoved Rishi's head hard to the side and rolled with him until she was on top again, her knee in his solar plexus, her knife blade poking the skin over his jugular.

"You were always better with a gun than a knife," she gasped, her voice tight and pained.

"We all have our talents," Rishi replied in a harsh whisper. In spite of the knife at his throat and the knee in his gut, his face suddenly relaxed. He almost looked like a kid again.

"They've never stopped looking for you, Meed," he said. "Kamenev won't stop until you're dead."

"Then he should have made me the target," said Meed.

There was a loud bang as a metal door flew open on the other side of the roof, followed by heavy boot steps. Meed rolled to the side and crawled behind a stand of grass, leaving Rishi in the open as the cops rounded the corner. He sat up slowly as the officers shouted their commands: "Don't move! Lie flat! Arms out!"

From where she was hidden, Meed could see the section of wall where Rishi's rifle was still leaning. It was just five feet away. Suddenly Rishi jumped up and dashed toward the edge. He paused there and turned back toward Meed. Then he gave her an eerie smile.

"Stop! Freeze!" the lead officer shouted. Meed crouched back down, expecting to hear a volley of gunfire. Death by SWAT. But no shots came. The next sound she heard was the sickening crack of a body striking the street far below. As boot-steps rushed forward from the other side of the roof, Meed faded into the garden. In seconds, she was gone.

# CHAPTER 33

HOURS LATER, MEED'S thighs were trembling and the muscles in her lower back were threatening to spasm. She had spent the long afternoon braced in a shadow of one of the building's side columns, waiting for the excitement to fade. It was after dark when she made her final descent, a few inches at a time. By the time she dropped the last few feet to the sidewalk, pedestrians hardly noticed. The security cordons were gone. The only remaining flashing lights reflected from the messy suicide scene at the front of the building.

As she walked back through the city, Meed kept her eyes down, her head low.

She knew Rishi had told her the truth. A save like this had been a huge risk. What if it had all been a lure? What if there were other assassins on other rooftops, aiming down at her? She tugged her beret tight over her hair and walked west, then south again. Twenty minutes later, when she was certain she wasn't being tailed, she headed for home.

The moment she walked out of the elevator into the loft, she saw a pile of chains lying loose across the workout bench.

She looked to the right. The professor was enjoying a protein shake in the kitchen, his feet up on the counter. As soon as he saw Meed, he lifted his hand triumphantly.

He was holding a hairpin.

"Lose something?" he asked with a self-satisfied grin. So proud of himself.

"I shouldn't have made it so obvious," said Meed. The professor's cheer faded a little. He held up the small cake of clay, with a hole where the fuse had been pulled out.

"And this . . ." he said, "this isn't really C-4, is it?"

"Silly Putty," said Meed. "The color should have been a giveaway." She pulled off her beret and let her copper curls loose. "What did they teach you at those Mensa meetings anyway?"

Meed was exhausted. But the events of the day had reminded her that she could not relax. Especially not now. And neither could Doctor Savage. She could see that he was learning, getting more resourceful and creative every day. More independent. But there were bigger challenges ahead. She had to stop going easy on him.

# CHAPTER 34

*Eastern Russia*
*14 Years Ago*

THE THIN COPPER coin was no match for concentrated nitric acid.

As soon as Irina let the disk drop into the beaker, the solution started to foam and bubble. Within seconds, all that was left of the metal was a cloudy green mist. At the next lab station over, Meed was working with magnesium, causing a bubbling hiss and a burst of orange vapor.

All along the rows of black-topped tables, the students tested their caustic mixtures on an assortment of materials—cloth, metal, plastic, wood—and watched with fascination as the powerful corrosives did their work. Ilya Lunik, the bearded instructor, paced along the tables, mentally scoring the teams on accuracy and laboratory technique.

Lunik, a fastidious man in his late sixties, was a master chemist, one of the most brilliant of his generation. His coursework included formulas he had perfected years ago for the Russian government. He still kept those formulas in his head. During the Cold War, he had also dabbled in sedatives and poisons.

But acids were his specialty, and his research had been widely respected in the darkest corners of the Soviet Union.

There had been no patents for his work, of course. No inventor's royalties or prestigious medals. Only personal pride. And the satisfaction of passing his knowledge on to those who could put it to productive use. He walked to the chalkboard and started scrawling a complex chemical diagram.

For once, Irina and Meed were not the first team to finish their assignments.

While the other students recorded their observations diligently in lab notebooks, the dark-haired girl and her partner were deviously searching for other items to destroy. A pencil eraser in hydrochloric acid. A strand of hair in sulfuric acid. A fingernail clipping in hydrobromic acid. Lunik had just finished his work on the chalkboard when he heard the room erupt in excitement. One of Irina's solutions had produced a thick white cloud, and the other students had abandoned their stations to observe the spectacle.

"Irina!" shouted Lunik from the front of the room. "Stick to the protocol!"

As soon as Lunik turned back toward the chalkboard, Irina thrust her hand at him in a rude gesture. The thick vapor blocked her view of a beaker on a tall stand. As she pulled her hand back, she accidentally knocked against the support. The beaker fell and crashed onto the lab table. The contents spattered on a bare patch of Irina's right arm just above her rubber glove. Instantly, her flesh reddened and bubbled. Irina fell to the floor, slapping her other gloved hand over the wound. She gritted her teeth, trying not to scream.

Lunik whipped around, his chalk crumbling against the board. He rushed to Irina's side, bent over her—and did nothing. As she writhed and twitched on the linoleum floor, Lunik looked down and said just three words to the class.

"Don't move. Observe."

This would be an object lesson, and a powerful one. The students were frozen in place. All except one. Meed lunged toward a side table and grabbed a gallon of distilled water. Lunik held a hand up to block her.

"No!" he said firmly.

Meed pushed past him. She uncapped the container and dropped to her knees at Irina's side, then poured the clear water in a torrent over Irina's forearm, which was now bright scarlet with ugly white patches. Irina arched and moaned with pain. The other students jumped back as the water splashed and seeped across the floor, afraid that the mixture might dissolve the soles of their shoes.

"Meed!" shouted Lunik, furious and red-faced. "Mistakes must be paid for!"

Meed set the water jug down and stood up. She grabbed a flask of hydrochloric acid from the lab table. She grabbed Lunik's collar and held the flask over his head.

"Are you willing to pay for yours?" she asked.

Lunik stepped backward, shocked into silence. In his career, he had dealt with Kremlin bosses, the KGB, and professional torturers. All of them paled beside this copper-haired girl.

She was barely sixteen. But she was truly terrifying.

# CHAPTER 35

*Chicago*

"FIVE MORE! RIGHT now! Don't quit!" I was doing hundred-pound leg presses with Meed shouting into my ear. Her heavy metal playlist blasted from the ceiling speakers. Top volume. It was hard-core, so loud that it felt like it was actually penetrating my organs. Screams. Aggression. Raw fury. That's what it took to get me through my two-a-day workouts, which had gotten more and more intense. I gritted my teeth and kept working the weight machine. I felt like a machine myself. My muscles were burning, almost exhausted. But Meed would not let up. She punched my shoulder—hard.

"That last rep was half-assed!" she shouted. "Give me an extra!"

I was into the fifth superset of my morning session. With my last rep, I was finished with legs, moving on to arms and back. I was panting, sweating, aching. I used to think a set of tennis was a solid workout. I had no idea. "Toy exercise," Meed called it. "Wimpy and soft." My soft life was definitely over. I'd almost forgotten what that life was like.

Now my world was a blur of preacher curls, lying triceps

extensions, cable pulls, dead lifts, and hang power snatches. I jumped rope like a maniac and swung fifty-pound kettle-bells. I balanced on a tilt board while holding sandbags in each hand. I was burning 400 calories an hour and replacing them with mass-gain supplements. I weighed myself religiously every morning, like a fighter in training. I was now up to 195. A twenty-pound gain in six months. All muscle. A whole new me.

"Let's go, Doctor!" Meed yelled. "Let out your inner savage!" I knew she liked that joke. But it wasn't a joke, not really. She was bringing out a side of me I'd never seen. Never *wanted* to see. She was turning me into her own personal monster. And I still didn't know why. No point in asking. Always the wrong question.

As I rested for a moment on the seat of the universal, I saw Meed glance up at the screen over the workout space. The TV was set to CNN, as usual. With Meed, it was all news, all the time. I looked up to see what was catching her eye.

At the start of a new report, a photo of a blue-eyed baby had popped up on a panel to the left of the anchor's head. Meed cut the music. The sudden silence left my ears ringing.

"Turn up the TV," she said.

I found the remote and clicked off the Mute button just as the anchor got into the meat of the story. His eyebrows were furrowed. His tone was concerned.

*. . . Evan Grey, eight months old, the only son of MacArthur Fellow Devon Grey and his wife, research physicist Anna Grey, has disappeared from his parents' remote campsite near Bend, Oregon. According to park rangers, the infant was napping in a portable playpen at the edge of a clearing in broad daylight yesterday, with*

*his parents nearby. The couple noticed him missing at approximately 2 p.m. and immediately contacted the local ranger station. Other campers and local residents of the remote mountain community have joined the search, while the parents are begging the public for any information about their missing child.*

The screen cut to a shot of the two young parents. They looked drained and scared. The mom spoke up, looking into the camera. Her voice was shaking. Her eyes were red.

*If you know anything about where our baby is . . . if you have our baby . . . we just, we just want him back. We need him back. We'll do anything. Please! Please contact us.*

Her voice trailed off at the end, and her husband wrapped his arms around her. When the report cut back to the anchor desk, there was an 800 number in bright red across the bottom of the screen. The anchor wrapped up the story:

*Anybody with information on the whereabouts of young Evan Grey, please call this anonymous toll-free tip line. For now, authorities are looking into all possibilities, including the chance that the baby may have been the victim of a rogue bear.*

And then it was over. The next story was about a flood in Missouri. Meed grabbed the remote and muted the TV.

"Bear, my ass," she said.

"It's possible, right?" I replied.

Meed pounded her fist on the weight rack. "Do you have any idea how many kids are taken in the world every year?"

"Thousands?" I guessed. I thought that might be too high.

"Eight *million*," said Meed. Her jaw was tense. It seemed like she was trying to keep herself under control. "In most countries, nothing happens without payoffs to the right people. No money, no investigation. After a year or so, the leads dry up, the case goes cold, the family moves on. The kid is just gone. Some of them pop up on sex-trafficking sites. Some of them get traded or sold. Many just vanish into thin air."

"Okay," I said. "But Oregon isn't some backwater country. Seems like they're on it, full force. They'll find him."

As usual, I could tell that Meed knew more than she was telling.

"Don't get your hopes up," she said. "That's a very valuable child."

# CHAPTER 36

IT WAS 3 a.m. But Meed wasn't even aware of the time. She sat alone in front of a crowded desk, scanning the screens in front of her. From her secure room behind the kitchen, she had a complete view of the entire loft. Cameras captured every angle with overlapping fields of coverage. No blind spots. With one click, she could shift to views of the elevator interior, the entrance hallway below, or the exit to the street.

One full screen was dedicated to the professor's cell, with a shot from a wide-angle lens mounted in the ceiling. Dr. Savage was asleep now under a thin blanket, exhausted from the day's workouts. He'd been down since 10 p.m. The professor's schedule called for a solid eight hours of rest. Not Meed's. Even after a hard day, her mind buzzed with activity. She'd always been a poor sleeper.

Meed leaned forward in her Aeron chair, focused now on a large computer screen in the center of the console. This was the heart of the system, with multiple windows displaying a constant flow of reports from every region of the globe. Custom software scanned for designated keywords and images, and elegant hacks opened the most secure government files. Meed hadn't cracked everything—not yet—but her reach was wide and deep. And the whole picture was becoming clearer.

Her fingers danced over the computer keyboard, bringing up image after image on the screen in front of her—scrapes from news sites, police investigations, Amber Alerts, and the darkest corners of the dark web. The reports and data scrolled by in dozens of languages. Meed tapped from one window to the next with a flick of her right middle finger, translating in her head as she went, report after report, headline after headline.

### INFANT MISSING FROM NEW DELHI SCIENCE COMPOUND

### YEAR-OLD SON OF FRENCH TECH MOGUL DISAPPEARS DURING CRUISE

### NORTH KOREAN CELLIST HOLDS OUT HOPE FOR LOST BABY

The reports and stories were spread over years and continents, too isolated and random to be connected. Some incidents, especially those from China and the Arabian Peninsula, had never been made public. The files started with blurry microfiche images, decades old, and accelerated through the turn of the millennium, with a spike over the past ten years. Babies with superior genes. Taken without a trace before fourteen months. All resulting in dead-end investigations.

The flickers on the screen reflected on Meed's face. She froze on a recent picture—the blue-eyed baby stolen from the Oregon campsite just thirty-six hours earlier. No blood. No body. No leads. No trail. Same pattern. Law enforcement had no clue how a baby could simply evaporate without leaving a shred of evidence. It seemed impossible. But it wasn't. It happened all the time.

After an hour in front of the screens, Meed pushed away from the console and flopped down onto the neat single bed against the opposite wall. Her gaze settled on the surveillance screen showing Dr. Savage in his cot. In fact, his cell was just a few feet away. If it weren't for five layers of cement, soundproofing foam, and tempered steel, she could have reached out and touched him.

Meed stared at the professor as he shifted and turned under his blanket. His physical progress had been impressive. His genes were even stronger than she'd hoped. But mentally, he still needed toughening. He wasn't nearly ready for what needed to be done.

Meed still didn't feel like sleeping, but she was determined to try. She wrapped herself around her pillow and forced herself to close her eyes.

# CHAPTER 37

*Eastern Russia*
*13 Years Ago*

THE STUDENTS STOOD in a circle, arms at their sides, eyeing each other nervously. The entire faculty sat on an elevated platform on the far side of the classroom, talking among themselves in a low murmur. Headmaster Kamenev sat at the center in a high-backed chair, saying nothing. Meed had heard that he always took a special interest in this particular final. His presence added a whole new layer of tension.

Like everybody else, Meed needed to pass this test to move on to the next level of training. And this was one course nobody wanted to repeat. It was mental agony. The preparation had consumed days and nights for weeks. The drills had been exhausting, and Meed's brain felt close to a meltdown. But in ten minutes, one way or the other, it would be over. Kamenev shifted in his chair. The conversation from the faculty trailed off. Then the headmaster waved his hand toward the circle of students.

"Begin," he called out. "And watch your words!" A few chuckles from the teachers, but not from the students. For them, this was dead serious.

Meed had drawn first position. She stepped to the center of the circle, chin up, projecting confidence, as if daring her classmates to do their worst. As her eyes moved around the circle, a tall Hispanic girl took a step forward to face her.

"*Nepovjerenje je majka sigurnosti!*" the girl said.

The language was Croatian. Not Meed's strongest. She knew that she had to replicate the phrase exactly. No hesitation. No flaws. No hints that she had not spoken the language from birth. That was the only way to pass.

"*Nepovjerenje je majka sigurnosti,*" Meed repeated. Out of the corner of her eye, she could see the language teachers nodding. Her pronunciation was impeccable.

She knew it. And so did they.

"Translation," the Hispanic girl said. Part two of the challenge. This was harder. Several Croat nouns sounded very close to Serbian. Meed cleared her throat and spoke out clearly, praying that she was making the right choice.

"*Distrust is the mother of safety,*" she said.

Meed got it right. She knew it the moment the Hispanic girl lowered her eyes. As she stepped back into the circle, a boy with fair skin and blond hair stepped forward.

"*Ferī bewīha wisīti'īnikuwanī labī yihonalī,*" he called out.

The boy's Scandinavian looks were a distraction, but Meed wasn't fooled. The language was Amharic, from the horn of Africa.

"*Ferī bewīha wisīti'īnikuwanī labī yihonalī,*" Meed parroted back.

"Translation," the blond boy said.

"*A coward will sweat even in water,*" said Meed.

With that answer, her confidence grew. One after another, her classmates stepped up to challenge her, faster and faster.

Time after time, she took in the phrase, then adjusted her jaw, her tongue, her lips, her throat, to deliver it perfectly, like a native speaker. After Croatian and Amharic, there was Urdu. Then German. The final challenge was from Irina.

*"Ek veit einn at aldrei deyr domur um dauoan hvern."*

It was Norwegian. Obscure and lyrical. To the rest of the room, the pronunciation sounded impossible. But Meed was fond of ancient poems. *The Aeneid. Beowulf.* And even the Old Norse *Hávamál,* where Irina had found the quote. Meed repeated the phrase syllable for syllable, careful to distinguish her Norwegian inflection from Swedish.

"Translation," said Irina.

Meed looked at her with a triumphant expression.

*"I know one thing that never dies—the dead man's reputation."*

Irina stepped back. That made five. All that was required. Meed was sure she had passed. She turned to take her place again in the circle. Then Kamenev stood up. Meed froze in place. The headmaster looked directly at her.

"One more, if you don't mind," he said.

Meed turned to face him. She straightened her back and took a deep breath. She nodded once.

Kamenev puffed out his chest, clearly relishing the moment. He rubbed his chin, considering his options. Meed clenched and unclenched her fists as the seconds ticked by. Kamenev cleared his throat, then spoke out, his diction crisp and precise.

*"Tantum est fortis superesse!"*

The phrase was Latin. That much was obvious. But Latin was a dead language, rarely spoken outside the walls of Roman churches. The pronunciation could be studied only by listening to recordings of Papal letters. Not many students went to that length. But not many students were as thorough as Meed.

*"Tantum est fortis superesse!"* she repeated forcefully. Kamenev turned to his language faculty. Heads nodded. Meed's pronunciation would impress a Vatican cardinal.

"Translation!" Kamenev called out.

Meed knew the phrase was a message to the class—and to her especially. She stared straight at the headmaster and delivered the answer in a calm, clear voice.

*"Only the strong survive."*

# CHAPTER 38

*Chicago*

"PROTECT YOUR DAMNED queen!"

Meed was right. I was getting careless. Maybe because we had been playing for five hours. Until I became a kidnapping victim, I had thought three-dimensional chess existed only in old *Star Trek* episodes, but it turned out it was a real thing. And Meed was a master.

Night after night, she brought out the chess set. It looked expensive—three teak playing boards mounted one above the other on a wrought-iron stand, with hand-carved playing pieces. Keeping track of three levels simultaneously took some getting used to.

"Focus," Meed told me. "You can do it."

And it turned out I could. Even though I'd never played chess before. I still didn't know if Meed was sneaking brain-altering chemicals into my protein shakes and injections, but I was starting to notice that my logic skills were sharper— sometimes almost magical. I could now solve a Rubik's Cube in four seconds. I could memorize playing cards so easily that I'd be banned from a casino. But all that added brain power couldn't help me figure out what was really going on, or what I was being trained for. In a lot of ways, I was still totally in the dark.

Chess was Meed's obsession. She loved the planning, the strategy, the practice of thinking two or three moves ahead. She was a fierce player and a demanding teacher. She made me more aggressive. Made me concentrate harder. She said it was good for my fluid reasoning and processing speed. Also, it was the only time when she actually answered anything I asked. As long as the topic was chess.

"Best player?" I asked.

"Carlsen."

"Better to give up a bishop or a knight?"

"Knight."

"Who taught you the game?"

"I learned at school."

"Where was that?"

Meed didn't even look up. Nice try.

"Your move, Doctor."

I'd started that game with the French Defense. It was a beginner's ploy, and Meed saw right through it. She'd anticipated every move and had embarrassed me up and down the boards.

But now that I'd managed to shield my queen on the top level, I could actually see an opening. In two more moves, I could make it happen. But only if Meed blinked. I shifted my knight and held my breath. Meed stared at the board for a full minute, then countered with her bishop. My heart started racing. I slid my rook forward two squares and looked up. "Check," I said.

I could hardly believe the word was coming out of my

mouth. Meed tilted her head and looked across all three boards, as if she couldn't believe it either. Then she tipped her king onto its side and reached across the table to shake my hand.

"Nicely done, Doctor," she said. I could see that she was annoyed—but also impressed. Part of her liked that I beat her. I could tell. So I decided to push my luck.

As our hands met, I slid two fingers under the cuff of her right sleeve. When she pulled back, I slid out the throwing knife she had hidden there. Before she could react, I held the knife up and whipped it at the man-shaped target across the room. It stuck hard in the left upper chest. Kill shot. My first.

I could tell that Meed liked that even better.

# CHAPTER 39

THE NEXT MORNING, I woke up with a strange voice in my head. Female. Chirpy. A bit nasal.

As I came out of my sleep fog, I realized that I had headphones over my ears. I didn't remember putting them on. What I was hearing was a series of repeated phrases about Chinese etiquette. When I blinked my eyes open, Meed was standing over me. She lifted the earphones away from my ears and asked me a question. In Mandarin. Without thinking, I gave her the answer. Also in Mandarin. My voice was doing things I didn't know it could do, making sounds I didn't know it could make.

I'd never studied Mandarin in my life, partly because everybody said it was the hardest language on earth to learn. But now, somehow, I could not only understand it, but *speak* it. How was that possible? I'd always been a quick learner, but now my brain was doing things that seemed way beyond reality. Freakish. I was absorbing information as I never had before, sometimes without even knowing it.

I pulled the headphones off. They were connected to an old-school disc player lying on my blanket. It looked like something Radio Shack might have sold thirty years ago.

"What the hell is this?" I asked. "What am I listening to?"

"I don't have time to explain everything," said Meed. "Some things I can teach you. Other things you need to learn for yourself, just like I did." She held up a pile of worn discs with handwritten labels. "You can absorb a lot during the REM stage. Why waste it?"

I tossed the headphones onto the blanket. I rubbed my eyes and swung my legs out from under the covers. This was crazy. Now she was even invading my dreams.

"What *else* have I learned in my sleep?" I asked.

"Wouldn't you like to know," said Meed.

I reached for my workout clothes at the end of the bed. "Don't bother with those," she said. "Just leave your shorts on."

"What? Why?" I asked. Wake. Health shake. Workout. That was the morning routine. I hated it, but I'd gotten used to it. I got nervous whenever she broke the pattern.

"Follow me," she said.

I pushed the blanket aside and put my feet on the floor. I got a tingle in my belly and I started to sweat. Meed opened my cell door.

"You know I hate surprises," I said.

"You really need to be more flexible," she replied.

She led the way through the kitchen, past the utility closet, and around a corner to a door that led to a back staircase. At least that's what I always assumed. The door had a heavy-duty alarm bar across the center. A small window with wire mesh showed a dim hallway on the other side. But when Meed disarmed the alarm and pushed the door open, I realized that the view of the hallway went along for the ride. It was simply an image set into the window frame. A trompe l'oeil. An illusion. What was behind the door wasn't a hallway at all.

It was a gigantic swimming pool.

# CHAPTER 40

"YOU HAVE *GOT* to be shitting me," I mumbled. The door closed behind us. We were standing in a sealed room with no windows. Just white brick walls and a narrow tile ledge around the edge of the pool. It was competition length, with three lanes. The bottom and sides were painted deep blue. A huge TV screen hung from a metal beam across the ceiling. I could hear the patter from a morning news team echoing off the walls.

As I took it all in, my stomach churned. It wasn't just the scent of the chlorine. It was pure, primal fear. Taking a dip in an ice bath was bad enough, but this was something else. I was absolutely terrified of pools. And lakes. And oceans. Because I'd never learned how to swim. While other kids were at summer camp, I was digging up artifacts in New Mexico. I didn't know what Meed had in mind, but it was going to take a shock wand to get me into that water.

"Have a seat," she said. She pointed to a narrow wood bench along the wall. Underneath was a plastic bin.

"What are we doing here?" I asked. I was trying not to

sound scared, but my voice was pinched and thin. The air in the room was warm and thick, almost tropical. But now I was shivering all over.

"We're testing your resolve," said Meed. "Among other things."

When we reached the bench, she pushed me down by the shoulders. Then she reached under and lifted the lid on the bin. I felt something being wrapped around my ankles. When I looked down, my feet were strapped together with thick nylon straps connected to lead weights.

"No!" I shouted. "Don't do this! I'll *sink*!"

Meed looked me right in the eyes. "That's correct," she said. "What happens after that depends on you."

My head was spinning. My mouth went dry. I pressed my back up against the tile, as if I thought I could push myself through it.

"Up we go, Doctor," said Meed, tugging on my wrists. When she pulled me to my feet, I was hobbled and off balance. She nudged me toward the pool. I tried to pull back.

"Meed!" I shouted. "Please! I can't swim!"

"I know," she said. "That's a serious gap in your education."

She wrapped her arms around my chest and swung me hard. I felt my feet fly out from under me. The next second I was in the water, dropping to the bottom. Ten feet down.

I thrashed my arms and tried to move my legs, but it felt like my feet were tied to a bowling ball. I started to panic. I flexed my knees and managed to press off the bottom, kicking like a wounded porpoise. I muscled my way to the surface and gasped for air. Meed was standing at the edge of the pool.

"Ten laps, Doctor!" she called out.

What was she *talking* about?? I threw my head back and screamed.

"I'm going to *die* in here!"

"After all I've done for you?" Meed called back. "That would be really inconsiderate."

The lead weight was pulling me down again. My head went under. My toes touched the bottom. My cheeks puffed out. My lungs burned. I could feel my brain starting to blur. For a split second, I wondered what it would be like to just open my mouth, breathe in, and end this insanity once and for all. How long would it take to drown? Would it hurt? Could it be any worse than this?

Then my body took over. I pushed off against the bottom again and shot back to the surface. I leveled my chest in the water and started to kick my legs out behind me. My feet were like a single unit, so I had to generate all the torque from my hips and knees, until I felt myself moving forward through the water. My vision narrowed and my brain went numb. I was conscious of the splashes behind me, the rhythm of my arms in front, and my head turning to breathe after each stroke. The weight on my ankles was still there, but now it felt like part of me. I stopped treating it like an obstacle and started using it as a lever to propel myself. Faster and faster.

I looked up and saw the end of the pool. Four yards away. Now *three*! I could have grabbed the ledge, held on, and hauled myself out. That's what any normal human being would have done. But I wasn't normal. Not anymore. I swung my feet against the pool wall and pushed off in the other direction.

One lap down. Nine to go.

# CHAPTER 41

MEED PACED CASUALLY along the edge of the pool. She was ready to make a rescue dive if necessary. She was even ready to perform CPR if it came to that. She was fully certified. But so far, she was impressed with the professor's adaptability. It looked like she wouldn't even have to get wet.

On the TV overhead, the hard-news block was over, and a young, doe-eyed culture reporter was talking about a gallery opening. Meed looked up.

*The event of the week is tonight's opening of the Armis Gallery in Pilsen, one of the city's trendiest creative centers. The exhibits include paintings and sculpture from American and European artists. Part of the admission for tonight's benefit opening will go to support arts programs in Chicago schools.*

As the reporter spoke, prerecorded footage showed the stylish gallery owner giving her a tour of the artwork on display in the sun-flooded space. The collection was first-rate. But it was the owner who caught Meed's attention. Handsome.

Impeccably groomed. Expensively tailored. With shockingly white teeth.

Meed felt a jolt deep in her gut. She never forgot a face. And certainly not this one. The gallery owner rested one hand lightly on the young reporter's shoulder as she delivered her wrap-up to the camera.

*"Join us tonight for great art, and a great cause."* The camera moved in for her close-up. *"For Chicago's Art Beat, this is Amy-Anne Roberts."* With that, the show cut back to the studio for a cooking demo.

Meed walked to the far end of the pool and knelt down to meet the professor after his last lap. He had done well. Even better than she expected. It occurred to her that she might have gone too light on the ankle weights. Dr. Savage thrashed his way to the edge. He was breathing heavily, too exhausted to speak. But Meed saw fierce pride and determination in his eyes. Which is exactly what she was looking for.

"Not bad, Doctor," she said. "Now climb out before you grow gills."

# CHAPTER 42

MEED HAD CHECKED her computer a dozen times during the day, waiting for the gallery segment to be posted on the Channel 7 website. Now, at 6 p.m., the link had finally appeared. She sat down at her console and got to work. Better late than never.

She stopped on a two shot of the reporter and the owner. She zoomed in on the face with the impossible smile and froze the frame. He might have had a lift or two since she saw him last, but it was first-rate work. Probably Mexico or Brazil.

With another click, she started running her facial recognition program. The software scanned through hundreds of documents and images a second, until it locked onto a series of matches. Over the past twenty years, that smile had been all over the world—anywhere death was profitable.

The man was a consummate chameleon, sometimes appearing in a business suit, sometimes a tunic or a Pashtun robe. He was frequently standing or sitting in the background of grainy group photos taken with telephoto lenses. In most of those pictures, weapons were in the foreground. Rifle crates, missile launchers, chemical cannisters. Some of the reports linked to images of carnage—bomb craters, leveled buildings, burned-out vehicles, charred corpses.

In more recent shots, the same bright smile stood out at a restaurant opening in Morocco and a ribbon cutting at a bank in Belize. Meed realized that both were convenient fronts for arms dealing. But nothing as highbrow as a big-city art gallery. Maybe the smiling man had taste. Or maybe he was just looking for a more elegant place to launder his blood money.

Meed took a deep breath. She had choices to make.

She pulled a small drawer out from under her console. She ran her fingers over the shiny cylinders inside and made an important selection.

Flamingo Pink would be perfect.

# CHAPTER 43

I WAS JUST finishing up my final bench-press routine when I saw Meed's door open. My arms still ached from the pool torture that morning, but I knew I'd catch hell if I didn't stick with the program. There was no time off. Even though Meed had been in and out of her room all day long, I could always feel her eyes on me.

When she stepped down into the kitchen, I wasn't even sure it was her. For one thing, the curls were gone. Now she had wavy black hair, parted in the middle. She was wearing a tight dress and a blue velvet jacket. And high heels. That was a first. I'd never seen her in anything but crew socks and sneakers. But the biggest change was her face. It looked like the face of a *Vogue* model. Her eyelids were blue and her lips were bright pink. Her cheeks and forehead sparkled with some kind of glitter. She looked spectacular, in a whole new way.

"Wow!" I said. "Is it prom night??"

Meed unlocked one of the kitchen drawers and put a small container in her purse.

"Something like that," she said. "And sorry, I already have a date."

"You look...like somebody else," I said.

"How do you know this isn't the real me?" she replied.

She had a point. Every time I thought I had something figured out in Meed World, something else happened to turn it upside down. I already knew her name was made up. Maybe the copper curls were fake, too. I wondered what else she wasn't telling me—or just plain lying about?

"I'll be out for a few hours," she said.

I suddenly got a sting in my gut. For a second, I was afraid she was going to chain me up again. Instead, she opened a cabinet and pulled out a bunch of audio discs. She put them in a little stack on the counter. Then she tapped them with her fingernail.

"Learn something new while I'm gone," she said.

"Like what?" I asked.

She walked to the elevator and pressed the button.

"Your choice," she said. "Surprise me."

# CHAPTER 44

THE CROWD ON the sidewalk outside the gallery was a mix of rich patrons and local bohemians, heavy on the under-thirty side. More vapers than smokers. Several sleek town cars idled at the curb. The exterior of the gallery was laced with thousands of tiny white lights. A well-curated music mix flowed out from the open door, along with the clink of glassware and the hum of lively conversation.

It had been a while since Meed had worn heels this tall or a dress this fitted.

But after a quick scan of the other guests, she saw that she'd blend right in. There was a small bottleneck at the entrance as a young hostess took entry donations with her iPhone card reader. When it was Meed's turn, she reached into her small evening purse and pulled out ten crisp hundred-dollar bills.

"I hope you don't mind a donation in cash," she said with a smile.

The hostess blinked as if she'd been handed wampum. But she recovered graciously and slid the money into a drawer under her hostess podium. "Would you like a name tag?" she asked.

"I think I'll stay anonymous," said Meed. She added a charming wink.

The main hall of the gallery was broken up by curved white partitions. The floor was some kind of exotic hardwood. The paintings and sculptures were illuminated with pin spotlights, while the rest of the space was bathed in amber light, the kind of glow that made everybody look their best. Beautiful people, beautifully lit.

The first person Meed recognized was Amy-Anne Roberts, the peppy arts reporter from TV. She was stick-thin, wearing a shimmery silver dress and a quirky tiara. She looked even younger than she did on TV, and her eyes looked even bigger. Meed turned to the right and saw another woman heading her way. She was carrying a neat stack of paper at waist level.

"Welcome to Armis," she said. "Would you like a guide sheet?"

She was a tall blonde in an elegant blue suit, as formal as a uniform. Meed looked up, started to smile, and instantly froze.

It was Annika.

Meed hadn't seen her school instructor for almost twenty years. One day, Annika had been leading the class—the next day she was gone. No explanation. And now, here she was.

"Descriptions and prices," said Annika, holding out an elegantly printed sheet. "Let me know what interests you, and I'll introduce you to the artist."

Meed held her breath and looked down as she took the cream-colored paper. She nodded, but said nothing. Annika moved on casually to the next guest. Meed turned and walked off in the opposite direction, trying not to flinch. Work the wardrobe, she told herself. Trust the illusion. Be the new you.

"Champagne?"

A young man paused in front of her, his tray filled with crystal flutes. "Thank you so much," said Meed, picking up a glass. It was exactly what she needed. The server smiled and moved away. Meed took a small sip and surveyed the room.

In a far corner of the gallery, the man with perfect teeth was chatting with an elegantly dressed couple in front of a huge canvas. He was about the same distance from her now that he had been when she first saw him on Kamenev's balcony. Even then, her intuition had told her that he had a dark soul. Now she knew just how dark.

The artwork the owner was showing off was bare white, except for a few oddly placed orange triangles near the center. To Meed, it appeared that he might have misjudged the couple's interest, because they quickly excused themselves and moved toward a grouping of more conservative works. For an awkward moment, the owner was left alone, sipping his red wine. Meed moved in quickly, placing her shoulder just inches from his as she faced the spare abstract on the wall.

"Derivative of Malevich, don't you think?" said Meed.

The owner turned and took a moment to appraise Meed's profile. Then he glanced from side to side and leaned toward her in a playful whisper, his lips almost touching her ear.

"I thought the same," he said. "But the artist draws a crowd."

"Well," said Meed, staring at the canvas, "it's too big for my apartment anyway."

"You live in Chicago?" asked the owner.

Not a pickup line, exactly. Just an opening move. Smooth, thought Meed. She expected nothing less. She took another slow sip from her glass.

"New York," she said. "Just visiting."

"Gregor Mason," said the owner, turning to extend his hand.

Meed turned toward him and returned his grip with a delicate squeeze of her fingers. When she looked into his face, her mind flashed on a review of his handiwork around the world. Terror. Destruction. Death.

"Belinda," said Meed. "Belinda Carlisle."

The owner's eyes crinkled. "Wait," he said. "Belinda Carlisle? As in . . . ?"

"The Go-Go's," said Meed with a wry smile, as if she'd made this explanation a thousand times before. "Yes. Blame my parents. Big fans." Meed leaned in toward him, taking in a whiff of his smokey cologne. "But trust me—I can't sing a note."

Mason smiled. Those teeth. Almost blinding. Meed let the guide sheet slip from her hand. It floated to the floor near her host's feet.

"Oh, *no*!" said Meed, looking down in playful alarm. "Now I won't know what anything costs!"

"Allow me," said the owner with a gracious smile. Meed knew he was charmed.

And that made him careless.

As he bent forward, Meed slipped her hand into her pocket. She put the toe of her shoe on the paper so that it took her host an extra half second to tug it free. In that interval, Meed dropped a tiny tablet into his wineglass, where it instantly dissolved.

"We need to get you a new one," he said as he straightened up, frowning at the scuff mark in the corner of his pricey matte paper. "Annika!" he called out. She was standing near a metal sculpture on the other side of the room. At the sound of her name, she turned and headed over.

"Sorry," said Meed. "Would you mind?" She handed her host her glass and pointed toward the ladies' room. "Too much bubbly."

"Of course," he said with a slight bow. Meed headed for the restroom, waited for the crowd to obscure the owner's view, then detoured into the back hallway that led to the kitchen. A catering van was backed up to the open door. Meed slipped out into the loading zone and headed through a narrow alley to a side street. In minutes, she was too far away to hear the screams. She knew that by now, the gallery owner would be vomiting blood all over his expensive floor.

She only wished she could have been there to see it.

# CHAPTER 45

"HEY THERE! *YOU!* You...are *stunning*!"

As Meed crossed the street a few blocks from the gallery, a frat boy in a Bulls T-shirt was hanging out the window of an Uber. She could hear the slurring in his voice. He was a harmless mess, just cocky and drunk and acting out for his buddies in the back seat. Meed stared straight ahead and kept up her pace as she reached the curb and headed down a side street.

She wanted to avoid crowds, but she needed the fresh air. And time to think. Her heart was still racing. She knew that her gallery mission had been dangerous, that it might attract attention in all the wrong places. Just like her encounter with Rishi. But she was tired of being afraid, tired of doing nothing. She'd spent more than ten years in hiding, pretending to be somebody she wasn't. More than a decade on her own, just watching the evil in the world grow, knowing where a lot of it was being sown. Mostly she felt helpless against it. But now she had to take action—just *had* to. No matter how risky it was for her. If they were coming for her, she had decided, let them come.

Meed tried to focus her mind on Dr. Savage. Her work with him was nearly done, she told herself. And then everything would change. At least that's what she was counting on. He was her secret weapon. He just didn't know it yet.

She rounded the last corner toward home and looked both ways before slipping through the back entrance. As soon as she stepped into the elevator, she pulled off her wig and unpinned her hair, shaking her copper curls loose. Then she kicked off her heels and stood in stockinged feet on the bare metal floor, wriggling her aching toes for the first time in hours. She couldn't wait to wipe her face clean—to wipe the whole evening off. The makeup felt sticky on her skin and the glitter was starting to itch. She pressed the Up button.

When the door to the loft slid open, Meed stepped out— then stopped. The loft echoed with music. *Live* music. It was coming from the living area. From Dr. Savage. He was sitting at the piano, his back to her, working the Steinway with so much concentration that he hadn't even heard her arrive. He was playing Rachmaninoff, and his technique was brilliant. Meed felt a pang in her stomach, and then a blind rage rose up inside her.

She dropped her heels and wig on the floor and walked over to the piano. The professor was on the second movement of the 3rd Concerto, executing a very difficult passage. Meed reached for the key lid and slammed it down hard. If the professor's reaction time hadn't been so sharp, she might have crushed his fingers. He jolted back on the bench and looked up.

"What the hell . . . !!" he shouted.

"Why are you playing that?" Meed demanded. "How do you know that?"

Dr. Savage pointed to the audio player and headphones lying on the piano top.

"You told me to surprise you," he said.

Meed reached for the player and ejected the disc. She held it in both hands and bent it until it shattered into bright shards. When she looked down, she realized that one of the sharp edges had sliced a finger. She let the blood run down her hand until it dripped onto the floor. The professor sat, stunned, not moving from the bench.

"Never that piece," said Meed coldly. "Never that composer. Not *ever.*"

# CHAPTER 46

*Eastern Russia*
*12 Years Ago*

IT WAS RACE Day—one of the most anticipated events of the school year, and one of the most dangerous. Meed's leather gloves rested on the throttle of her growling black ATV. She tested the brakes, but she wasn't planning to use them much. Speed was everything. The engine vibration rattled her hips on the leather seat. Standard racewear was a nylon jumpsuit with a single zipper from neck to crotch, plus a pair of goggles. Meed had added a red bandanna for style. As always, helmets were optional, and it was a school tradition to refuse them. Some students also considered safety harnesses a sign of weakness. But not Meed. She had hers buckled tightly, intending to stay one with her machine.

To reach the day's competition, every student had already survived a course in evasive and tactical driving in high-powered sedans, pickups, and SUVs. Brutal and demanding. But the ATV race was the crucible—a no-holds-barred competition among the senior students. Rule number one: Last machine moving was the winner. There were no other rules.

The oval dirt track was rugged and uneven. It had been

carved by bulldozers and left rough on purpose. The quarter-mile circuit route was interrupted by dirt mounds and wooden ramps at random intervals, adding to the perils. The infield was dotted with a few equipment hangars and an open-sided white medical tent. Spectators—younger students and school instructors—watched from a set of crude bleachers.

The outer edges of the track were ringed with bundles of hay staked to the ground with metal bars. All around the perimeter, flaming torches had been jammed into the bales. The torches gave off streams of oily black soot, which mixed with the bluish ATV exhaust fumes. The effect was hellish.

Meed had spent weeks working on her ATV, tuning the carburetor for the optimal mix and swapping out the clutch for a heavy-duty design. Her wheels were extra-fat, with high-performance treads, and the chassis was low and stubby. The machine looked lethal just sitting still.

Sitting at the starting post, riders revved their engines aggressively, sending fresh plumes of exhaust into the air. At one end of the track, the head mechanics instructor stood on a high platform with a pistol in his right hand. With his eyes on the pack, he raised his arm and fired a bright green flare into the sky. The engine noise rose to a thunderous din as tires bit into the dirt. Within seconds, all twenty-four ATVs were careening around the track, and drivers were picking their targets.

As Meed cranked her throttle, Irina slid her blue ATV into position just behind her on the right—the wingman slot. Irina's job was defense, keeping attackers at bay while Meed concentrated on the action in front. They planned to switch positions after two circuits.

Meed had studied the videos of the previous year's competition and calculated the most effective strategies. She was determined to strike early, while her machine was in peak condition. She crouched low in her seat, leaning forward, copper curls blowing behind her. Just ahead, one of the senior boys was already showing off, standing on the floorboards of his ATV as he drove, harness-free, stupidly raising his center of gravity. First victim.

Meed goosed the throttle and whipped her machine to the left in order to get a better angle, then turned hard right, cutting through the crowd. The show-off didn't even see her coming. She banged into his left front tire with her thick steel bumper. The impact knocked the boy sideways. As he clung desperately to the steering wheel, his ATV spun wildly and tipped onto its side, sending him flying hard into a hay bale. One down. Meed swerved back to the center of the track as Irina held her position six feet to the rear.

Suddenly, Irina heard a fresh roar behind her. She glanced back. A boy with a blond crew cut had zoomed up from the rear in a dark green machine. He was making a move to pass. Irina swung left to block him. The pack was now moving at fifty miles per hour on the straightaways. The track was a blur. The intruder yanked his steering wheel to the right. Irina leaned forward to check her distance from Meed. In that split second, the pursuer banged hard into Irina's rear bumper. A few yards ahead, Meed dodged a two-foot mound in the middle of the track. Irina swerved a split second later. Too late. She hit the hump hard with her right front tire and went airborne. Meed glanced into her rearview just in time to see Irina's ATV crashing onto the infield. Irina flew from her machine, bounced, and rolled across the grass. Meed was another hundred yards around the track when she saw a team of white-jacketed medics rush out of their tent.

Meed had two choices. She could pull off onto the infield and help her partner. Or she could keep going and avenge her. Her foot inched toward the brake. Then, above the roar of the engines, she imagined Irina's voice, low and even. Just like on the mountain.

"Stop being weak," the voice said.

Meed hit the throttle.

# CHAPTER 47

FIVE MINUTES LATER, the track was Armageddon. Students were ramming each other from every direction, causing spectacular spinouts and flips. Engines sputtered, transmissions whined, tires squealed. A few wounded ATVs limped to the side on bent rims. Others were left as smoking wrecks in the middle of the track, creating a fresh set of deadly obstacles. Out of two dozen starters, only a handful were still running. Meed was one of them. So was the crew-cut boy in the green machine.

He had vaulted past Meed to weave through what was left of the pack, so far evading every hit. Meed dodged a pair of ramps and accelerated toward him. A bright orange ATV knocked into her from the right, but only managed to bat her slightly off center. Meed straightened out and rocketed forward with just a minor dent. Her engine was still solid, her transmission tight and responsive. Her mind flashed to Irina, picturing her broken—or dead. But she shook it off and concentrated on the task at hand. *I have only myself,* she kept thinking.

About fifty yards ahead, two other drivers were working as a team to close in on the green machine from both sides. The boy with the crew cut waited until his pursuers were parallel to his rear wheels, then slammed on his brakes. As he dropped back, he knocked into the ATV on the right, causing it to career into the machine on the left. A two-for-one hit. But costly, because now the two damaged machines had him blocked on the track.

Meed dropped her head low as she rounded the corner, sighting the center of the green ATV as it tried to maneuver around the wreck in front. She feathered the throttle, adjusting her speed to inflict maximum damage on the other machine without demolishing her own—a critical balance. Just as she made her final attack run, a mound of dirt obscured her view of the target. She leaned right in her seat, straining to see around it. Suddenly, she felt a violent shock on her left rear bumper. Her machine went spinning out of control. As she crashed hard into the side barrier, she caught a flash of orange. Her attacker sped by and hit the mound ahead at high speed, launching into the air.

The boy in the green ATV put his machine in reverse, but his wheels locked up. He unstrapped his harness and started to lift out of his seat. The orange ATV had become a 500-pound missile. It landed hard and bounced once, turning on its side as it flew forward. In less time than it took the crew-cut boy to blink, the roll bar caught him in the chest, knocking him fifteen yards down the track. He landed like a heavy sack, blood pouring from his mouth. The green and orange machines crumpled together in a single, smoking heap.

Meed glanced around the oval. In every direction, ATVs littered the track, but none of them were moving. She tested her throttle to see if her machine had anything left. It lurched forward, shaky and sputtering. There was a loud scraping noise from underneath, metal on metal. Meed worked the clutch and the shift lever. The whole transmission felt balky. It felt like she had only one gear left. But that was one more than anybody else had. She knew that all she needed to do to secure the win was to thread through the smoke and the wrecks and cross a white line fifty yards ahead.

Mead revved her engine. The sound reverberated around the track like a wounded animal. Every spectator and driver turned in her direction, expecting her to roll forward. The instructor on his platform readied the blue flare to signal victory.

Instead, Meed swerved directly across the track and bounced onto the infield. It was twenty yards to the medical tent. When she got there, she jumped out of her seat and ran to the open side—just as Irina burst out.

Irina's driving suit was torn and stained with grass and blood. Her eyes were wild. Meed leaned forward, exhaling a sigh of relief. Irina grabbed her by the shoulders, pulled her up, and shook her hard.

"Why didn't you *finish*?!" Irina shouted into Meed's face. *"Why??"*

Meed stared back in stunned silence. She realized that she had no answer—at least not an answer that Irina would ever accept.

# CHAPTER 48

IN THE SMOKEY aftermath of the race, Meed and Irina headed across the rutted track toward the school. They walked side by side, but not speaking. Irina could barely *look* at her partner. All around the dirt oval, students stood on top of their wrecks or tried to rock them upright. One boy kicked his dead machine with his boot, again and again. Two boys with huge wrenches had already started to cannibalize parts.

Several students sat on the grass while medics tended to bloody gashes and twisted limbs. Meed looked to the left, where the boy from the green machine lay still on the grass, a blanket pulled over his face, his crew cut showing at the top. His hands, now bluish-white, were clawed at his sides.

Meed yanked off her gloves and wiped the mud from her face with the back of her hand. Irina pulled a few stray strands of grass from her jet-black hair. She was limping slightly, but Meed knew better than to offer help, even when they reached the rise that separated the track complex from the main campus. She slowed down to match Irina's pace.

When they crested the hill and looked down the other side,

they saw Kamenev standing at the edge of the main school-yard, hands behind his back. It was not unusual to see the headmaster outside, especially on the day of a major event. The girls nodded respectfully as they approached. Then it became clear that Kamenev was not just out for a stroll. He was waiting for them. Meed and Irina stopped, suddenly nervous.

"I see you both survived," said Kamenev.

"We both failed," said Irina—brutally honest, as always.

Meed looked down, not wanting to make things worse. No use in trying to explain her motivation at the end of the race—why concern for her partner was more important to her than winning. That was a conversation she could never have, not with anybody at school. And definitely not with Kamenev. But the headmaster did not seem concerned with the outcome of the race. He pulled a folder from behind his back.

"This is your final test," he said.

Meed and Irina looked at each other, hearts pounding. From the age of five, they had been told this moment would come. They just didn't know exactly when or how it would happen. But they instantly knew what it meant.

With those five simple words from the headmaster, they understood that their classwork was over, competitions done, a lifetime of training complete. There was only one more thing to accomplish. The last assignment. The final test.

Over the years, Meed had managed to tease out a few details about finals from Lyudmila Garin during her piano lessons. She knew that every final was different, meant to reveal each student's strengths and weaknesses. Some finals were solos, others paired. Meed glanced over at Irina and felt a sense of relief. In spite of their conflict over the race, there was nobody alive that she trusted more. Nobody had more determination.

If they'd been assigned to their final as a team, Meed had no doubt that they would both succeed, no matter how impossible the task appeared.

"There's a village six miles to the east, over the mountain," said Kamenev. "A matter there has been festering for years. It needs to be cleaned up once and for all."

A village? To Meed, it felt odd to realize that there was any other kind of civilization nearby. For as long as she could remember, all she had known of the world was what she experienced at school and what she'd seen in videos and photographs. There had been nothing else. No other contact. The final was a huge step from theory to reality. Meed knew that it was meant to be disruptive, even shocking. Students never spoke about a final test after it was completed. That was an ironclad law. But she knew that they came back changed— and that, soon after, they usually left the school for good.

Kamenev held out the dossier. Irina took it and opened it. Meed leaned in to see the contents. She had expected a complex file, filled with data and background information. It was nothing like that. The file was bare bones. A simple hand-drawn map was clipped to the inside cover. A single sheet of paper showed an address and photo scans of two people. Just faces. A man and a woman. Total strangers. There were no names on the paper, just four digits and a letter, repeated twice. The assignment codes. Meed knew the codes. They were death warrants.

Meed felt her adrenaline start to pump as her mind shifted. She *forced* it to shift. Because whoever these people were, they were not human to her anymore. They couldn't be. They were simply targets.

"Final test accepted?" asked Kamenev.

Both girls nodded.

"I need to hear it," Kamenev said.

"Final test accepted," said Irina, closing the folder.

"Final test accepted," said Meed softly.

Meed understood that there would be no further clarifications or explanations. They had the assignment. The rest was theirs to decide. She knew that from this point on, anything they asked would receive the same reply: "Wrong question."

# CHAPTER 49

IT WAS ONE o'clock the next morning when Meed and Irina first saw the village. They were still half a mile up the mountain. The whole place looked smaller than the school grounds. In fact, from this height, the buildings looked like a set of toys.

"Wait," said Irina, tugging Meed down behind a fallen tree. Irina pulled out a set of binoculars and scanned the streets below. They were too far up to see address numbers, but the map left no doubt that they were headed for the right place. It was the only human settlement for miles around. Irina stood up and started angling her way down the slope. Meed followed close behind, placing her feet in Irina's footprints.

They both knew how far sound could carry in the mountains. From here on, there would be no talking. Meed was grateful for that. She was afraid that her voice would reveal her shakiness about the assignment—the fact that she was about to graduate from student to killer. If Irina had any concerns like that, she wasn't showing them.

As they got closer, a winding trail spilled onto a small field at the far edge of the village. Now the girls could see the actual scale of the place. It looked cozy, with neat two-story frame houses and tree-lined streets—like a place that hadn't changed in decades.

The streets were empty, but the main route was well lit. On the side streets, the street lamps were placed only on the corners, spaced far enough apart to create shadows at the center. Irina led the way, glancing at the map, picking her way block by block. Meed followed at her elbow, so close that anybody looking might have seen one shape, not two. After scouting for a few minutes, they huddled by the side of a dark drugstore and peeked out across the side street. Irina pointed to the brown house directly opposite. Meed squinted at the porch and saw three numerals lit by a small bulb above the door. 4-6-6. That was it.

The girls wound their way all the way down the block through backyards and alleys before crossing to the other side. Meed tried to tamp down her emotions and focus on the task. Her brain was pulling her two different ways. Part of her hoped that something would happen to force them to abort the mission. The other part just wanted to get it over with.

As the girls passed behind a corner house, the door to the rear porch opened, slamming hard against the outside wall. They crouched down and held perfectly still. Two men came through the door holding beer bottles. They were laughing loudly and almost tripping as they stepped. One man rested his bottle awkwardly on the porch rail and lit a cigarette. The other man tucked his bottle under his chin, unzipped his fly, and urinated off the porch. Irina tugged Meed's sleeve. They melted back into the shadows, picking their way toward the brown house farther down the row.

When they arrived, they sat on the soft ground behind a

low wood fence and watched for a full ten minutes, looking for any movement. On Irina's signal, they moved forward. The fence had a simple latch gate. Irina opened it and slipped through. As they walked softly across the small backyard, Meed suddenly stopped. Her stomach roiled and her mouth felt sour. She bent over a bush and vomited. Irina quickly scanned the house and the neighbors for any reaction. Meed wiped the spittle from her lips. Irina leaned in close.

"What's wrong with you?" she asked. She didn't speak it. She mouthed it.

Meed made one final cleansing spit into the bush and looked up. "I'm fine," she mouthed back. Even though she knew she wasn't.

The porch looked old and likely to creak. Irina climbed the steps on all fours, distributing her weight. Meed followed her up the same way. When they reached the back door, they found it secured with two sturdy locks. Top quality. Professionally installed.

It took Meed a full twenty seconds to get them open.

# CHAPTER 50

THE INSIDE OF the house was as modest as the outside. Neat and well organized.

No children's toys on the floor to avoid. No sign of a dog. No security cameras. A lingering aroma of vegetables and herbs hung in the air. Potatoes. Onions. Garlic. Rosemary. Meed felt the bile rising in her throat again. She swallowed it.

The girls moved through the kitchen and into a hallway intersection. One path led to the front of the house. They could see a small living room to the left and a dining room to the right. The other path led lengthwise across the back of the house. The bedroom corridor. The door to the left was open to a small empty room with bare wood floors and a solitary window. The door in the middle of the hallway was ajar, revealing the corner of a porcelain sink. The door at the other end of the hall was closed. Meed jabbed her finger toward it. It was the master bedroom. She felt it.

They moved slowly down the hall, hugging the sides, where the floorboards were less inclined to squeak. When they reached the door, Irina turned the knob slowly and pushed it open. It gave a tiny groan near the end position. By then, Meed and Irina were both inside. Meed held her breath. Her heart was pounding so hard she was afraid Irina could hear it.

The room was simply furnished. Dresser. Dressing table. Double bed. End tables on each side, with matching picture frames. Two people asleep in the bed. Male on the left, female on the right. A shaft of moonlight came through the small window over the headboard. Irina stood on tiptoe to get a better angle on the faces. She nodded and held up two fingers, close together, then dipped them forward. Confirmation.

Meed's head felt spacey and light. She fought to keep her focus. All her training told her not to hesitate, not to judge, not to worry, not to think. But she couldn't help it. Who were these people? Why were they chosen? Why did they deserve what was about to happen to them? And could she really do it? She thought back through all the death she had seen. She understood that it had all been meant to harden her for this exact moment. Now. Or never.

On the street in front of the house, a truck banged over a pothole, causing a loud metallic shudder. The girls shrunk back. The man in bed stirred and rolled over onto his side. Then, suddenly, he sat up. Early fifties. Bearded. Slightly built, wearing a light-blue T-shirt. For a split second he froze in place, peering at the two shapes against the wall. He settled back down, facing the outside of the bed, as if he thought he'd been dreaming.

Irina was not fooled. As she took a step forward, she saw the man's hand snake into the open drawer of his side table. Suddenly, he was upright again, wide awake, his upper body thrust forward, a black pistol in his hand. The barrel was pointed at Irina's head.

"Don't move!" he shouted. "What do you want?"

At the sound of his shouts, the woman jolted awake. She stared toward the foot of the bed and grasped her husband's shoulders. The woman had dark hair and a lined face. She looked older than her picture.

Meed instinctively stepped to the side to split the man's attention. Give him two targets instead of one. Make him choose. As she moved, the barrel of the pistol followed her. She heard the hammer cock, then a quick swish and a thud. The man fell back against the headboard, eyes wide and frozen. Irina's throwing knife was buried in his heart. Meed jumped back in shock. The woman screamed and reached for the gun as it fell onto the blanket. She picked it up. Her finger found the trigger. Meed pulled a knife from her sleeve. For a split second, she hesitated, her hand trembling. She felt Irina grab the knife out of her hand. All she could hear was the woman's voice.

"Stop!" she was yelling. "Whoever you are, just..."

Another swish. Another thud. Another kill shot. The woman's gun hand dropped limply onto the bed. The other hand flailed out and knocked into an end table. A framed photograph flew off the table and landed at Meed's feet as the glass shattered.

Meed looked down. In the pale light from the window, she could see the picture clearly. It showed an infant girl sitting against a white pillow. Meed gasped. Her mind reeled. Kamenev's office. Garin. The file. The photograph. The infant girl in the bassinet. Same age. Same copper-colored curls.

Oh, dear God!

Meed looked up from the picture to the bleeding shapes on the bed. That was the instant it all clicked. Irina stepped forward to pull the knives from the bodies. Meed put her hands over her mouth, suddenly feeling sick again.

"My *parents*!" she screamed. "Those were my *parents*!"

# CHAPTER 51

MEED LURCHED TOWARD the bed, reaching out with both arms. Irina grabbed her hard and wrestled her toward the door, whispering harshly into her ear.

"It's over!" she said. "There's nothing to be done."

Meed shook free and staggered down the corridor. Disoriented, she turned right past the living room and jerked the front door open. She ran down the front steps and into the middle of the street. Not thinking about exposure. Not caring. She dropped to her knees and started retching onto the dark pavement. Irina was at her side, tugging her to her feet. Meed swung wildly with her fists, her blows glancing off Irina's shoulders, mostly striking empty air. She started screaming again.

"No!" she wailed. *"No, no, no!!"*

Up and down the street, lights began to pop on. Silhouettes appeared in second-floor windows. Halfway down the block, a front door cracked open. Meed couldn't walk, couldn't move. She felt Irina's arms tight around her shoulders, supporting her, holding her up. And then she felt the sharp sting of a needle in the side of her neck.

In two seconds, Meed was limp and unconscious, unaware that for the second time in her life, she was about to be carried up a dark mountain.

# CHAPTER 52

MEED'S EYES DIDN'T flicker open again until 4 a.m. She was in her bed. Her lids were heavy and her vision was slightly blurred. The sedative had not fully worn off. But as her mind flashed to what had happened just hours earlier, the fury burned off the fog. In her rage, Meed was clear about what she had to do. The events in that bloody bedroom would not be her final test.

*This* would be.

Meed turned her head from side to side to check around the dormitory. The other girls were sleeping soundly. She slipped out from under her blanket and rested her feet lightly on the wood floor. She slowly slipped on socks and boots. Then she reached under her thin mattress and pulled out a three-foot strand of knotted rags. It had taken her weeks to collect and prepare them. They had been hidden under her mattress for months. She never knew exactly when she would need them.

It was now.

Two beds over, Irina lay curled under her blanket, her head facing the opposite wall. Meed walked quietly to the sink, turned on the tap, and let a slow trickle of water soak the cloth. She twisted the excess water from the whole length and snapped it tight. It could have been a noose or a garotte. But it was neither. It was a science experiment.

Meed tiptoed to the window, an arched opening with a hinged frame of thick glass. Meed flicked the latch and slowly pulled the window open. Behind the frame were sets of vertical metal bars set into the stone, top and bottom. The water was starting to activate the acid mixture with which she'd infused the cloth, giving off wisps of white vapor.

Meed knew she had to work quickly. She wrapped the rag strip around the two center bars, close to where they were set into the granite sill. The iron began to steam and sizzle. As the reaction intensified, Meed pressed her body up against the window. Sparks from the melting metal sprayed onto her forearms, leaving small searing marks on her skin. She winced. Her eyes teared with pain. But she did not make a sound.

In just a few seconds, the cloth had dissolved. The bases of both bars were now withered and shaky. Meed pried the loose bars out of the bottom sill and pushed them out as far as she could, creating a gap barely ten inches wide. It would have to be enough.

She looked back at her sleeping classmates, and then wormed her way through the opening. The rough stone scraped her thighs through her thin cotton pajama pants. Her arms burned with pain. She clung to the two remaining bars as she slid her shoulders and head through, and then hung dangling against the outside of the building. She was twenty feet off the ground. If she fell the wrong way, she would break an ankle or a leg. Her training had made her both an athlete and an acrobat, and she would need both skills now.

The grass at the bottom of the wall sloped slightly away from the building. Meed braced her feet against the stone and kicked away as she let go with her hands. As she landed, she tucked in her arms and rolled to the bottom of the slope, coming to rest on her belly on level ground. The coarse grass scraped against her burns, now a pattern of swollen red welts on each arm. As she lay flat, breathing hard, Meed dug into the ground with her fingers, then rubbed cool dirt onto the wounds. It was all she could do. It was a pain she could deal with.

The dawn light was just beginning to stripe the horizon to the east, toward the village. Meed rose to her feet and started to run in the exact opposite direction—slowly at first, then full-out, feet pounding, hair flying. She had no map, no weapons, no tools. She was leaving the only place she had ever known, and there was nobody in the outside world that she could trust. Nobody she even knew. Not a single human being.

She had only herself.

# CHAPTER 53

*Chicago*

"READY TO BE dazzled?" asked Meed.

"I'm not sure," I said.

That was the truth. I was nervous. I didn't know what to expect. For six months, I hadn't once looked in a mirror. Meed hadn't allowed it. One of her many rules. Since the day I'd been kidnapped, I'd never seen a single picture or video of my new self. I'd learned to shave my face by touch.

Of course, I knew how I looked in bits and pieces. I could see the changes when I checked out my arms, my chest, my legs, my abs. I knew that I was bigger and stronger than I had ever imagined. I could recite my new measurements to the centimeter. But I didn't have the whole picture. I had no clue how I looked to anybody else. Only Meed did. So she'd decided that tonight was the big reveal. Tonight, I was being introduced to myself.

She was holding a full-length mirror turned backward against her torso. I was standing in my gym shorts and bare feet. I was still pumped and sweating from my workout. For some reason, I guess she thought this was my best look.

"On the count of three," said Meed. She wiggled the mirror in a little tease. "One...two...*three!*" Then she flipped it.

When I saw the man looking back at me, it was like looking at a stranger.

"Holy shit," I said softly.

"Mr. Universe competition, here we come," said Meed.

This was crazy. Over the past couple months, I'd felt my development accelerating. It wasn't just the extra training or the protein shakes or the mass-gain powder or the endless brain exercises. Something had fundamentally shifted in me, physically and mentally. I felt myself progressing in leaps, not just steps.

"Look," said Meed, tipping the mirror, "even your hair is better."

I leaned forward and ran my fingers over my scalp. She was right. I still had my widow's peak, but the hair on top was now thick and full. The little bald patch on the crown of my head had completely filled in. The last time I had hair like this, I was in high school.

"Go ahead," said Meed, twirling her index finger in the air. "Take in the rear view."

Now I was really self-conscious. But also kind of curious. I did a three-quarter turn and looked over my shoulder into the mirror. Jesus! My traps and lats were carved like marble. My waist was narrow and tight. My external obliques looked like thick straps. My glutes bulged like two solid rocks under my shorts.

"Work of art, right?" said Meed. She turned the mirror around and leaned it against the wall. "Hold on. I have another treat for you."

I never knew when to take her literally. She always kept me

off balance. Usually, when Meed said she had something special for me, it turned out to be pure misery. But sometimes, she actually came through with something great. Like Kobe steak for dinner instead of tofu. Or letting me choose the playlist.

She bent down and reached into a cooler. I stepped back.

"That better not be another pig head," I said.

"Give me some credit, Doctor," she said. "We're celebrating."

Sure enough. When her hand came out of the cooler, she was holding two frosty bottles of Blue Moon Belgian White beer. I almost started panting. I hadn't tasted any liquid besides protein shakes and bottled water since last November. Just the thought of that cold beer hitting my throat made me tremble.

She knocked off both caps on a corner of the weight machine. Little dribbles of foam spilled out of the necks. She handed me one of the bottles and tipped the other to her lips. I felt the frosty sensation in my hand then took my first delicious sip. Sweet Lord. Heaven.

I heard Meed shout. It was earsplitting. I saw a flash in front of my face as she knocked the bottle out of my hand and into the side of the treadmill. I heard it crash and shatter.

"What the *fuck*!!" I shouted.

She rammed her elbow into my gut with enough force to rock me. Instinct took over. I put my arms up and lunged at her. She stepped back, then moved in for another punch, this time to my mouth. I felt the flesh split and tasted blood. She came at me with a chop toward my neck. I knocked her hand aside with my forearm. She used the momentum to spin on the ball of her foot and whip her leg around. The instant before her heel was about to hit my temple, I grabbed her ankle and twisted it hard. She screamed and went face-down onto the mat. When she flipped face up, I was on her. Her hand whipped up and I saw the flash of a blade coming straight at me. I knocked it away with one hand and pinned her wrists to the side. I had one knee across her thighs and the other knee jammed into her solar plexus. For the first time—the very first time—I realized that I had her. She was done, and she knew it. In that instant, I felt all the fight go out of her. I let go of her wrists and backed off. I sat back, breathing hard.

"What the hell was *that*?" I asked, dabbing blood from my lip.

She winced as she sat up.

"That was your final test," she said. "You passed."

"I could have killed you just then," I said. "You know that, right?"

She actually smiled a little. "That's all I've ever wanted."

I shook my head. I was starting to feel like a trained monkey again—totally manipulated. Was I supposed to feel great about being able to murder a woman with my bare hands? Meed reached over and tapped my arm. She leaned closer.

"Ask me something," she said.

"What do you mean?" I replied.

"Anything you want," she said. "No wrong questions."

"Bullshit," I said.

"Try me," she said.

I was fed up. But if this was another mind game, I was going to swing for the fences. I didn't go for anything new. I went straight to two questions I'd asked her a hundred times—questions she'd never come close to answering.

"Okay, Meed," I said. "What's your real name? And why am I here?"

She tipped her head back and took a deep breath. Then she

looked me straight in the eye. Over the past six months, I'd seen this woman mislead me, trick me, and lie to my face over and over again. But we had just crossed some kind of border. I could feel it. And somehow, in that moment, I knew she was about to tell me the truth.

"My name is Kira Sunlight," she said. "And I need you to save my life."

# PART 2

# CHAPTER 54

*SUNLIGHT?!* MY GOD!

That was the last name I expected to hear—or *wanted* to hear. But in that instant, at least I knew I wasn't some random kidnapping victim. And my kidnapper wasn't some local psycho. This woman and I were deeply connected. I suddenly realized that this whole setup had been decades in the making. Maybe a century.

*"Sunlight?"* I repeated. "You're related to..." I stopped and let her finish the sentence, just to be sure I was right.

"John Sunlight," she said. "Yes. He was my great-grandfather."

I'd known about John Sunlight my whole life. And not in a good way. He was a part of my family's past that I'd tucked away, further than the rest of it, thinking it would never surface again. But here it was, staring me in the face, three generations later.

I was amazed that this woman and I would ever be in the same room. Stunned, in fact.

Because her ancestor and mine had been determined to kill

each other. Now I had to wonder about her intentions all over again. The change in her name changed everything. She was a Sunlight. I was a Savage. It was a bad combination.

"You realize that if John Sunlight had had his way," I said, "I would never have been born."

"Think how *I* feel," she said. "It's kind of like being related to Hitler."

From what I knew, it was a fair comparison. Because back in the 1930s, John Sunlight had also wanted to rule the world. And, like Hitler, he almost succeeded. He built his own private army and tried to corner the market on the world's most devastating weapons. The only thing standing in his way was *my* great-grandfather, Doc Savage. Which is why John Sunlight tried to wipe him off the face of the earth. But all that was in the distant past, done and buried long ago. Ancient history. I'd heard about the battle between Doc Savage and John Sunlight from my parents before they passed. But it wasn't something I ever thought about. As far as I was concerned, it had nothing to do with me.

"Your great-grandfather has been dead for decades," I said. "So has mine. I need to save your life?? Who the hell wants to kill you?"

She didn't seem scared. But she did seem nervous. I'd never seen that before.

"Let's just say my past is catching up with me," she said. "So is yours."

# CHAPTER 55

*Gaborone, Botswana*

EIGHT THOUSAND MILES and eight time zones away, in a small neighborhood bistro, sprinter Jamelle Maina was on her first wine spritzer of the evening. The cool chardonnay was easing her guilt—slightly.

She was really enjoying the company of her fellow runners, but she had a definite twinge about leaving her infant daughter with a new sitter. Jamelle was so in love with that baby— the baby the trainers had told her she should never have. She hated to be away from her, even for a minute. But this evening was special. Her *friends* were special. And her apartment was just down the street.

She had *earned* this evening, she kept telling herself. After all, how often does a single mom from the African bush get to compete in the Olympics?

"Jamelle! Where is your *mind*??" It was her teammate Luanna, the tall runner. She reached across the table and snapped her fingers in Jamelle's face.

"Sorry!" said Jamelle, coming back to the moment. "I'm here!"

*   *   *

Half a block away, in Jamelle's tidy apartment, Irina was busy wiping down everything she had touched since she arrived. Light switches, refrigerator, toilet handle. It was an unnecessary precaution, since her fingerprints were not on file anywhere in the world. But she had been trained to be thorough. And it was her nature.

She could hear the music from the bistro down the block as she walked softly into the nursery and lifted the tiny black baby from her crib. The doctored formula had done its work. The baby would not stir for hours. Irina just hoped the diaper would hold out.

As she picked up the limp infant, she wondered if she would feel anything this time. She didn't. Not really. No more than she would feel about any other piece of valuable merchandise. It was just another assignment. Get in. Get out. Deliver the goods. It did occur to Irina that the baby would not remember anything of this room, or this apartment, or her mother. That was probably a mercy, Irina thought. From now on, this little girl would have only herself. And someday, she would serve a bigger purpose.

Irina wrapped the baby in the blanket from the crib, then found another to add an extra layer of cushioning. She folded the top of the second blanket lightly over the baby's face. She checked the Mother Goose clock on the nursery wall. Time to go.

The transfer team would be waiting.

As Irina stepped into the stairwell leading down to ground level, a couple passed her heading up. They were young and tipsy, interested only in each other. When the police interviewed them the next morning, along with all the other residents of the small apartment complex, the couple would only remember seeing a young woman with a duffel bag, looking as if she were leaving for a weekend trip. The surveillance video would be no help. For a few critical intervals, it would show nothing but static.

# CHAPTER 56

*Chicago*

I WAS ON my own again. After telling me the truth about who she was that afternoon, Kira had disappeared into her room. I just kept on with my training routine. What else could I do? Whatever had gone on in Kira's past, she wasn't ready to get into details. Not yet. So I just kept pumping iron and thinking about all the other questions I needed answers to. What was the threat? Who was coming for her? Would it ever be over? Was I ever going to get my life back again?

I finished my last workout at about 8:00 p.m. and took a shower. I was getting ready to lock myself in for the night, following the rules. I put on some old sweats to sleep in and sat down on my bed. That's when I saw Kira standing outside my cell, holding a bottle.

"Join me in the kitchen," she said. So I did.

In six months, my kidnapper had never poured a glass of wine without quizzing me about tannin levels, complexity, and region of origin. She never let me drink. Just taste and spit. But tonight was different. Maybe because she wasn't pouring wine. She was pouring mezcal.

"Sip it. Don't shoot it," she said. Good advice. The taste was smokey and fierce. I almost coughed it back up. My eyes were watering.

"How long has this stuff been aging?" I asked.

"About a hundred years," she said. "That's why it's so mellow."

I picked up the bottle. The glass was thick and heavy, and the label was all in Spanish. The vintage year was handwritten. Sure enough. *1922.*

"Did you steal this from a museum?" I asked. She shook her head.

"From a private collection."

I took another sip. This one went down easier. I started to feel warm all over. Anybody looking at the two of us would have thought that we were just a regular couple enjoying a quiet evening together. Not quite. For one thing, I was still adjusting to my companion's name. Her *real* name. As I looked at her across the counter, I pictured a giant *K* on her forehead so I wouldn't slip up and call her Meed. There were so many blanks I needed to fill in that I didn't know where to start. But she beat me to it.

"How much do you know about Doc Savage?" she asked.

It was a loaded question. I'd basically spent my life trying to pretend the guy never existed. It was a pain in the ass to be descended from a legend as big as my great-grandfather. Genius. War hero. Crime fighter. Soldier of fortune. You name it, he did it. Hard to live up to. Even harder to live down.

"I know he was brilliant," I said, "and a great inventor. But I think he depended on brawn over brains too much. From what I've heard, he was a pretty violent guy. After my folks died, I thought about changing my last name to get rid of the connection once and for all. Fresh start."

"So why didn't you?" Kira asked.

The reason was pretty embarrassing.

"Because *Savage* was already on all my diplomas," I said.

Kira gave a quick laugh. "Right," she said. "I guess all that calligraphy would be a bitch to redo." I realized that I'd never heard her laugh before. Maybe it was just the mezcal, but it sounded terrific.

"Look," I said, "I know there's probably a ton of exaggeration in the old Doc Savage stories. Pirates? Ghosts? Phantom cities? Evil hunchbacks? That stuff can't be true. It sounds like pure fantasy."

Kira took a slow sip and raised her eyebrows, like she was holding back another secret. I leaned toward her over the counter.

"Wait," I said. "How much do *you* know?"

Kira put her glass down on the counter.

"Follow me," she said.

By this time, the rest of the loft was mostly dark, except for a dim glow from inside my cell and a few under-counter lights in the kitchen. And with all that mezcal on board, my vision wasn't super-sharp. Kira led the way through the kitchen and stopped at the metal door that said UTILITY. I'd never paid much attention to it. Why would I?

Nothing but circuit breakers and HVAC equipment inside, I figured. Besides, it had a pretty sophisticated electronic lock. Kira tapped the lock with her finger.

"Open it," she said.

Open it? I could barely *see* it. "I have no idea how to do that," I said.

"Sure you do," said Kira. "You learned it in your sleep two nights ago."

I didn't remember the session, but I suddenly recalled the content, every single detail. Even with the Mexican buzz in my brain. I ran my finger over the lock face, then reached into a kitchen drawer and pulled out a butter knife. I pried off the small screen that was meant for displaying the pin code. Underneath was a set of very small circuit boards.

At that point, I was as focused as a surgeon. I pried off the top board to get at the one underneath. I pulled two small wires loose from the second board and pressed the bare ends against two metal leads, one on the board itself, the other on the inside of the lock casing. I heard a small click.

"Told you," said Kira.

I grabbed the thick metal handle and gave it a tug. Sure enough, the door was loose. But I almost didn't want to open it. Something told me that whatever was behind that door was going to change my life in a major way. Probably more pain. I looked at Kira.

"This isn't really a utility closet, is it?" I said.

"It was mislabeled," she replied.

# CHAPTER 57

I OPENED THE door. An automatic sensor turned on a bank of industrial lights overhead. As my eyes adjusted, I suddenly felt totally sober again. I couldn't believe what I was looking at.

We were in a huge room with a high ceiling and no windows. It was filled with metal shelves in long, neat rows. It looked like a natural history archive. It had the smell of old paper, old chemicals, old leather.

"Welcome home, Doctor," said Kira.

She stood by the door as I started walking through the room. At first, there was too much to take in. Stacks of journals. Jars of sand and soil and dried plants, all neatly labeled. Topographical maps with notes and arrows drawn all over them. Files with TOP SECRET government stamps. And that was just the first row. It was overwhelming.

"What the hell *is* all this?" I asked.

Kira walked down the other side of the shelf and looked at me through the gap. She ran her hand over a pile of thick dossiers tied with twine.

"This whole floor belonged to Doc Savage, your great-grandfather," said Kira. "Everything in here was his."

"I thought Doc Savage lived in New York," I said. I remembered some lore about a hideout on the eighty-sixth floor of some Manhattan skyscraper.

"That's true," said Kira. "He had an apartment there. But after a while, too many of his enemies knew about it, so he just kept it as a decoy." She looked around the room. "*This* is where he did his experiments, and perfected his training, and worked on his inventions. Right here."

At the back of the space, there was a long lab table with gas outlets and cartons of unused test tubes and petri dishes. One end was filled with dark brown chemical jars. The other end was piled high with lab notebooks.

Another corner of the room was filled with electronic devices, some finished, some half assembled. There were coils of wire and bins filled with parts—knobs, switches, dials, and a lot of stuff I didn't recognize.

It looked like the secret lair of some mad scientist, but there were some personal items, too. A watercolor painting of a small boat with *Orion* on the stern. A theatrical makeup kit. A pair of boxing gloves. And leaning up against the wall, a battered violin case. Along with everything else, I'd heard that my great-grandfather was a musical prodigy. Maybe it was true.

On the floor was an old wooden liquor crate, top ripped off, with one bottle missing. Now I knew where the mezcal came from. I squeezed past the memorabilia and peered into the far corner.

"Jesus!"

I was staring at an antique arsenal. Shotguns. Pistols. Hunting knives. Military rifles. Bayonets. Hand grenades. Just about every possible way to kill another human was sitting right there. It felt weird. I turned to Kira.

"Don't tell me this was all for self-defense," I said.

Kira shrugged. "Dangerous times. Dangerous tools."

I turned away from the weaponry to a small table. There was a black and white photograph sitting on top. It was Doc Savage himself, no doubt about it. I'd seen the illustrations from the pulp stories, but this was the first actual photo of him that I'd ever laid eyes on. I spotted the family resemblance right away. Same widow's peak, for one thing. In the picture, my ancestor looked strong and fit. Totally buff. In fact, he looked a lot like me.

There was another picture underneath. Another man. Same era. Same features. Except this guy was no great physical specimen. He was stooped and awkward-looking. Kind of like I looked before I was taken.

"Who's this?" I asked.

Kira walked over to meet me at the table. She ran her finger across the picture.

She hesitated for a second before she answered, like she wasn't sure how to break the news.

"That's Doc Savage's brother, Cal," she said.

I shook my head. Wrong. That made no sense.

"You don't know what you're talking about," I said. "Doc Savage was an only child."

"No," said Kira, looking straight at me. "Doc Savage was a twin."

# CHAPTER 58

I STARED AT the two pictures side by side. Out of nowhere, a new branch of my family tree had just been added. Suddenly, I had a great-uncle.

"Why didn't I know about this guy?" I asked.

"Because your family was really messed up," said Kira. She took the pictures and put them down on the table. She pulled out a ledger and opened it to a middle page. It was filled with anatomical stats—heights, weights, muscle measurements— along with nutritional data and athletic performance records. Running, swimming, hiking, boxing, marksmanship. All noted in painstaking detail, like lab notes.

"Doc Savage was a human science project," Kira said. "He was part of a twenty-year experiment conducted by his father. The goal was to create the perfect physical and mental specimen—a man who was the best at everything. The twin brother was the control. Their father turned one brother into a superman and let the other brother fend for himself. That's why you've never heard the name Calvin Savage. Nobody has."

She walked over to another row of shelves and came back

with a thick leather binder. The title stenciled on the cover was "Sunlight." She handed the binder to me. I opened it. Stuck between the cover and the first page was a photo of a man in a lab coat. Bursting out of it, actually. Because his build was almost as big as Doc Savage's.

"John Sunlight," I said. Who else could it be? I looked for any similarity to Kira. Definitely not the hair. Her great-grandfather was totally bald.

"Let's sit," said Kira. She cleared off two leather armchairs against the wall. The chairs looked like they belonged in a men's club. They even smelled like cigars. I sat down. The leather was soft and worn. Pretty comfortable, actually. I felt like I should be wearing a smoking jacket. Kira tugged her chair around to face mine. Our knees were almost touching.

"Listen," she said. "My great-grandfather was a genius. Close to Doc Savage's level. But he was twisted. Delusional. Probably a sociopath. He had all these insane theories about how to reorder the world. He even managed to steal some of Doc's technology and weapons. But he realized that to get *all* the secrets, he needed an inside man. So he reached out to Cal, who didn't have much going for him. He and Cal made a pact. That's how John Sunlight got his hands on the manual for Doc Savage's training."

"There was a *manual*?"

"Absolutely," said Kira. "The full regimen, from fourteen months of age to twenty-one. It was all written down. Physical training. Mental challenges. Martial arts. Languages. Science. History. Music."

"So after Sunlight stole the manual," I asked, "what did he do with it? Use it to train his mercenaries?"

"No," said Kira. "He used it to start a school. With himself and Cal in charge."

"A school?" I asked. "Like what? A college?"

"A secret academy," said Kira, "based on the Doc Savage methods. Strict discipline from infancy on, every minute programmed, no outside influences. My great-grandfather took the Doc Savage training and corrupted it, turned it into something else."

"Turned it into *what*?" I asked.

"Into something that would help him extend his influence and take over the world," said Kira. "Espionage. Infiltration. Psyops. Murder."

"How do you know all this?" I asked. "How can you possibly...?"

Her look stopped me in mid-sentence.

"Because I was raised there," said Kira. "I was trained there. In eighty years, I'm the only student to leave without authorization. I escaped when I was a teenager."

I leaned back against the wall. Suddenly a lot of things were adding up. But not everything.

"Wait," I said. "So you mean you put up with that evil shit for all those years and then decided to run away? Why? What changed? Did you suddenly grow a conscience?"

Kira's eyes dropped. Her voice got soft and low.

"I can't talk about that," she said.

Something in the way she said it told me to leave it alone.

"Okay," I said. "But where did you go? You're not a teenager anymore. Where have you been all this time? What were you doing—kidnapping innocent college professors?"

"I promise," she said, "you're my first. I've been all over the world. Made plenty of money. I've been lots of different people, and I've covered my tracks pretty well. But the school is still operating, still pumping out graduates. They're getting better, and smarter, and more dangerous. You cannot believe the amount of evil they are responsible for. It's everywhere."

"And that's why you needed my help?" I asked.

She nodded. "I knew you had the right genes," she said, "but I had to bring out your full potential. I couldn't tell you the truth until you were ready. Until I knew I could trust you." She leaned toward me in her chair. "I'm sorry." That was the first time she'd ever uttered those two words. And somehow, in that moment, I felt sorry for *her*. I reached over and put my hand on top of hers. I expected her to pull away, but she didn't.

The effects of the mezcal had mostly worn off, but now there was something else. I felt like I'd stepped into a different time and place—a world where only one other person knew what was going on. Over the past six months, I'd been afraid of her, I'd hated her, I'd admired her. And now I was having *other* feelings. Maybe stuff I'd been suppressing. I wondered if maybe she was feeling the same thing. Kira stood up.

"I think we need to release some tension," she said.

Finally, it sounded like maybe we were on the same page.

# CHAPTER 59

"STOP BEING SUCH a baby!"

I'd never been touched like this in my life. The pain was intense. But Kira said it was all for my own good.

I was lying on a massage table behind a set of linen curtains in a corner of the loft. My face was poking through an oval in the table cushion and all I could see through it were floorboards. I was naked except for a towel across my backside. That part didn't bother me. I'd gotten over my self-consciousness around her a long time ago. But my body was definitely going through some new experiences. Kira's elbow was buried in the muscles that ran along my spine. I could feel her leaning in with the full weight of her upper body. She slid her elbow up and down, from the base of my neck to the top of my sacrum. I flinched from the pressure.

"What are you *doing* to me?" I asked.

"I told you," she said. "Deep-tissue massage and myofascial release. Just breathe through it."

"I'm trying." More of a groan than actual words.

I felt her applying more warm oil to my back, spreading it

in a diamond pattern, her palms moving across my shoulders, down my back, and over the top of my hips, then back up again. When she stood at the head of the table, I could see her black tights and bare feet through the opening. Then she was gone again, moving around to another part of my anatomy. Neck. Arms. Hips. Calves. Feet. She used her knuckles, thumbs, and knees. She pressed deep into my muscles and tendons, probing for every knot.

"Don't fight me, Doctor," she said. "Let go."

Slowly, bit by bit, my body stopped resisting and gave in. At some point, I crossed the boundary between pain and relief. By the end of an hour, I felt warm and loose from head to toe. More relaxed than I'd felt in a very long time. *Years,* maybe. Maybe my whole damned life. I could hardly speak.

"Where the hell did you learn *that*?" I mumbled.

"Like I said," replied Kira, "I've been lots of people."

Her last big move was a rolling motion with her forearms up and down my back. Like she was ironing me out. Then I saw her feet through the hole again. I felt her hands resting lightly on my head. She curled her fingers through my hair and massaged my scalp. I could feel the skin moving over my skull. It was heaven. After a minute of that, she gently lifted her hands away.

"We're done, Doctor," she said softly. "How do you feel?"

"Amazing," I sighed.

I gripped the towel around my waist and slowly turned face up on the table. I raised myself up on my elbows. Kira was closing the top of her oil bottle and slipping back into her shoes. She looked down at the same instant I did—and saw my erection poking up under the towel. Kira put the oil bottle down on the side table.

"Autonomic reflex," she said. "Totally normal." Then she disappeared behind the curtain. I flopped back down onto the table. I felt flushed and embarrassed.

Autonomic reflex. It sounded so clinical. So scientific. Maybe that was all there was to it, I thought.

Maybe.

# CHAPTER 60

THE NEXT MORNING, breakfast was a little awkward. One reason was the menu. I'd gotten used to Kira's weird nutrition repertoire. Goji berries, chia seeds, flax, maca, and the rest of it. Some of it I'd learned to like. Some of it I'd learned to tolerate. Some of it I still had to choke down. But now I was staring at a plateful of wet green weeds.

"What in God's name is *this*?" I asked. "And don't say 'wrong question.'"

"It's kelp. You're low on antioxidants."

Now that she said it, it looked exactly like stuff I'd seen in nature documentaries, waving around underwater. It was seaweed, pure and simple. I pushed the plate away.

"Thanks," I said, "but I draw the line at algae."

I was a little surprised when she didn't push back or try to force feed me. She downed the last of her smoothie and wiped her lips with a napkin. She looked serious. She put her elbows on the butcher block.

"Doctor," she said, "we need to have . . . the talk."

More awkwardness. I figured this was about my display the night before. Had to be. I cleared my throat.

"Right," I said. "I'm sorry about the . . ." I glanced down at my lap. Kira shook her head.

"It's not about that," she said. She leaned toward me over the kitchen island. "I have a confession to make, Doctor. It's about me. About you and me. *Our* history."

"Our history?" I said. "I've seen our history, remember? Our history is you stalking me, stealing my mail, hacking my router, and spying on me from the bushes."

"You're absolutely right," she said. "And that's what I can't really explain. I think I **liked** watching you from a distance. I could see how awkward you were. The way you kept to yourself, lost in your own little universe. No friends. No relationships. No adventure."

She was right, of course. Her little film had proven the point in spades.

"I'm a loner," I said. "Always have been."

"To be honest," said Kira, "I found the whole package kind of irresistible."

I sat up in my chair. Was she playing another game? I'd never felt the least bit irresistible. To *anybody*. I never expected to have a stalker with some strange long-distance crush. Especially one who looked like Kira.

"And what *about* now?" I asked. "Now that you've turned me into this . . . this physical masterpiece."

She shrugged. "That's the weird part," she said. "Now you're just another guy."

I guess I should have been hurt. Or insulted. Or disappointed. But mostly I was confused. What Kira seemed to be saying was that back when I thought I would *never* have a chance with a woman like her, I actually *did*. And now that I looked like somebody who might *actually* have a chance with her, I *didn't*. It was a head-spinner. Over the years, I'd been attracted to plenty of women who had stuck me permanently in the friend zone. But this was a whole *new* zone. The Kira zone. And I was totally lost.

"Don't feel bad," said Kira. "I'm no prize, believe me. I have baggage. I'm not easy to be with."

At that point, all I could do was laugh. "Tell me something I don't know," I said.

And that was it. No meaningful looks. No hugs. She'd said what she needed to say, and then she shifted gears. She took the plate and scraped the seaweed into the garbage, where it belonged. At least *that* was a relief.

"Come with me, Doctor," she said. She headed back toward the door that said UTILITY. "I've got something else to show you." I got up from my chair as she pulled the door open. She had a strange smile on her face. "You probably shouldn't have too much in your stomach for this anyway."

# CHAPTER 61

A FEW MINUTES later, we were standing on a narrow ledge that projected from the side of the building and I was preparing to die. We were about sixty stories up, wearing silver overalls over our clothes and helmets on our heads. Kira said the overalls were fireproof. But fire was the least of my worries. I was way more afraid of ending up as a bloody speck on the sidewalk.

"Adjust your straps, Doctor," said Kira. "Like this."

The straps were attached to big chrome canisters on our backs. They looked kind of like old vacuum cleaners. I looked over as Kira pulled the loose ends of her front straps down tight across her chest. I did the same. Then I tightened the belt around my waist. I felt the canister press even harder against my back.

I looked over at Kira like she was nuts, because I truly thought she was. This whole project seemed suicidal. But she wouldn't back off.

"Don't worry," said Kira. "I've bench tested these things a dozen times. Doc Savage knew what he was doing. The thrust and aerodynamics all add up."

I'd read about some of my great-grandfather's inventions. Fluoroscopes for night vision. The first hi-def TV. Ejection seats for airplanes. But I never knew how much of it was real. And I definitely never expected to be standing on a ledge wearing one of his 1930s-vintage jetpacks. That part felt absolutely *insane*.

Kira took a step forward. She was standing right next to me, just one foot from the edge.

"Trust me," she said. "Trust your great-grandfather."

I didn't. Not for a second. Not when it came to a 600-foot drop. I felt like throwing up. Kira reached over and made a small adjustment to a dial on the side of my jet canister.

"What are you doing??" I asked.

"Giving you a richer mixture," she said. "More power."

"Is this another one of your manhood tests?" I asked. "I thought I'd already passed!" My voice was shaky. I sounded desperate, and I was.

"I no longer doubt your manhood," she said.

"I can't do this!" I said. I backed up against the wall. "This is *crazy*!"

Kira pulled me forward again and stood right behind me. Her hands were on my shoulders. She spoke right into my ear. Her voice was calm and reassuring. I thought maybe I could still talk her out of it.

"Wait! I just need a little more time!" I could feel my palms sweating.

Her voice was calm and reassuring. "No rush, Doctor. I know you're nervous. Totally understandable. We'll go when you're ready."

I took a deep breath. She shoved me off the ledge.

# CHAPTER 62

I MIGHT HAVE screamed. I don't really remember. What I *do* remember is the feeling of my heart thudding and the air rushing up against my face. I was falling straight down, head first. I could see the street and all the traffic zooming closer in a blur. Then I heard a loud bang and a roar behind me. I felt a tremendous jolt. And suddenly I wasn't falling anymore. I was shooting up into the sky like a rocket, so fast it felt like my stomach was being pressed down toward my feet.

I looked over. Kira was right alongside me. I saw a bright tear-shaped flame blasting out of the bottom of her jetpack. Her hair was whipping out from under her helmet in little copper-colored waves.

She flexed her legs and leveled out until she was flying parallel to the ground. I copied her exactly. Got the same result. I was a bad judge of heights, but it looked like we were a couple thousand feet up. We were soaring over the center of Chicago, with skyscrapers stabbing up and all the other buildings laid out like a giant puzzle. The streets were a neat crosshatch pattern. The Chicago River was like a blue ribbon winding through the city.

It probably took me a half minute to adjust to the reality of what was happening—the fact that we were flying with machines built sixty years before I was born. And that they actually worked. There was no use trying to talk, or even shout to each other. The wind was too loud. But I could read Kira's body language in the air.

She was having a ball. And once I realized that I wasn't going to drop out of the sky like a stone, I started to have a ball, too.

At first, Kira took the lead, and I followed what she did. She was like a ballet dancer in the air. A total natural. I wasn't quite as smooth, but I was getting the hang of it. I realized that I could control my position in the air by dipping my head and adjusting my arms. When I tucked my arms tight against my sides, I swooped down. When I lifted my arms out to the sides, I rose back up. After I got a little confidence, I straightened out and shot out in front. The sensation was unbelievable. It was a mix of lightness and speed and amazing power. I had to hand it to my ancestor. I'd never felt anything like it.

Lake Michigan was off to the east, looking like a big green carpet. I banked to the left and headed out over the water. Kira was right behind me. I tucked myself into a dive and plummeted down until I was about thirty feet above the surface. When I passed over a lake freighter, I was close enough to see the crew looking up and pointing. The lower I got, the faster it felt like I was going. It was a total rush, and I was loving it. I lost all sense of time. I wanted it to last forever.

Suddenly I felt a lurch from my rocket pack. Instantly I dropped about ten feet. I looked over at Kira, who was flying right next to me. The flame from her rocket was coming out in short bursts, with little belches of smoke in between. I felt another lurch, then a loud pop. Then I started to spin like a pinwheel, end over end. My vision flipped between sky and water. Sky and water. And then only water. I hit feet first.

I sucked in one last breath, and then I went under, sinking fast. I saw Kira plunge in a few yards away. She sank down in a cloud of bubbles until she was out of sight in the murky lake. I couldn't see the bottom. But I knew that's where I was headed. With fifty pounds of metal strapped to my back, it's not like I had a choice.

# CHAPTER 63

I STARTED TO panic. The light was fading above my head and the water under my feet was getting blacker. My lungs were on fire. I wrestled with the straps around my chest and middle but they wouldn't budge. I lost all sense of space. There was nothing but murk all around me. I tried to swim up, but it was no use. With my jetpack attached, I was dead weight.

About five seconds later, my boot landed on a long piece of metal. I had reached the lake bottom. I spun hard to the left. Something caught on the strap behind my back. I felt around with my bare hands and realized that I had fallen onto a pile of cement and rebar. Pure terror shot through me. After everything, that's where I was going to end up—wrapped around a pile of construction debris at the bottom of Lake Michigan.

I saw a blast of white in the distance. Then I saw Kira swimming toward me out of the dark. Her jetpack was gone. So was her helmet. Bubbles were blowing out of a device attached to her face.

When she got close, she went blurry. I was starting to pass out. She grabbed at my strap fasteners and yanked them open.

I felt the weight of the jetpack drop away. I was loose. But still drowning.

Then Kira was in my face, holding up a set of nose plugs attached to something that looked like a toothpaste tube. She yanked off my helmet. She jammed the plugs into my nostrils and twisted the top of the tube. I felt a rush of air into my lungs. I clamped my mouth shut and inhaled through my nostrils. My head instantly cleared. I was breathing again. Kira gave me a thumbs-up. I think I nodded. I wasn't sure what was happening. I only knew that I was alive.

Kira started kicking her way through the water. I followed right behind, trying to keep her in sight in the murk. After a few minutes, the water started turning green again.

Suddenly there was a ripple of light above. A few strokes later, my head broke water. I opened my mouth and took in the fresh air. Deep, long breaths of it.

"Pretty ingenious, right?" Kira's voice, yelling from a distance. I twisted around in the water. She was about twenty feet away, holding up her breathing apparatus.

"Thank your great-grandfather for these!" she shouted.

All I could do was shake my head and spit out some lake water. I was starting to wonder how many lives I had left. We were still about fifty yards from the shoreline. I could see a modern building with white pillars overlooking the lake. The Oceanarium of the Shedd Aquarium. We started swimming toward it.

As we approached the shoreline, I could see crowds of families on the curved sidewalk in front of the building. There was some kind of water festival going on. I saw kids and balloons and costumed characters dancing around. The outdoor sound system was blaring Disney music.

We climbed over the ribbed cement wall between the lake and the sidewalk. Water drained out of our fireproof suits. I still had my breathing tube dangling from my face. The whole crowd turned in our direction. A little girl holding a toy lobster started bouncing on her toes and laughing. She poked her younger brother and pointed at us. Then they both started clapping. Their parents joined in. So did the rest of the crowd. They thought we were part of the show. I looked at Kira and pulled the apparatus out of my nose. I was exhausted and mad.

"You planned that whole disaster, didn't you?" I said.

Kira wasn't looking at me. She was looking at the crowd. She had a big smile on her face.

"Wave to the nice people," she said.

# CHAPTER 64

*Gaborone, Botswana*

THE OFFICE OF private investigator Jaco Devos was small and cluttered. It was also sweltering. The only moving air came from an anemic desk fan pointed mostly in his direction. Jamelle Maina sat across from the sweaty PI, an Afrikaner with a grayish complexion. The smoke from his cigarette spun in the vortex created by the fan blades. Jamelle's thin cotton dress stuck to the back of her metal chair. Devos flipped through the thin file in front of him on his desk, pretending to study it intently.

"Can you help me?" Jamelle asked, her voice soft and pleading.

"I have the police report right here," said Devos, cigarette ashes dropping onto the papers. "Your babysitter's credentials were impressive forgeries. No surveillance footage. No forensics. Not a single hair. In terms of a conventional investigation, this woman does not exist."

"She took my *baby*!" said Jamelle, tears brimming in her eyes.

Devos closed the file and squinted at his prospective client. "There are no reliable witnesses, other than yourself. Nothing else to go on." He paused and looked up, as if searching the heavens for a solution. "But..."

Jamelle leaned forward. "Yes? *What?*"

"Remind me," said Devos. "Who referred you?"

"My friend Luanna. Luanna Phiri."

Davos reflected for a second.

"Yes! The other runner," he said. "I remember. Boyfriend issue. Nasty man."

"Can you help me?" Jamelle asked again, her hands stretched out toward him on the desk.

"Miss Maina," said Devos. "Let me be clear. The authorities have done all they can. They will keep your case open and say reassuring things. But frankly, after a month or two, they will lose interest and move on. I will not. I have connections in places they don't. The people I talk to are people who will not talk to the police. That is my value to you."

"Yes!" said Jamelle. "Anything you think might work! *Anything!*"

Here Devos took another pause. Another salesman's trick. He sighed. "I'll have expenses, of course," he said. His voice conveyed resignation, even regret.

Jamelle nodded quickly. "I understand. I do."

Luanna had told her to bring cash. She reached under her chair and pulled up a nylon gym bag. She unzipped it and dumped a pile of money on the desk. It was all the money she had in the world. She would pay anything—*do* anything—to get her baby back.

Devos began stacking the bills and gave Jamelle a tight smile through a haze of smoke.

"Right," he said. "Good for a start."

# CHAPTER 65

*Chicago*

I WAS STILL pissed off at Kira for almost killing us. Putting me in mortal danger was getting to be a pattern with her. I didn't appreciate being treated like a guinea pig—or like some kind of new-and-improved version of my ancestor. But our near miss didn't seem to bother Kira in the least. As soon as we got back to the loft and dried off, she took me back into the Doc Savage archive for more research. I held my tongue. I was afraid of what I might say if I let loose.

"All right," said Kira, clapping her hands together. "Time to get serious."

That did it. Was she kidding? I grabbed her by the shoulder and spun her around. I shook her.

*"Serious??"* I said. "A flameout over Lake Michigan wasn't serious enough?? Kira, we almost *died* out there!"

"Those were toys," she replied calmly. "We need protection."

I felt myself getting red in the face. I was getting tired of the runaround and the cryptic hints. "I thought *I* was your protection," I said. "For Christ's sake, you've turned me into Captain America! You've made me a mental marvel! Isn't that *enough*??"

Kira pulled away. "No, Doctor," she said, "you're *not* enough. Neither am I. Not with what we're up against. We're not ready yet. We need to pick Doc Savage's brain a little more. And this is where we do it."

She walked off and started rummaging through the shelves, sorting through parts and devices, pulling things aside and piling them on the lab table. I had no intention of helping. Not today.

"Pick away," I said. "Be my guest." I was feeling surly, and this room was starting to give me the creeps.

I wandered off into the corner and found myself staring at the Doc Savage arsenal. I ran my finger over the blade of a long cutlass. It still felt sharp enough to slice a man in half. I reached into a corner and picked up a rifle with a huge barrel. It was as heavy as a ten-pound weight. I realized that I'd never held a gun before in my life. I lifted the rifle up to my shoulder and pointed it at the brick wall across the room, aiming at a small stripe of mortar. Kira looked over.

"That's an elephant gun," she said. "Five-seventy-seven. Too heavy to carry. Forget it."

"I wasn't planning to put it in my pocket," I said.

I squinted down the barrel and tried to picture an actual human being in the sights. If it came right down to it, I wondered, would I actually be able to pull the trigger? Even if my life depended on it—or Kira's? I put the gun back in its place.

"Try a pistol," said Kira, nodding at the handguns. "Much more practical." There were about twenty of them, all shapes and sizes, hanging from wooden pegs. Some looked like they came straight from the O.K. Corral. Others looked like World War I vintage. I wondered if any of them still worked. I didn't really care. Just looking at them made me queasy.

"No thanks," I said.

Kira was dumping items out of containers and sorting them out on a small table. I could see her flipping through journals and reference books, trying to put the pieces together. I wondered how many days she'd spent in this room by herself. How many nights. How many *years*.

As I moved through the rows of firearms and ammunition, I picked up a sharp odor. I stopped and looked down. I realized that I was actually smelling the gunpowder from inside the cartridge casings. Was that even possible? My head started throbbing. I was sweating all over. The ceiling lights flared. I squeezed my eyes shut. That only made it worse. I suddenly felt weak and sick. I fell backward against a metal shelf.

The next second, an image flashed into my head. I was standing next to my great-grandfather in a jungle. It felt as if I could reach out and touch him. I could feel the heat radiating off his body. He had a gun in each hand and a wild look in his eyes, like he was facing down some kind of danger. Suddenly, he went into a crouch and started firing away through the thick foliage. I couldn't tell what he was shooting at. Animals? Humans? Ghosts? Flames shot out of the gun barrels. Shredded leaves and branches flew into the air like confetti.

Each shot was like a hammer hitting my skull. The smell of gunpowder was overpowering. Smoke was everywhere. My knees buckled. Everything went dark. I felt my body hitting the ground.

Was I shot? Was I dead? Was it over?

# CHAPTER 66

"HEY! HELLO? YOU in there, Doctor?"

I felt my eyes being pulled open. It was Kira. She was pressing my lids up and staring deep into my pupils. I was sitting on the floor with my back against the kitchen wall. It felt like my brain was coming out of a fog. I pushed her away.

"What the hell was *that*?" I asked. "What happened?"

"Not sure," said Kira. "Migraine maybe?"

"I've had migraines," I said. "That was no migraine. It was that goddamn *room*!"

"You might be right," said Kira. "There's some strange energy in there."

"No shit," I said.

I wondered about a Doc Savage curse. It sounded like something out of the old stories. Too crazy to be true. But what I felt was definitely real.

"Don't move," said Kira. "I'll be right back."

She stood up and walked into the kitchen. I squeezed my eyes shut and opened them wide to bring my vision back into focus. I heard the blender whirring, which was the last thing my throbbing head needed. When Kira came back, she was carrying a thick green smoothie.

"Let's get your blood sugar up," she said. "You didn't eat enough today."

She had a point. I was hungry. Starving, actually. But Kira's high-fiber slurry was not the answer. The sight of it turned my stomach.

"Pass," I said.

"You need protein," she said.

"I don't need it *that* bad," I replied.

She put the glass down. I could see her turning things over in her mind. I knew she was reading my mood, trying to figure out a way to get me back into the game.

"I have an idea," she said.

Naturally, I was suspicious. "What *kind* of idea?"

"What if we went out for dinner?"

I rubbed my temples and looked up. Was this some kind of trick? I sat forward.

"*Out* out?" I asked. It sounded too good to be true. "You mean to an actual restaurant—with normal food?"

"Why not?" said Kira. "My treat."

"Tonight?" I asked, still not believing it. "We can go out *tonight*?"

"If you're up for it," she said.

Maybe she was feeling sorry for me. Maybe she was manipulating me. I didn't care. Suddenly, my head was clearing. I could breathe again. The queasiness was gone. In fact, I was already thinking about a fat, juicy cheeseburger. I could almost taste it.

"You're on," I replied. "It's a date!"

Kira gave me a slight smile and patted my arm.

"Let's not use that word," she said.

# CHAPTER 67

*Lake Trasimeno, Italy*

AS PREDICTED, CLOUDS covered the moon by 10 p.m. The water in the cove was still and inky black, with no reflections. The two people in the small boat looked like a high-school couple out for a romantic rendezvous.

The boy cut the engine and turned off the running lights as the girl readied herself in the prow. Silent and nearly invisible, the skiff drifted toward the dock below a small hillside villa. The home was modestly impressive and slightly run down, the kind of lake estate that stayed in families for generations. The boy and the girl exchanged strange smiles. They were on time and on target.

Inside the dimly lit villa, chemist Angelo Chinelli was toking away his disappointment at missing out on the prestigious Antonio Feltrinelli Prize. Short-listed, but no win. Second year in a row. "Goddamn politics!" he muttered bitterly. But the bitterness was quickly fading. The weed he was smoking was top-notch, cultivated by one of his lab assistants. After just three hits, he was already feeling relaxed and drowsy. The two goblets of Barolo he had downed earlier contributed to the stupor.

As he eased back into the large worn sofa, his wife, Lucia, came down the hall from the nursery. She was wearing a cotton robe and her dark brown hair fell loose around her shoulders.

"She good?" Angelo asked, his lips barely moving.

"Sleeping like a baby," Lucia reported with a soft smile.

Angelo smiled back. His daughter, Carmella, was the true prize of the year, he told himself. Just eleven months old and as beautiful as her mother. Brilliant, too. He could tell already.

"I'm heading in the same direction," said Angelo, eyelids fluttering. Lucia flopped down next to him on the huge soft cushions and plucked the joint from his lips. She took a deep drag, held it, then exhaled a purple plume into the candle-light. She nuzzled up against him and gave him a warm smile.

"Next year, the Nobel," she said, stroking his cheek.

"Next year," Angelo replied with a soft laugh and a touch of pride. He knew that it might actually happen.

Lucia dropped the roach into a ceramic ashtray. She swung her leg over Angelo's lap, then pressed forward to deliver a warm, lingering kiss. She tasted of smoke and red wine. Angelo gently tugged the top of her robe open.

The next twenty minutes went by in a haze, but a very pleasant one. When it was over, Lucia rolled to the side and curled up. Angelo slid a pillow under her neck and gave her a soft kiss on the forehead. She was asleep already. Angelo looked at his watch, then slid off the sofa and walked back toward the nursery for one last check.

In the semi-darkness, it looked like little Carmella had burrowed under her blanket again. But when Angelo stepped closer, his dulled senses suddenly blasted back to life.

The blanket was there. The baby was not.

# CHAPTER 68

*Chicago*

I WAS FEELING almost normal, which felt totally amazing. The sidewalk café was trendy and hopping. The street traffic was a little noisy, but nobody cared. It was exciting to be out in the middle of the city. We were sitting in a small grouping of tables on the wide patio just outside the front door. By 8 p.m., every table was filled. It seemed like the kind of place people went to kick off an evening.

I remembered going to places like this after work by myself, with my nose buried in a research paper. But tonight was different. Tonight, I actually had female company. It felt nice. Even if the female was my kidnapper. Even if she was totally not attracted to me.

Kira was wearing skinny jeans and a flower-print blouse. Her hair was tucked under a black cap. She looked like an art history grad student. She looked great. I saw a few guys checking her out as they passed, but they lowered their eyes as soon as they noticed me. I realized that I now looked like the kind of boyfriend who might punch their lights out just for looking.

I was wearing the new white shirt and khaki pants Kira

had ordered to fit my new physique. Larger neck size. Smaller waist size. In addition to everything else, Kira was now my personal shopper. It had been a long time since I made any real decisions for myself. She picked up the little card that listed the evening's wine specials.

"Are we drinking tonight?" I asked.

"We certainly are," said Kira. "And I won't even drill you on the vintage."

She ran her finger down the choices. I looked over the appetizer options. I realized that, for the first time, I could read a menu without my glasses. New eyes. New body. New clothes. New everything. Mostly, it felt good to just pretend that I had an actual life again, even if it was only for a few hours. I tried to put Doc Savage and his blazing guns out of my mind.

Kira was still reviewing the wines when a blond waitress walked over and set a red votive candle down in the center of the table. The flame wobbled slightly and then settled. Kira looked up to order the wine, but the waitress was already gone.

Kira shrugged. "I guess she's just the official candle placer." I went back to the appetizer list. But only for a second. Something was off. A smell. Like bleach from a table cleaner. No. Stronger. Sodium hypochlorite. I jumped out of my seat.

"Bomb!" I shouted.

I grabbed the votive off the table. I glanced toward the street and saw a stake-bed truck passing by. I hurled the votive into the back of the truck, then dove across the table and threw Kira to the ground. I heard a huge blast and felt the shock wave pass through me, shaking my insides. The café windows shattered. Tables flipped, and people were blown out of their seats onto the patio.

I turned my head back toward the street. It was filled with smoke and ash. The truck bed had absorbed most of the blast. The wooden frame had exploded into a thousand chunks and splinters. The driver staggered out of his cab, blood pouring from his nose. All over the patio, people were crawling and reaching for one another, covered in blood and debris. My ears were numb. All I could hear was a high-pitched hum.

I grabbed Kira under one arm and pulled her to her feet. There was a rip in the back of her blouse and she had a scrape on one cheek. But other than that, she seemed okay. As I tried to recover my balance, she patted me down for damage. All I was missing were a few shirt buttons.

Kira turned toward the restaurant and looked down the alley that ran beside it. The hum in my ears was still too loud to hear what she was saying. But I could read her lips.

"The waitress!"

# CHAPTER 69

WE HEADED DOWN the alley at a dead run, dodging dumpsters and wooden pallets. Halfway down, I saw a blond wig sticking out of an open trash can. The noise in my ears had dissolved into a mild buzz. I could hear shouts and screams and sirens behind us.

A block ahead, I saw a female figure running away. She was slender and agile. When we reached the end of the alley, she was gone. Kira looked left and right down the busy street. Then she looked back and saw a fire escape ladder hanging off the side of the building we had just passed. She grabbed onto the rungs with both hands and started climbing.

"Up here!" she said.

"How do you know?" I asked.

"I know," she said, scrambling higher.

As soon as she cleared the first floor level, I followed. In about twenty seconds, we were both crawling over a low wall onto the roof. The sunset was casting long shadows over the whole city. We were in a strange landscape of massive AC units and satellite dishes. We ran across the rooftop to the other side of the building. I caught a flash of movement from the roof on the other side of the street.

"There!" I shouted.

Kira spun around and ran halfway back across the roof. Before I could react, she bounced on the balls of her feet and then headed toward the edge at top speed. When she was about four feet away, she launched herself across the gap, four stories up. She landed in a somersault on the other side and jumped to her feet. She looked back at me.

"Let's *go!*" she shouted.

I wasn't sure I had it in me, but there was no way I was letting her go on alone. I gave myself plenty of room for a head start and then jumped off from the same spot she did. But I misjudged my bulk or the distance, or both. As soon as I was in the air, I knew I was coming up short.

As I fell, I grabbed for the bars of a window guard on the top floor. The rusty metal cut into my hands and my knees banged into the bricks below. I gritted my teeth through the pain and pulled myself up. When I rolled over the low wall onto the other roof, Kira was already on the move.

The rooftop was a maze of bubble-shaped skylights and old water tanks. We threaded our way through until we could see across to the next building. A woman with dark hair was hanging from a stone parapet just twenty feet away. As she muscled herself up, her right sleeve fell back to her elbow. Her forearm was red and scarred. Kira immediately dropped down behind the low wall on our side.

"Oh my God," she muttered to herself. She looked pale and stunned. I watched as the woman flipped herself over the parapet like a gymnast. She crouched low for a second, staring right back at me. Then she ran off and disappeared behind a mass of metal ductwork.

"C'mon!" I said. "We can catch her." I started to psych myself up for another jump. But Kira didn't move.

"No," she said. "That's exactly what she wants."

I looked down. Kira had her fists balled against her forehead and she was rocking back and forth, muttering to herself over and over again. "Not her, not her, not her..." She looked scared. I'd never seen that in her before. *Never.*

"Wait," I said. "You *know* her?"

Kira nodded slowly. She sounded numb. "Her name is Irina," she said. "We were classmates. I haven't seen her for more than a decade."

"What does it mean that she's here?" I said.

"It means we don't have any more time," said Kira. Her voice was strong again, and when she looked up, her expression had changed. There was no more fear in her eyes. Just rage.

# CHAPTER 70

WHEN WE GOT back to the loft, Kira was quiet and focused. All I saw was cold determination.

"Hang on a minute," she said, then disappeared into her room. Actually, it was less than a minute. When she came out, her casual clothes were gone. She was back in athletic gear. All black. Her hair was pulled back tight. She looked like a commando.

I was watching the news report on the TV over the workout area. Explosion outside a Lakeview restaurant. Twenty injuries. Three people in critical condition. So far, no motive, no suspects, no leads. Terrorism could not be ruled out.

Kira glanced up at the screen. "I was careless and stupid," she muttered. "I felt sorry for you, and look what happened."

"So this is my fault now?" I asked. "This is on *me*??"

She opened the door marked UTILITY. "We don't have time to argue."

Inside the vault, Kira moved quickly. She grabbed a small backpack and tossed me another one. She started throwing in canisters, packets, and tools off shelves and tables. She grabbed a pistol from the rack and handed one to me. As soon as my hand touched the grip, I started to twitch. Kira grabbed my arm—hard.

"Hold it together, Doctor," said Kira. "Now is when I need you."

I stuffed the pistol into my backpack. She tossed me an extra box of ammunition, then took one last look around the vault.

"That's it," she said. "Let's go."

"Where are we going?" I asked.

Kira slung her backpack over her shoulder and walked straight out toward the elevator. She glanced at me over her shoulder.

"Back to school," she said.

# CHAPTER 71

WHEN WE GOT to the street, Kira scoped out the traffic and speed-walked to the nearest intersection. I saw a cab idling at a stoplight. Kira ran in front of the car and slapped the hood. The cabbie shook his head. She moved around and rapped her knuckles against the driver's window. The glass slid down two inches. I heard the cabbie say, "Off duty." The light turned green. The cab started to move. Kira moved right along with it. She pulled out a hundred-dollar bill and slapped it flat against the window.

"How about now?" she shouted.

The cabbie stopped and unlocked the doors. Horns were blaring from the cars behind. Kira yanked the rear door open and we slid into the back seat.

"Where to?" asked the cabbie. He accelerated before the door was even shut.

"O'Hare," said Kira. She pulled out another bill. "And here's another hundred to ignore the speed limit."

"You got it," said the cabbie, glancing down at his dashboard clock. "What time is your flight?"

"As soon as we get there," she said.

I didn't think we had a flight booked. I didn't even know where this mysterious school was located. I also didn't know how Kira planned to get us on a plane carrying a bunch of metal devices and two loaded pistols. But at the moment, I was more worried about dying in a car crash.

The cabbie shot through River North traffic, running two yellow lights and one red before turning onto I-90. The car rattled and roared as he pushed it up past seventy on the highway. Kira twisted herself backward to look out the rear window, her hands gripping the headrest. Suddenly, she whipped back around.

"Damnit!" she shouted. "Get *down!*"

"Get down where?" the cabbie shouted back. "I'm fucking *driving!*"

"Lower your head! *Now!*" shouted Kira. She looked at me. "She's back," she said.

The cabbie slid down in his seat until his eyes were barely at the level of the steering wheel. A second later, the rear window exploded into a million pieces. I dropped down in my seat as hard pebbles of safety glass rained through the cab.

I turned and looked up—just far enough to see a black sedan weaving through traffic behind us, approaching fast. A dark-haired woman was leaning out the driver's window, arm extended. Irina! I saw the muzzle blast and heard two loud metallic bangs inside the cab.

"Son of a *bitch!*" shouted the cabbie. "Who *are* you people??"

"Do not stop!" Kira yelled back. "Do not slow down!"

Kira shoved me down on the seat. She reached into her backpack and pulled out a small metal oval. It looked like an egg. She leaned out the rear window and tossed it onto the roadway. I heard a huge bang and screeching tires. I jerked my head up again to look. The black sedan was spinning off to the side of the highway. The front end smashed into the guardrail, and I saw the airbags deploy. Cars careened around the wreck. A truck slammed into a Prius, and they both ended up crosswise on the interstate as cars piled up behind them.

We were way ahead of the wreckage, coming up on the Canfield exit.

"I'm getting off here!" shouted the cabbie. "I gotta find a cop!"

Kira pulled the pistol out of her backpack and pointed it at the rearview mirror.

"You're going to the airport," said Kira. "You're not stopping anywhere."

"Okay, okay," said the cabbie, raising one hand. "No more shooting!"

He crouched as low as he could behind the wheel and sped up again. I looked out the window and saw signs for the departure terminal. Kira stuffed the gun in her backpack and braced herself on the edge of the seat, ready to move. The driver sped up the ramp, cutting in line. He swerved toward the curb and jammed on the brakes.

"Out!" he screamed. "Get out now!"

I shoved the door open and scrambled to the curb, brushing bits of glass off my clothes. Kira followed right behind. She leaned through the front window and tossed a wad of bills at the cabbie.

"For your back window," she said. She looked up at the two holes punched through the cab's roof. She pulled out a few more bills and tossed them in. "And the rest of it." The cabbie didn't even reach for the money. He just let it flutter onto the floor mat as he pulled away. I watched him dodge a traffic guard and bounce hard over a speedbump. Then he sped off toward the airport exit. He didn't look back.

"Let's go," said Kira.

She was heading toward the bank of sliding doors at the terminal entrance. Suddenly she stopped and pulled me down behind a low cement divider. All around us, people were moving through the doors with their carry-on bags and rolling suitcases.

"Don't move," she said.

"What?" I asked. "Irina's gone. You bombed her off the road."

Kira jerked her head in the direction of an entrance door about twenty yards down the row. I poked my head over the barrier. I didn't see anything strange—just a bunch of neatly dressed teenagers near the door, ten or twelve of them. They looked like an international youth group. Maybe a choir.

As I watched, one of the guys pulled out his cell phone. He glanced at the screen, then gave a hand signal. The other kids gathered around him and looked at one another with weird robotic smiles. Kira pulled me back down and leaned in close to my ear.

"Irina didn't come alone," she whispered. "She brought a whole damned class."

# CHAPTER 72

"JESUS!" I WHISPERED back. "Somebody must really want you dead."

"You and me both," said Kira.

She pointed toward the entrance door closest to us. Then she glanced toward the curb and gestured for me to wait. An Uber had just pulled up and a whole family was spilling out— mom, dad, and four young kids, all chatty and excited, hauling color-coordinated luggage. As they walked past us, we stood up and blended in with them, like a friendly aunt and uncle.

The automatic doors parted and then we were all inside. I looked back. The students had passed through the door on their end of the terminal. They were glancing in our direction, trying not to be obvious. The happy family headed toward the ground-floor elevator, leaving us alone and exposed. Then the students started to move. Not like a youth group. More like a military squad, or killer robots. They fanned out, slow and deliberate. No rush. I got a sick feeling.

"Damnit!" I said. "How many of them *are* there??"

"Look around, Doctor," said Kira. "Or do you need your glasses back?"

She tugged me toward the escalator that led to the upper level. We walked quickly, weaving through the crowd. One team of students followed us, matching our pace. Another group suddenly emerged near the escalator at the other end of the terminal. Kira was right. They were *everywhere*. We stepped onto the metal stairs and jostled past the other passengers as we headed up. When I looked back, I could see the pursuit team right behind us.

We stepped off onto the second level and started speed walking, trying to open the gap. The team was about ten yards back. Three male, two female. They looked eighteen, maybe twenty. They moved as a unit, slipping between other travelers, excusing themselves with strange smiles. I started looking for places to duck into, but this part of the terminal was wide open. Like a target range.

"They won't shoot in here," said Kira. "They don't want the attention."

"Are they planning to *smile* us to death?" I asked.

"They'll try to separate us," said Kira, "then get close enough for a needle stick—make it look like a heart attack."

I nodded toward her backpack. "Don't you have any escape tricks in there?"

"Nothing that's any good in the open," she said. "We don't want any attention either." She glanced back. "We need to get out of here. *Now!* Keep moving."

The second team of students stepped off the other escalator, moving along the right side of the corridor in a neat line, just waiting to pick us off. Kira headed toward a young attendant in a United Airlines uniform.

"Hang back," said Kira. "When this guy starts talking to me, bump my elbow. Make sure I feel it."

Kira sped up. I slowed down. She stepped up square in front of the airline attendant and waved her hand in his face.

"Sorry," she said. "I'm all turned around. Which way is Terminal C?"

The attendant gestured toward the TSA checkpoints to his left. "That way," he said. "There's a moving sidewalk once you get through security."

That's when I bumped Kira, knocking her forward into the attendant. She whipped around and glared at me.

"Watch where you're going, idiot!" she said.

"Sorry!" I said, looking back. The attendant recovered quickly. He was already turning to answer another traveler's question. Kira caught up to me.

"What was *that* for?" I asked.

"For this," said Kira.

She opened her hand. I looked down. The attendant's plastic key card was in her palm. I looked back. The class was closing in.

Kira headed toward a nondescript metal door in the right-hand wall. It had a square Plexiglass panel at eye level and a metal alarm bar across the middle. The students to our right were moving past the TSA podiums. If we didn't speed up, they'd get to the door first.

"Go!" said Kira.

We started running. So did the students. They got tangled up with a tour group and started pushing their way through. That bought us a few seconds. When we got to the door, Kira waved the key card over a plastic panel on the wall. She pushed the alarm bar. The door opened with a loud beep.

I heard a rush of footsteps behind us. We slipped through the door. I rammed it shut with my shoulder—just as a bunch of faces mashed up against it from the other side. They looked agitated and fierce. Kira looked back at them and lifted her middle finger.

"Hey, kids!" she said. "Who's smiling *now*??"

# CHAPTER 73

WE DUCKED OUT of sight behind the door and moved down a short hallway. Kira keyed us through another exit door and we stepped outside into the night air. It smelled like jet fuel. There was another long terminal building glowing brightly a few hundred yards to the right. I looked back over my shoulder.

"Did we lose them?" I asked.

"No," said Kira. "We just pissed them off. They'll find a way out."

"Should we get help?" I asked.

"Help?" Kira just stared at me. "You still don't get it, do you? There's only one person in the world that I can trust right now. And that's you."

She led the way across a grass border onto a large section of asphalt. I looked past the end of the other terminal and saw the outlines of three sleek executive jets.

"Don't tell me you have a plane," I said.

She stared straight ahead. "Not yet."

It was another few hundred yards from the corner of the far

terminal to the edge of the runway. We hung tight against the terminal building as airport workers buzzed back and forth on their little carts with their warning lights blinking.

The jet closest to us had its boarding stairs down, and the interior lights were on.

The pilot was walking underneath doing his preflight check. As he moved toward the tail section, a white stretch limo approached from the rear. The pilot straightened his jacket and walked toward the car.

"Now!" whispered Kira.

It was a thirty-yard dash. We ducked underneath the fuse-lage and hung there in the shadows for a few seconds. Twenty yards behind the tail, the limo doors were opening. The pilot shook hands with a man in an expensive suit. Two stylish young women slid out of the back seat.

Kira yanked the chocks away from the jet's front wheel. We came out on the other side of the fuselage and raced up the six steps to the main door. We stepped inside and looked left and right. Empty. The cabin looked like a luxury lounge. There were six huge passenger seats and a sofa in the passenger section. Lots of leather and expensive wood trim. No economy class here.

Kira ducked into the cockpit and slipped into the left-hand seat. It took me a second to realize what was happening.

"We're stealing a *jet*??" I asked.

"Fastest way out of town," Kira replied. She was already flipping switches. I heard a loud hum and saw the stairway being pulled up into the fuselage.

"Lock it!" Kira called out.

I cranked the locking lever hard in the direction of the big red arrow. There was a satisfying **thunk**. Two seconds later, we started rolling forward.

I peeked out one of the cabin windows to where the pilot and limo passengers were sorting baggage on the tarmac. They looked up. The pilot blinked in disbelief and then started chasing after us, waving his arms like crazy. Kira made a hard turn to the left. I fell against one of the leather seats.

"Get up here and strap in!" she shouted.

I scrambled forward and dropped into the copilot seat. I pulled the harness over my shoulders and fastened it. Kira was already turning onto the runway. I could see the long stretch of asphalt reaching into the distance. Back near the terminal, red lights started flashing. Workers in coveralls were climbing into emergency trucks. Guys in white shirts ran out of the terminal with walkie-talkies. I saw a couple of security guards with their guns out.

"No way we're getting away with this," I muttered.

Kira looked over at me. "Hold my beer," she said.

She had her hands on two large white handles on the divider between us. She pushed the handles forward. There was a strong vibration and a roar from the back of the jet. We started rolling down the runway. In a few seconds, we were at highway speed. The ground started to blur.

"Let's go, let's go!" Kira muttered, low and intense, as we ate up the runway. At that moment, the nose lifted and suddenly the windshield filled with sky. I looked back to my right and saw a cluster of red lights circling the end of the runway like angry fireflies. I let out a huge breath and looked for something to hold onto. This was *nuts*!

"Aren't we supposed to talk to the tower or something?" I asked.

"Don't be such a goody-goody," said Kira.

She put the jet into a steep climb. I felt myself being pressed back against the seat. I looked down at Cook County disappearing below. My heart rate started to settle, but my brain was still buzzing. Kira was cool and calm, like she was taking a drive to the mall.

"You should have told me you knew how to fly," I said.

Kira tapped a few buttons on the console. We started to level out.

"Don't look surprised," she said. "So do you."

She nodded toward the screen in front of my seat. "Set a course 330 degrees northwest," she said.

I had no clue how to make that happen. For a few seconds, I just sat there, staring at the console.

"I'm not kidding, Doctor," said Kira. "*Do* it."

I reached out and put my fingers on the screen. Suddenly, the whole navigation protocol popped into my head. Every single step.

I must have learned it in my sleep.

# CHAPTER 74

"KAMCHATKA," I SAID. "Never heard of it." That was the destination readout that popped up on the screen as we got closer. "That's where we're going?"

We'd already been flying for five hours.

Kira nodded. "It's a tiny piece of Russia, like a finger poking down along the Bering Sea." I looked at the map on the screen. That's exactly what it looked like.

"Why would anybody put a school there?" I asked.

"My great-grandfather was Russian," said Kira, "or *said* he was. Nobody really knows. But that's where he built his little empire. Up where he knew nobody would ever find it."

"What happens when we get there?" I asked.

Kira stared out through the windshield. "We save the world," she said, "starting with a few hundred kids."

Okay, I thought to myself. One step at a time. First step— land in one piece. I looked out my side again. We'd crossed over western Canada and the lower edge of Alaska. Now we were cruising over open water.

"Are you sure we've got enough fuel?" I asked. The gauges looked low to me.

"We're cutting it close," said Kira. "But we're not stopping at a Shell station."

I stared out through the windshield. At this point, there was nowhere to land anyway. There was nothing outside but dark sky and even darker water.

Suddenly, a bright orange streak shot past my window like a comet. Before I could even register what I was seeing, I heard Kira shout.

"Damnit! Missile! Air-to-air!"

I whipped around in my seat.

"Are you *shitting* me??" I yelled. I'd actually started to feel cozy in our luxury ride. Now somebody was trying to blast us out of the sky.

"Who the hell is shooting at us??" I yelled.

"Does it matter??" Kira yelled back.

She banked hard to the left. My head banged against the side of the cockpit. A second streak passed by her side, close enough to shake the whole body of the jet.

I felt trapped, terrified, helpless. My mind flashed to ejection seats and parachutes. But I knew better. We were in a cushy executive jet, not an F-16.

I heard a loud bang and felt a huge jolt on my side. The fuselage rocked. I saw another orange flame going by, but this one was fragmented into separate flares. The nose started to drop, and the horizon disappeared.

*"Sonavabitch!"* Kira shouted. "It clipped the wing!" The jet wobbled and started doing crazy corkscrews. Kira kept punching controls and pushing forward on the throttle handles. The

engines whined and rattled behind us. Everything through the windshield was black. I felt a sick drop in my belly. I was losing all sense of direction.

Down was up. Up was down. I braced my arms against the top of the console. I looked over at Kira. I couldn't believe this was happening.

"Is this another one of your goddam *tests*??" I shouted. The sound of the engines was so loud I could barely hear myself.

"This time you might be on your own," Kira shouted back. She was doing everything she could to regain control. But none of it was working. I stared at the altimeter. 1,000 feet. 500 feet. Blood rushed to my head. My vision clouded over. Then another woman's voice filled the cockpit, sounding like a very stern Siri.

"Pull up!" she kept saying, "Pull up!"

That's the last thing I remember.

# CHAPTER 75

THE FREEZING COLD brought me back. Or maybe the pain in my head. I woke up floating in black water with a sharp stabbing sensation over my left eye. When I touched my forehead, I felt a long gash. My fingers came away covered in watery blood. My legs were numb, but I could move them. They were all that was keeping me from going under. I had no memory of the crash, no idea how long I'd been out.

I twisted around, looking for Kira. Or wreckage. Or land. But there was nothing. The night was so dark that the sky blended with the water.

*"Kira!"*

I shouted her name, over and over. It felt like hours. Until my voice gave out and I couldn't shout anymore. My body was getting stiff. My brain was starting to shut down. As I stared into the darkness, small waves started to look like fins. I just hung there, trying not to thrash around. I knew there was blood in the water. It was mine.

I squinted to sharpen my vision. My heart started to pound, and I got a jolt in my gut. There was a small lump floating in the distance, maybe fifty yards away. Was it human?? *Please, God!*

"Kira!" I shouted again. By now, my voice was barely a squawk. I started swimming as hard as I could. The lump, whatever it was, kept disappearing behind the waves and popping up again.

When I was about twenty yards off, I took a deep breath and did a surface dive. I knew I could move faster underwater. Just as my breath ran out, I stretched my arms forward and grabbed. I was praying that it was Kira, and that she was alive. Instead, I felt a small bundle of leather and cloth.

My heart dropped. It was my backpack.

It was floating because of a small inflated sack in the lining. A Doc Savage invention, no doubt. I opened the flap and looked inside.

I saw some rope. A coil of thin wire. A pair of goggles. A bunch of loose buttons. A small water bottle. One energy bar in a foil wrapper. But no life vest. No signal flares. And no mini underwater breathing device. I should have known we'd used up the last two in existence.

I reached into the bottom of the bag and felt hard metal. The pistol.

I pulled the gun out and pointed it into the sky. Three shots meant SOS. Kira didn't teach me that. I learned it in the Boy Scouts. I squeezed the trigger. There was nothing but a loud click. The shell casings were soaked and useless. At that point, the gun was just deadweight. And it felt like the worst kind of bad luck. I dropped it into the water and watched it sink.

I was shivering all over. My lips were trembling. I tried to blink the salt out of my eyes. Then I saw something new in the distance. At first, I thought it was just another line of whitecaps. But it wasn't moving. It just sat there. I couldn't tell how far away it was. I had no reference point. A mile maybe?

I wasn't sure I could make it that far. Then I thought about the ice bath. The swimming pool. The plunge into Lake Michigan. In my head, I could hear Kira yelling at me, pushing me, *shaming* me. I felt fresh energy flowing into my limbs, and my mind started to clear. I realized that the old Doctor Brandt Savage would have been dead already—broken to pieces or drowned. But somehow, I was still here.

I wrapped the backpack strap around my shoulder and started kicking like a porpoise toward the white something in the distance. I thought it might be a mirage, just my mind giving me false hope. But I kept going. What else could I do?

It was the only hope I had.

# CHAPTER 76

*Eastern Russia*

AT THAT HOUR, the school was mostly dark. But underground, the warm nursery ward still glowed. A long row of rocking chairs lined one whole wall. Seated in each rocker was a stone-faced woman with a baby at her breast. The wet nurses were stout, red-faced Slavs, but the babies were of every race and complexion. It was a multinational feeding station.

The woman at the end of the row sat alone, rocking more slowly than the others. The door from the corridor opened. The nurse looked up. A female attendant walked in, carrying an infant wrapped in two blankets.

"Two-day trip from Africa," said the attendant. "She's weak."

The nurse reached up and took the small bundle into her arms. She peeled back the blanket to expose the baby's face. Dark brown skin. Huge brown eyes. Tiny puckered mouth. The baby mewed softly, not enough strength to cry. The nurse looked up at the hovering attendant.

"Get out," she said bluntly. "Let her feed."

The attendant turned and walked back into the corridor. The nurse opened one side of her blouse to expose a large, elongated breast. She teased her nipple around the baby's lips until the little girl latched on.

As the infant suckled, the wet nurse started to rock in sync with the rest of the row. When she looked up again, there was another figure in the doorway.

It was the headmaster.

Kamenev caught the nurse's eye and nodded approvingly. Odd, thought the nurse. It was unusual for Kamenev to check on a new arrival. He obviously had high hopes for this one.

# CHAPTER 77

THE WATER WAS getting choppier. It took me twenty minutes to get close enough to realize what I'd been swimming toward. It wasn't some hallucination after all.

It was an iceberg.

The part I could see was about fifty feet long, with a couple of jagged peaks jutting up toward the sky. I felt a sudden surge of relief. I figured if I could get there and climb on, at least I wouldn't have to die from drowning. I could just die from hypothermia. I'd read that it was like going to sleep.

I breast-stroked the final fifty yards or so, then used my elbows to haul myself onto a low ledge just above the waterline. I rolled onto my side and lay there for a few minutes, catching my breath. I flexed my fingers to get the feeling back in the tips. I stared up at the sky and watched the vapor clouds blow out of my mouth.

I realized that my wet clothes were starting to freeze in the open air. Before long, I'd be covered in an icy shell. Part of me just wanted to close my eyes and let go. That would be the easy way out. No pain. No fear. But I couldn't do it. Something inside made me start moving.

I rolled over and pressed against the ice to push myself up. It felt strange. I pounded on the surface. I scraped at it with my fingernails. I leaned closer. I scraped again. I realized that what I was feeling wasn't ice at all. There was nothing natural about it. It was some kind of manufactured material, made to look like ice from a distance—like a gigantic Hollywood prop.

What the hell was going on? I looked up and saw a series of indentations in the white surface, leading up the side of one of the peaks. From out in the water, they'd looked like natural formations. From where I stood now, they looked like steps. I started to make my way up.

Even though the ice was artificial, it was covered with a layer of actual frost, slick and dangerous. One wrong move and I'd be back in the water. I felt for handholds as I moved up the steps. Just ahead was a large overhang, dripping with icicles. I reached up and touched one. A convincing fake.

I peeked under the overhang and saw a hard vertical edge—some kind of hatch. It looked rusted shut. I scraped through the thin coating of frost until I found an indented metal handle. It wasn't much of a grip. I hooked my fingers in and pulled. The hatch groaned slightly and the gap widened a few millimeters. I tried again. My fingers slipped off. They were stinging from the cold and scraped raw from the rough metal.

I was getting nowhere.

I pulled the backpack off my shoulder. I unfastened one of the straps and slid the metal buckle into the small gap between the hatch door and the frame. Then I pulled the strap up until the buckle caught underneath. I gripped the strap with both hands and tugged. The hatch groaned some more. The gap got wider. Now I had enough space to jam my hands underneath. I strained and pulled until the hatch door gave way.

I leaned over and peeked inside. I saw the top edge of a rusted ladder. There was light coming from below. I flipped onto my belly and put my foot on the top rung, then slowly backed through the opening. I pulled the hatch closed behind me.

I was inside a translucent tube. The ladder stretched down about twenty feet. My feet were still so numb I could barely feel the rungs. When I got to the bottom, I was below sea level, in a room about half the size of a football field.

I couldn't believe what I was seeing.

Of all the stories I'd heard about my ancestor, this was the one I thought had *zero* chance of being true. Even the name I'd heard for this place seemed overblown. But it was obviously real.

I was standing in the Fortress of Solitude.

# CHAPTER 78

I LOOKED AROUND for a minute, barely moving. It took that long to absorb the scale of the place. The whole interior was supported by a framework of wooden beams, running up, down, and crossways. The ceiling was nearly as high as the peaks outside, maybe thirty feet up. The floor was made of thick planks, like a boardwalk or dock.

When I started walking around, the planks creaked and groaned. There were cracks in the walls where seawater had leaked in, and I saw big puddles and salt stains on the floor. If this place had actually been around since the 1930s, it was amazing that it hadn't sunk. Even more impressive, some of the lights still worked. They looked like primitive fluorescent tubes, dim but still glowing. They gave the whole place a tunnel-of-doom look. Which reflected exactly how I felt.

In the center of the space, there were long wooden tables covered with all kinds of electronic devices and tools. Most of the stuff looked corroded and useless. I walked over to a row of rusted metal bins against one wall, each one as big as a washing machine. I lifted one of the lids and got hit with a horrible odor. I held my breath and peeked inside. There was a layer of black sludge lining the bottom. I figured it used to be food. Now there was nothing but stench.

At the far end, there was a kitchen with a propane stove and an open cupboard with pots, dishes, and coffee mugs. Against one wall, there were long shelves filled with books— an impressive private library.

A lot of the bindings were falling apart, but I could still read some of the titles, mostly science textbooks and literary classics. *The Complete Works of William Shakespeare,* the *Iliad, The History of the Decline and Fall of the Roman Empire.* I picked up a couple leather-bound books from the end of the row. The first one was *Twenty Thousand Leagues Under the Sea,* by Jules Verne. The second one was by Robert Louis Stevenson. *Kidnapped.*

I winced—and thought about Kira.

# CHAPTER 79

I SLID THE two books back onto the shelf. My head felt light. I was achy and exhausted. I leaned against the wall and tried to organize my thoughts. They were scattered, and pretty dark.

I was alive, but I wasn't so sure that was a positive. I'd been trained for a mission, and the mission had failed. It was my job to protect Kira, and I hadn't done it. And somewhere on the Kamchatka Peninsula, her school was still pumping out smiling killers. It felt strange to think about it, but after all these years, John Sunlight's vision was actually taking over the world. And there was nothing I could do to stop it. *Nothing!*

All of a sudden, the anger and helplessness boiled over. I started screaming at the top of my lungs. I grabbed a hammer off a workbench and threw it into a glass cabinet. It shattered with a loud crash. I ran my arm along a crowded benchtop and knocked everything onto the floor—machine parts, chemical bottles, piles of loose papers.

A book tipped off the edge of the bench and landed with a heavy thud. I don't know why, but something made me reach down and pick it up. It was as thick as a Bible, with brown leather binding. I brushed off the dust and saw a name embossed on the cover. It took me a second to understand what I was looking at.

*Dr. Clark Savage, Jr.,* the lettering read.

Doc Savage's full name.

My hands actually started trembling. I set the book on the workbench and started leafing through the pages. The paper was yellowed, but the contents were totally readable. I realized that I was looking at my great-grandfather's journal. The famous Doc Savage genius was right there in front of my eyes. There were plans for X-ray cameras, fluoroscopes, and desalinization units. There were sketches for gyroscopes and flying wings and crazy pneumatic tube systems. It was like paging through one of da Vinci's notebooks.

One page near the end stood out from all the scientific scrawls. It was some kind of personal manifesto, handwritten in bold lettering. I ripped the page out and put it on the bench. Then I flipped to the last page of the journal. Glued to the inside back cover was a small sepia photograph. It showed two infant boys, no more than a couple months old. They were lying side by side on a thick blanket. At the bottom of the picture were two names written in bold script: *Clark & Cal.*

I stared at the picture. Kira had been right. The twin story was true. I carefully pulled the photo loose and put it on top of the ripped-out page. In that instant, I felt a weird sensation come over me. My whole body started shuddering. It was as if everything I'd gone through was catching up with me at once. My legs buckled and my head started spinning. I staggered down the length of the workbench, holding on to the thick wooden top for dear life. I managed to reach a wooden bulwark a few feet from the end. I looked around the corner and saw a row of military cots, each one with a small pillow and a folded blanket. As I eased myself around a support post, I caught a glimpse of myself in a shaving mirror. It was not pretty.

I had a day's growth of beard. My eyes looked hollow, and my skin was pale. The gash on my head was red and angry looking. I'd have a scar there for sure. Not that anybody would ever see it. Nobody was going to find me. Not here. Not *ever*.

I stripped off my clothes and lay down on the nearest cot. I pulled the wool blanket over me. I realized that I'd never felt so alone. I thought back over the last six months—about how Kira had changed my body, and my brain, and my life.

For what?

Maybe I should have hated her for leaving me in this position, but I didn't. Somehow, I felt that I'd let her down, and I couldn't believe I'd never see her again.

It wasn't possible. It wasn't fair. After all we'd been through together, how could she go and die without me?

"Wrong question," I could hear her saying. And then, "You have only yourself."

I turned my face to the pillow and started sobbing like a baby.

# CHAPTER 80

*Eastern Russia*

THE MAIN GROUNDS OF the school compound were dark, except for the glow of security lights from the main building. After his stop in the nursery to admire the new enrollee, Kamenev walked across the yard toward the far edge of the property, beyond the firing range and the oval dirt track. There, at the end of an asphalt strip nearly half a mile long, he waited. Before long, he heard a low whistle in the sky and saw a set of navigation lights beaming through the cloud cover in the distance. Kamenev reached into a metal junction box and flipped a switch. Rows of bright blue lights came to life on both sides of the asphalt, forming bright stripes.

The compact fighter jet touched down at the far end of the runway at 150 miles per hour. By the time it reached the apron where Kamenev was standing, it was rolling to a gentle stop. The engine shut down. The cockpit hood folded back. Irina unfastened her harness and pushed herself out of the pilot's seat.

Her face was bruised and she favored her left leg as she walked across the tarmac. Kamenev stepped forward, expecting his usual thorough debrief, but Irina brushed past him without even looking up.

"Target destroyed," she said numbly. "No survivors."

# CHAPTER 81

*Gaborone, Botswana*

IT WAS JUST past noon when Jamelle Maina finally opened her eyes. She rolled to the side and tossed back her top sheet. Her body was covered in sweat. Since her baby had been taken, she'd had an impossible time getting to sleep. But last night's pills and wine had finally knocked her out. Now the midday heat was bringing her around.

She swung her long, muscular legs out of bed and walked over to the boxy air conditioner in the window of her tiny bedroom. The machine was rumbling, but the fan wasn't blowing. With her bare feet, Jamelle could feel a small puddle of warm water on the floor underneath. She banged the unit with her fist, but that just made the rumbling louder.

She walked to the bathroom, turned on the sink tap, and wiped her forehead and neck with a wet towel. She stared into the mirror. Her face was drawn, and her eyes were red. She felt like she looked a decade older than her twenty-three years.

Another week had passed without word from the police—and without contact of any kind from the private investigator.

In the beginning, Devos had returned her calls and texts, but now all she got was his voice-mail greeting.

Jamelle flopped back onto the bed and turned toward the wall, staring at a photo she kept taped at eye level, so close she could touch it. Her little girl. Jamelle ran her finger over the picture and imagined the feel of her baby's skin, the smell of her hair, the sound of her laugh. As tears dripped down her cheeks, Jamelle called her daughter's name softly, over and over again. Like a prayer.

# CHAPTER 82

*Eastern Russia*

ON THE REMOTE peninsula two continents west, dawn was still several hours away. In a small room buried beneath the school's main building, security officers Balakin and Petrov were eight hours into their shift, their eyes bleary from staring at screens all night long. It was boring work. The only activity had been a solitary fox crossing the perimeter, its eyes glowing yellow on the night-vision camera. Everything else was quiet and secure, as usual.

Balakin pulled a cigarette from his pack and lit it. He leaned back in his chair, took a deep drag, and exhaled toward the ceiling. A forbidden pleasure. This was the one place on the property he could smoke with impunity, in violation of Kamenev's strict prohibition. The room's powerful vent filters removed every trace of smoke and odor. Petrov used the soundproof room to indulge in a vice of his own—one that drove Balakin to distraction.

"How can you *stand* it?" Balakin shouted. He was referring to the German techno music blaring from Petrov's Bluetooth speaker.

"Keeps me awake," Petrov called back, bobbing his head in time to the pounding beat.

"Hey!" Balakin shouted.

"All right, all right!" said Petrov. "I'll turn it down..."

"No!" said Balakin. *"Look!"*

He was leaning over the console, his nose just inches from one of the monitors—the one showing the outside of the explosives shed on the far side of the property. "Shed" was a misnomer. It was a pillbox-shaped building with walls two feet thick and six feet of solid steel descending into the ground to prevent burrowing, animal or otherwise.

Balakin dropped his cigarette through a metal floor grate and rolled his chair forward. The shed was just a blocky outline in the darkness, but there was a bright flare around one side of the heavy metal door, so strong it almost whited out the camera lens. Petrov shot his partner a look. Balakin nodded.

Petrov reached to the far side of the console and pounded a red alarm button. They both stood and tightened their gun belts. Balakin turned the handle to open the vacuum-sealed door. Outside, they jumped into matching black ATVs and raced toward the location.

By the time they arrived, the whole scene was swarming with a dozen other ATVs, their headlights shining across all sides of the shed. The student squad on call had responded to the alarm in record time. They seemed excited that, for once, it was apparently not just a drill. When Balakin pulled up, the students greeted him with unsettling wide-eyed smiles. He nodded back. He avoided the students whenever possible. They made his skin crawl.

Petrov pulled up right behind. He jumped out of his vehicle and walked to the building. He placed his hand on the seam of the metal door. It was blackened and pitted, but otherwise intact. No intrusion. No structural damage. All around the building, ATV engines revved and roared, blocking out any other sounds. Balakin rolled his ATV forward and swiveled the powerful spotlight beam across the thick woods in the distance.

He saw nothing but trees.

# CHAPTER 83

*The Bering Sea*

I THOUGHT THE banging noises were part of a dream, but when I woke up, they were still there. I didn't know how long I'd slept. Maybe hours. Maybe days. The only light came from the fluorescent tubes overhead. No clue about the world outside. My whole body felt bruised and sore. My skin was still crusty from the salt water, and my throat felt like sandpaper.

I reached into my backpack and pulled out my lone bottle of water. As I guzzled it down, I heard the sounds again. They were coming from the other side of the fortress.

I rolled my aching body off the cot and walked around to the other side of the partition into the main space. I started following the sounds. They had more definition now. Rhythmic. Hollow. Metallic. I looked up and down for something that might have come loose, maybe something knocking into a beam. Nothing. I looked for pumps or heating units. Again nothing. Except for the sleeping area, the fortress was wide open.

The sounds reverberated through the space. I froze in place and tried to triangulate the source. Then I took a few steps forward. The sounds were louder now. Closer.

I was almost at the other end of the vast room when I felt a vibration under my feet. The planks I was standing on trembled in sync with the noise. A few steps farther, I saw a metal hatch set flush with the floor. There was a handle near the top. I pulled on it, but the hatch door was rusted to the frame. I braced my legs and pulled again. The handle ripped off in my hand. I leaned down. No question now. The banging was coming from underneath the hatch. Like somebody or something was trying to get in.

I was out of patience. I grabbed a crowbar and jammed the edge under the floorboards on one side of the hatch. I worked the bar back and forth, splintering the wood until I'd exposed the edge of the metal. I took a deep breath, hooked my hands underneath, and ripped out the entire hatch, frame and all. It fell back onto the planks with a huge bang, leaving a gaping hole in the floor.

I looked down through the opening. I was staring at a black metal object floating in a large chamber of seawater right below the level of the floor. It was about twice the size of an oil drum. One side was banging against an underwater support post. That was the noise.

I dropped to my knees for a closer look. It wasn't a drum—more like a stubby tube, with tapered ends and a round lid in the center.

A submarine.

# CHAPTER 84

*Eastern Russia*

"I SHOULD HAVE been called sooner," said Irina, her voice steely.

She stared straight ahead as Petrov and Balakin led her to the front of the explosives shed. Irina was running on two hours of sleep and she was in a dark mood. As she approached the building, students were still circling it in their ATVs. When they recognized Irina, they cut their engines and stiffened in their seats.

Dawn was just rising over the mountains, and the west-facing half of the structure was still in shadow. Irina stared at the damaged door. She leaned in and stroked her index finger over the sooty residue on the metal. She sniffed it.

"Old-school thermite," she said. "*Very* old."

Thermite was no match for titanium. Even the weakest students would know that. The intrusion attempt had been amateurish. Almost like somebody was playing games, or trying to attract attention. She turned to Petrov.

"You have video?" she asked. He nodded.

Back in the basement security center, Balakin watched

nervously as Petrov cued up the segment from the early hours. Irina had her chair rolled up tight against the console. The image was dark, the outlines of the shed barely visible. Suddenly, the explosive flare illuminated one side of the building, blowing out the picture for a few seconds before fading back into darkness.

"Stop it there!" said Irina.

Petrov hit the Pause button. Irina leaned in.

"Toggle the last two frames."

Petrov switched back and forth. Irina's jaw clenched. At the far-left edge of the second frame, a figure was partially silhouetted by the dying flare. It was a woman's figure. The head was surrounded by a halo of copper-colored curls.

Irina's fists clenched the console in disbelief. Her jaw tightened. She wasn't just angry. She was humiliated. And that was worse. She realized that for the first time in her entire life, she had failed to complete an assignment.

As Irina shoved her chair back, the wheels hit the metal grate in the floor. She glanced down and spotted a flake of ash hanging on the edge. She looked over at Petrov, then at Balakin.

"Somebody's been smoking in here," she said evenly.

Both guards blanched, but Irina noticed that Balakin's eyes blinked faster. She stood up and walked to his chair. She crouched behind him, hands on his shoulders. She could feel him trembling. She leaned in close to his ear and whispered.

"Smoking will kill you," she said.

Balakin released a nervous laugh.

"Don't worry," said Irina. "I won't say a word."

Balakin exhaled in a heavy rush. Irina felt his whole upper body relax under her touch. She cupped her forearm around his chin and yanked violently, breaking his neck in an instant. The pop of his vertebrae sounded like a whip crack.

Petrov flew out of his chair and stood shaking against the wall. Irina released her grip and let Balakin's body slide onto the floor. She advanced slowly toward Petrov.

He reached down and fingered his gun holster. Irina rested her hand lightly on top of his. She was smiling now, strangely polite and composed.

"Plant him in the woods," she said, "or sink him in the lake. Your choice."

# CHAPTER 85

*The Bering Sea*

FOR A SOLID hour, I went back and forth in my mind. I was so hungry I couldn't think straight. I was getting weaker by the minute, and my mind was getting foggy. I knew I had to make the most of my body and my brain cells while they were still functioning.

The way I saw it, I had two choices, both of them bad. I could resign myself to dying a slow death inside my ancestor's artificial iceberg. Or I could take a chance on getting out—in a machine that might kill me. I paced around the gaping hole in the floor, looking down into the chamber of seawater, watching the submarine bobbing in its berth. The more I stared at it, the more I felt like Doc Savage was taunting me—or daring me.

Then I thought about Kira again, and about the battle we were supposed to face together. She'd never told me her plan. Maybe she didn't have one. Maybe she assumed that we'd figure it out as a team. I definitely didn't feel up to saving the world on my own, but I realized that if I had a chance to complete the mission, I had to try. For her.

In other words, I didn't really have a choice.

I grabbed my backpack. I tossed in a hammer, a screwdriver, and a pair of pliers. I grabbed a butcher knife from the kitchen and the wool blanket from the cot. I rustled through the rusty devices on the worktables, but nothing else looked useful.

I stood for a minute at the edge of the hole in the floor, then stepped onto the top of the sub. The metal shell was curved and slippery, and the whole thing shifted under my weight. I grabbed the edge of the lid. I figured that opening it was going to take all my strength. But it flipped up with no effort, as easy as popping a beer can. There was a thick steel wheel on the inside of the lid. I used it to steady myself as I lowered myself into the cabin.

Once I was inside, I could barely move. Even with my old physique, it would have been a tight fit. The only light came through the hatch from the space above. I took a chance and flipped a row of switches on the inside curve of the submarine wall. A row of light bars popped on along the sides, casting a weird bluish glow. I felt a sick wave of claustrophobia. The whole idea seemed suicidal. *Suck it up, Doctor,* I told myself.

I reached up and pulled the hatch shut. I cranked the wheel to the right and heard the opening seal tight. I felt like I had just locked myself in a tomb. The sub was still banging against the support post, but now I was hearing it from the inside—a metallic echo. Like a bell tolling.

I wedged myself into the single seat and looked around. For all I knew, I was sitting in an unfinished model or a decoy. I wasn't even sure it had a working engine. I looked around, trying to read Doc Savage's mind from the distance of a century. Some of the controls seemed obvious. I assumed the metal stick in front of me was the speed control, and that the foot pedals turned the rudder.

I ran my fingers over the maze of buttons and switches on the small console in front of me. A few of them actually had labels. One said *PWR*. I hovered my finger over it, then pressed. I heard a low whine behind me, then loud thumping. The thumping got faster and faster until it turned into a throbbing hum. The whole sub vibrated and I could see white bubbles blasting up from underneath.

I took a guess that *RLS* meant "Release." I pressed the button. I heard metal parts grinding and felt something give way. Suddenly the sub dropped a few feet lower in the water and rolled to the left. I pushed forward on the stick between my knees. The engine hum turned into a growl. The sub righted itself and began to glide forward out of the chamber.

All I could see through the small porthole in front was greenish-blue water filled with whitish fragments, like dandruff falling from the underside of the fortress. In a few seconds, I could see that I was emerging from under the far edge of the structure into the open sea. The water turned a lighter shade of green. I exhaled slowly.

If this was my tomb, at least it was moving.

# CHAPTER 86

*Eastern Russia*

ON THE FIRST floor of the school's main building, an austere lecture hall now doubled as a ready-room. It was crowded with students, the school's most senior and seasoned, the ultimate survivors, male and female. They were all dressed in tactical gear. Nobody sat. They were all too nervous and eager. The news of the attempted intrusion had spread through the student body, but only the elite—these twenty—had been chosen for primary pursuit. The room hummed with anticipation.

The side door to the classroom flew open and Irina walked in, her face grim. The room instantly fell silent. Irina walked to the front and looked over the class. She had trained most of these students herself, and she knew they were ready. She clicked a controller and brought up an image on the monitor at the front of the room. It showed a close-up of the blackened metal door.

"You all know we had an attempted breach early this morning," she said. "Unusual. And unacceptable. But we also happen to know who's responsible." She paused. "It was somebody who lived here and trained here."

The students eyed one another nervously. Was this a setup? A test? Was there a traitor in the room?

Irina clicked to the next image—the grainy frame of the woman's silhouette. The students leaned forward, trying to digest every pixel of information. Irina let them stew for a few seconds, then clicked again. The next image was sharp and clear. It was an enhancement of a surveillance photo taken in Chicago. It showed Kira alone on a city street. Her copper curls glowed in the light.

"Her name is Meed," said Irina. "She's brilliant and she's dangerous. She is a danger to this school's existence, and to our power throughout the world. She is a threat to me and to Headmaster Kamenev and to each and every one of you."

She zoomed in on the image until Kira's face filled the screen.

"This is your target," said Irina firmly. "This is your final test."

# CHAPTER 87

*The Bering Sea*

ACCORDING TO THE dials on the console, I was moving at about ten knots. I'd found the switch for the forward-facing spotlight, and the beam cut through the water for a distance of about twenty feet. Beyond that, it was all haze.

My depth was twelve meters. And if I could believe the compass, I was headed due west—directly toward the Kamchatka Peninsula, ten kilometers away. The hull was making terrifying noises, creaks and thuds that were even louder than the hum of the engine. Heat blasted through the cabin. I could smell motor oil and fuel and my own sweat. Every muscle in my body was tense. I was taking quick shallow breaths and keeping my movements to a minimum. I felt like I was in a very fragile egg, and I prayed that it would go the distance.

Suddenly a loud squawk filled the cabin. My adrenaline shot through the roof. A red light on the panel was blinking. A second later, I knew why. I looked down and saw water seeping through a seam on the floor. I pulled the ballast lever to lift the nose angle, but the sub wasn't responding. There was no way to surface. I felt a sudden rush of ice water over my feet, then my ankles.

I scanned the controls and flipped the switch marked *PUMP*. Somewhere behind me another motor fired up, and I could hear water being sucked out through a vent. But not fast enough. The flood was rising up my calves. The nose of the sub was tilting down. I was descending fast. Twenty meters. Now thirty.

The creaking got louder. I heard a rivet pop, then another. Like gunshots. I looked around the cabin. I started pressing every button, hoping something might seal the leak. I looked behind me. The only thing I saw was a hand-cranked radio mounted to the rear of the cabin, like something out of a museum. The sub tipped almost vertical and picked up speed. I knew I didn't have much time. I was riding a rocket to the bottom of the sea.

# CHAPTER 88

*Eastern Russia*

THE ATVS WERE even louder than Kira remembered.

She covered her ears and held perfectly still as the search party bounced over a ridge and down a rocky slope at the bottom of a steep 200-foot cliff. Kira knew the riders would be jostling for position, each one hoping to spot the target first. She knew they'd be pumped with energy and bent on speed. Her hope was that they'd scan the trail ahead but ignore the perimeter.

Huddled under a pile of brush, covered with a thin mesh net that make her look like part of the landscape, Kira lowered her head and held her breath. The riders passed so close to her that the tires threw sharp bits of stone against her head and back. She did not flinch.

Her body was already bruised and aching from the night before. She had no memory of the crash, and no idea how long she'd been unconscious in the water, only that her backpack had somehow kept her afloat until she'd washed ashore. She'd spent a desperate hour in the dark searching for the professor, hoping he'd been carried in on the same current. But there was no trace of him. She'd lost the one person on earth who could help her, the one person she could depend on. No matter how unlikely, the professor had become her partner. Now she was on her own again.

Kira was furious with herself for her clumsy attempt on the shed early that morning. She should have known that the thermite had been degraded by age and by the salt water. She realized that she might as well have left a fingerprint. But she was desperate for weapons, something to even the odds—something beyond the meager supplies in her backpack. She'd hoped that she'd retreated far enough to avoid the dragnet. But she now realized that they were looking everywhere.

As the roar of the ATVs faded into the distance, Kira shrugged off the camo net and stuffed it into the backpack. She needed to move, improvise another plan, accomplish the mission, no matter what. The mission was everything. She stood up, legs aching, and started to head back in the direction of the school.

She'd gone just a few yards when a single ATV crested the hill in front of her.

The rider was slender, with black hair and a bruised face.

Irina.

Kira gasped. She felt bile rise in her throat. She froze in place, but she was no longer camouflaged. She was trapped in plain sight.

Irina froze, too, but only for a second. Then her mouth curled into a strange smile. She revved her engine.

Kira made a dash across the trail for the cliff, about twenty yards away. She saw Irina begin to roll down the hill on her ATV. She was in no rush. She was enjoying this.

The cliff face was nearly vertical, but it was laced with

narrow cracks. Kira reached into her backpack and pulled out a handful of steel climbing pegs. She jammed them into small cracks and began to pull herself up the rocks. She looked back as Irina rolled to a stop at the base of the cliff. As Kira found another handhold, an incendiary bullet spattered flames and stone fragments inches from her head. She swung herself around a ledge and nearly lost her grip. Another shot exploded just below her feet. Kira knew that Irina was an expert sniper. She wasn't going for a kill shot. She was just playing with her. For now.

Thirty feet up, Kira plunged her hand into her backpack again and pulled out a large button. She slammed it against the rock face. In a second, she was enveloped in a thick gray cloud. For the moment, she was invisible again. She ducked behind a protruding section of rock and hung there motionless. When the cloud cleared, she looked down. Her heart was pounding.

Irina was nowhere in sight.

# CHAPTER 89

*The Bering Sea*

THE SUB WAS resting on a ledge forty meters down. I heard the engine sputter and die. The water in the cabin was up to my chest. The pump was no match for the surge. The electronics under the console crackled and sparked like underwater fireworks. I was about to be drowned or electrocuted, maybe both.

My heart was thumping and my mind was racing. I flailed around and grabbed the wheel on the inside of the hatch lid. I turned it to the left as hard as I could. I managed to loosen it, but I couldn't push the hatch open. The water pressure from above was too much. I heard more rivets popping. It was like the entire Bering Sea was out to crush me. My lungs burned. I was floating inside the cabin now, kicking off the back of the seat to keep my head above water. The water bubbled up to fill the last air pocket. This was it. I tilted my chin back and took one final gulp of air.

As my head went under, I heard a series of muffled beeps, about one second apart. Like a countdown. My only thought was that the sub had been programmed to self-destruct.

Which meant I was about to be blown to pieces. I closed my eyes tight and waited for the blast. I wondered if I'd feel it, or if it would just be over. In that moment, I wasn't afraid anymore, just frustrated and mad. I let out one last scream as I went under.

Suddenly, the hatch blew off. The impact rocked me back against the inside of the hull. In less than a second, the pressure equalized. There was a hole above me—and open water. I grabbed my backpack, pushed myself through the hatch, and started kicking toward daylight.

# CHAPTER 90

*Eastern Russia*

EXHAUSTED, KIRA PULLED herself over the top of the cliff. She lay flat on the rock ledge, breathing hard. When she turned her head, she was staring across a narrow plateau covered with dirt and grassy stubble. The tree line was about twenty yards away. That was the cover she needed. She got to her knees and steadied herself.

Suddenly, a violent kick to the ribs knocked her backward, almost over the edge.

"Welcome home, Meed," said Irina.

Kira looked up. This close, Irina's face showed the years. But the voice was the same—and it took Kira back. For a second, she flashed back to that bedroom fifteen years ago. The terror in her parents' eyes. The blood on the bedsheets.

"This is not home," she said.

Kira got back onto her knees and took another kick, this one to the head. As she went down again, her backpack slipped off her shoulder onto the dirt. She reached for it, fingers stretched out. Irina booted the bag off the cliff.

"No toys," said Irina. "Just us." She bent down and lifted

Kira's head roughly by the hair. Kira spit a string of saliva and blood and wrenched herself free. She rolled hard to the left and struggled to her feet.

Irina was circling, knees bent, arms flexed and ready. Kira aimed a kick at her knee and heard cartilage pop. Irina didn't even react. She stepped forward and swung her leg at Kira's midsection. It connected—hard. Kira crumpled as the breath was knocked out of her. She raised her arms to block the next blow, but Irina blasted through her defense, throwing her onto her back. In a blink, she had her hands around Kira's throat.

With her last surge of strength, Kira hooked her leg under Irina's left knee. Irina grunted as Kira flipped her and pinned her wrists to the ground. As Irina struggled to lift her head, her eyes shifted. Kira turned and saw a tall boy in tac gear emerging from the edge of the tree line. His right arm was raised in a throwing position, a knife in his hand.

Kira waited for his release, then rolled hard to the side, carrying Irina along with her. The knife buried itself in Irina's thigh. Irina's lips tightened, but she didn't make a sound. She pulled the blade out and slashed it toward Kira's throat. Kira knocked it away. They rolled again. With a powerful shove, Irina pushed herself loose. Her momentum carried her over the edge of the cliff. At the last second, she grabbed tight onto Kira's wrists, dragging her across the rocky ledge.

Kira lay flat and dug her shoes into the dirt, but Irina's weight pulled her forward, until they were face to face, with Irina dangling in the air. Irina's sleeve was ripped open, exposing her angry scar. She stared up at Kira, eyes bright with fury.

"Your parents were weak," said Irina, spitting out the words. "And the weak need to be weeded out."

Kira felt her arms and back straining from Irina's weight.

"Their blood is my blood," said Kira. "Does that make me weak, too?"

Irina glanced down the cliff at the boulders below. She looked at Kira.

"Not weak," said Irina. "Just needy. We could be stronger as a team, Meed. We could be unbeatable."

"Sorry," said Kira. "I have only myself, remember?"

She wrenched her wrists free and let Irina drop.

Kira rolled onto her back, gasping. In an instant, she saw the glint of a knife swinging down toward her chest.

# CHAPTER 91

THE BOY SMILED as he went for the kill.

Kira batted the knife away with one arm and brought her knee up hard against his temple. The kid dropped onto his side, stunned and groaning. Kira picked up the knife and wiped Irina's blood off it. She took a step toward the boy and instinctively visualized his carotid artery. One quick stroke was all it would take. He looked about sixteen. She hesitated, then slipped the knife into her belt and headed for the woods. The trail she'd taken from the school last night would be too dangerous now. She'd have to make her way back cross-country. As soon as she moved through the tree line, the forest closed in around her. The tall firs formed a canopy. White birches shot up everywhere in vertical stripes, and the undergrowth was daunting. After just a few hundred yards, Kira's hands were scraped and bloodied from pushing through the tangled brush. As she tugged aside another prickly branch, she froze. Then she tilted her head slightly and listened. She was not alone.

A twig cracked in the distance, then another. Fifty yards

ahead, a line of students appeared through the trees. It was a foot patrol, moving slowly and deliberately. Younger students, Kira figured. Not yet worthy of ATVs. The automatic rifles looked incongruous against their narrow shoulders. But she had no doubt that they were deadly shooters. That skill was taught early.

Kira was in a thicket of birches. She realized that her black outfit was a poor disguise against the white trunks. She kicked herself mentally for not putting her camo net in her pocket, instead of in her backpack, which was lying somewhere at the bottom of the cliff. She ducked down as the patrol moved toward her. Suddenly, she heard footsteps coming from the opposite direction. Then, a shout.

"She's here! I saw her!"

It was a boy's voice, calling out from a few yards behind her. Kira pressed her face into the brush, thorns stabbing her cheek.

"*Evanoff??*" A voice called back from the approaching patrol. "Where the hell have you been?"

Kira heard steps behind her, coming closer. Her hand tightened around the handle of the knife. The boy passed within ten feet of her as he hurried to reunite with his squad. It was the boy from the cliff. Kira gritted her teeth. This is what I get for showing mercy, she thought.

Kira held still as the boy joined the other students. She could hear their voices, but the sentences weren't clear. The boy pointed in the direction he came from, then turned to lead the way back. The entire squad moved with fresh intensity, spreading out in formation, with students a few yards apart.

Kira rolled slowly to the side, trying to stay low. Her hip

bumped the trunk of a thick birch. She crouched behind it, searching for a path out. In every direction, she saw ground cover that would rustle and crack if she made a run for it. The patrol was getting closer.

She reached slowly into a pile of deadfall and picked up a thick branch about two feet long. She pressed herself against the backside of the birch then swung her arm in a high arc and let the branch fly. It sailed end over end and landed in the brush with a loud crunch about twenty yards away.

"Target left!" a voice called out sharply. She heard steps moving quickly in that direction. Kira grabbed the birch trunk with both hands, braced her feet against it and climbed. Fifteen feet up, she reached a section where the white bark was mottled with gray. It was the best she could do. She rested one toe on a knotty stub, hugged the trunk, and held on tight.

A half minute later, the near wing of the squad swept by underneath her. Kira's foot was starting to slip off the tiny protrusion. The coarse bark was scraping the inside of her wrists. She adjusted her grip and tried to ignore the fire in her biceps and thighs.

Through the light scrim of birch leaves, Kira watched the patrol moving off in the direction of the cliff. When the last figure disappeared, she began to ease herself down the birch, a few inches at a time. Suddenly, she felt herself slipping down the slick bark. She scraped her left shoe wildly against the trunk, feeling for a new foothold. Her toe hit a slick patch of moss. Her weight shifted, too far to recover. She clawed at the tree with both hands, but too late.

She landed hard. Her right shoulder separated with a loud pop and she felt a blinding stab of agony—even more painful than she remembered. She jammed her mouth into the crook of her elbow and bit down on the fabric of her sleeve. She did not scream. After the initial shock passed through her, the pain came in nauseating waves. Kira folded her bad arm across her chest and rose to her knees. Then she stood up. Each shift brought a fresh blast of agony.

She staggered over to a twin birch, with two trunks that split about four feet off the ground. She slid her wrist into the V and made a fist to wedge it tight. She rotated her torso to face the tree. She took a deep breath and jerked her body backward with all her strength. She heard the snap of the ball popping back into the socket. She saw bright sparks. She fell to her knees again and pulled her hand out of the wedge. Tears of pain streamed down her cheeks. Her body was telling her to stay still and conserve her energy. But she wouldn't listen.

As soon as the flashes in her eyes eased, Kira backed away from the thicket, found a small gap in the underbrush, and headed west.

# CHAPTER 92

*The Bering Sea*

I SWAM FOR an hour through cold, choppy water. Even while I was doing it, I couldn't believe my own strength. It was more than adrenaline. More than Kira's training. I felt like I had left my old body behind, almost like I had turned into a different species.

When my feet finally touched bottom, I was still about twenty yards off the peninsula. I could see waves curling around huge rocks at the shoreline. A steep hill rose just beyond, covered in brownish grass and stubby bushes.

I sank calf-deep into cold muck as I half-walked, half-swam toward the beach.

For the last few yards, I was tripping over jagged rocks. I fell on my face in the water and crawled the rest of the way. When I finally got to shore, I crawled behind a craggy boulder and pulled my backpack under my shoulder for a cushion against the hard rocks.

The beach was just a narrow strip. It was littered with boulders, blasted from some ancient volcano. Back in the years when I was doing my doctoral research, I would have been scouring the site for signs of life, traces of lost civilizations. Now I was looking for a school of killers. And my only advantage was that they probably thought I was dead.

I heard a roar in the distance, coming from the south end of the peninsula. At first, I thought it was a chainsaw. But it kept getting louder. Then I spotted movement. It was a pack of ATVs, moving single file in the narrow space between the hillside and the beach. Four of them.

For a second, I thought about backing out into the water and waiting until they passed by. But I was tired of running. In the past two days, I'd been firebombed, shot at, and blasted out of the sky. I'd almost drowned. Twice. But Kira had taught me to survive, no matter what. She'd given me the power to fight. I decided it was time to start using it.

I reached into my soggy backpack and pulled out a roll of wire. I unspooled a few feet of it between my hands and tugged on it. It felt as strong as piano wire, but as flexible as fishing line. The ATVs were still just specks in the distance, bouncing over rises, kicking up dust. The sound of the engines rolled up the steep hill and echoed back down.

I darted from boulder to boulder until I was at the edge of the trail. I wrapped one end of the wire around a rock the size of a dumpster. Then I made a quick dash across the trail and wrapped the other end around a thick tree stump. I lay down on my belly in the low grass and waited. The sound of the machines got louder and louder. They were moving fast, and I could hear the riders yelling back and forth above the engine noise.

I ducked low as the first ATV flew by. As it passed the stump, the wire caught the front of the chassis and the whole thing flipped end over end. The rider flew out and landed hard about fifteen yards away. The other three riders jammed on their brakes, but they couldn't stop in time. One after the other, they spun out and piled up. I heard yelps of pain and crunching metal.

I knew I had to move fast, while the riders were still in shock. I got up and made a dash for the last ATV in the pile. It was the only one still running. The kid behind the wheel had a bloody lip and his eyes were glassy. He looked startled and confused as I grabbed him.

"Who the fuck are *you*?" he mumbled.

"Nobody you know," I said.

I yanked him out of the driver's seat and hopped in.

By now the kid from the flipped ATV up front was struggling to his feet, and the other two drivers were sliding out of their seats. They both looked banged up and dazed. I put the ATV in reverse and cranked the throttle. The tires spun in the rocky sand, then bit. I shifted into low gear and did a full 360. The water was at my back. I had no idea who else might be coming down the trail. So I headed in the only direction I had left—straight up the hill.

In a few seconds, I was bouncing up the slope at a forty-five-degree angle. I heard a rattle behind me. I turned and saw a rifle fly off a rack on the ATV and slide down the hill. No way I could stop to pick it up. If I lost my momentum, I'd stall or flip over backward.

Suddenly, a bullet ricocheted off my front fender. The kids below had recovered enough to shoot. I ducked forward to make myself a smaller target. I hit a patch of loose rock. My rear tires started to spin. I cranked the wheel left and picked up traction again on the grass.

Another shot blasted into the metal frame. I felt hot

fragments dig into my leg. The engine was whining and smoke was pouring out from underneath. The summit was just a few yards farther. But now the slope was even steeper. I gave the machine more gas.

Another shot grazed my roll bar just as I flew over the top of the hill. I landed hard on the other side, and started swerving down the slope, weaving through bushes and boulders.

I'd never driven an ATV before in my life. Turns out, I was damned good at it.

# CHAPTER 93

KIRA DIPPED HER face into the clear mountain stream and wiped the sweat from her face and neck. She held her bad arm across her torso. The pain radiated from her shoulder to her collarbone and across her ribs. The fingers on her right hand were tingling, mostly numb.

She lifted her head, took a few deep breaths, and then bent down again to take a few short sips of the cold water. She sat back on the bank and looked around. The setting felt strangely familiar. The bend of the stream. The angle of the hill. Then it came to her. She realized that she'd crossed this stream before, close to the same spot, fifteen years ago, heading in the other direction.

She closed her eyes and thought back to that desperate morning. Her plan had been simple. Find the shore. Then find a port. Then find a ship. The destination didn't matter. All she wanted was to forget everything she'd seen, and everything she'd learned, everything she'd turned into. It took her more than a decade to realize that she *couldn't* forget, couldn't leave the past alone. She had to go back. The evil had to be stopped at its source. Even if she had to do it by herself.

Now that she'd figured out exactly where she was, the rest of the route unfolded in her head, as clear as a line on a GPS screen. She wiped the water off her face and waded through the stream to the other side.

An hour later, she huddled at the edge of the tree line and looked across the grass at the main wall of the school compound. She'd scaled that same wall the night before to reach the explosives shed. But now it was broad daylight, and she had only three working limbs.

She ran to the outside of the wall and crouched against it, then started moving around the perimeter, hugging the stone as she went. She still needed weapons. And she knew one more place to find them.

Moving a few feet at a time, it took her another ten long minutes to reach the firing range. It was located at the bottom of a wide depression, about twenty feet below the level of the school buildings. The range was empty and quiet. Nobody there. Probably because by now the whole school was out looking for her.

Kira slid down the slope on her back, cradling her bad arm. She crept toward the long metal weapons bin near the firing stations. The lock was new. Electronic. Kira plucked a spent cartridge clip from the ground and pulled the spring out. She used the sharp end of the thick wire to pry off the small LED screen. She cracked the lock in seconds and flipped the metal clasp. Then she used her left arm to raise the heavy metal lid. She looked inside.

The box was empty.

Then she heard the sound of metal clicking above her. Rifle bolts.

# CHAPTER 94

KIRA LOOKED UP. The rim of the hill was lined with students in tac gear. All with high-powered weapons. All aiming directly at her. Another squad was rounding a wall on her right flank.

Kira dropped the lid on the weapons box. She turned and sprinted toward the closest mound on the target range. Shots rang out as she dove behind the huge earthen barrier. Dirt splattered up beside her.

Kira could hear the squad advancing toward her from two directions. She knew the students were angling for position, looking for the honor of blowing her head off. She wondered if being hit by a bullet could be any worse than the pain in her shoulder.

Suddenly, there was a crackle from the PA speakers mounted on poles overhead. A voice boomed out.

"All students! Weapons down! I repeat, weapons down!"

Kira hadn't heard that voice in a very long time. Her whole body tightened at the sound. Kamenev! She squeezed her eyes shut and clenched her fists. Her mind flashed again to the bodies of her parents in their bloody bed, and pure fury swelled inside her.

"The target is isolated!" the headmaster called out, his voice echoing across the range. "Your new assignment is to take her alive!"

Kira took a quick look around the side of the dirt mound. The students had lowered their rifles and pulled out their truncheons. They were advancing like machines, smiling as they came.

Kira braced herself against the back of the dirt pile, then made a run for the next mound, about ten yards away. Then the next. Her chest was heaving. Her arm was throbbing. She thought maybe—*maybe*—she could reach the trees beyond the perimeter. She had to try. As she ran, she spotted a horizontal ridge about twenty yards in front of her. Kira thought she knew every inch of the grounds. But this was new.

As she ran, the ridge seemed to get longer and higher. When she reached it, she stopped short and gasped. The ridge was the top edge of a deep ditch, filled with broken glass, rusted metal, and coils of razor wire. Too wide to jump and impossible to crawl across.

Kira looked back. The students were closing in from two sides. A slow, deliberate pincer action. She realized that she was out of time and out of tricks. She had tried and failed.

She had only herself. And that was not enough.

# CHAPTER 95

THE STUDENTS MOVED slowly toward her, scores of them now.

Kira looked down into the ditch and thought about diving in. With luck, a sharp scrap of metal would slice an artery and she'd bleed out before they could get to her. At least she'd be spared whatever Kamenev had in mind. He'd have to make an example of her—the school's one and only dropout. Even if he didn't kill her right away, he'd make sure that she never escaped again. One way or another, Kira knew, she was going to die at this school.

The speakers were silent now, except for a low crackle of static. But there was a quiet buzz from somewhere in the distance—getting louder by the second.

Kira looked to her right. Her line of sight was blocked by a huge target mound, tall enough to absorb a grenade blast. Suddenly an ATV vaulted over the mound, twenty feet in the air. It looked like a giant insect. The roar was deafening now.

The machine landed hard on the packed dirt. The driver

bounced in the seat, then stood up as he cranked the wheel, kicking up a cloud of dust, riding the machine like a bronco.

Impossible! Kira couldn't believe what she was seeing. *Who* she was seeing. The professor's shirt was ripped open to his waist and his pants were torn. He vaulted out of the ATV and pushed Kira behind him, placing his body between her and the menacing crowd. For a second, she couldn't move, couldn't speak. Then she threw her good arm around his chest and leaned into his ear.

"You're *alive*??" she said. "I thought . . ."

"I know," the professor replied. "Me, too."

All around them, the students were massing for the final push, pounding their truncheons against their palms in unison. And smiling. Always smiling.

"Why aren't they shooting?" asked the professor.

"They want me alive."

"No problem. So do I."

In another second, the first wave of students was on them. Doctor Savage took them as they came, tossing them aside in bunches, blocking punches and the blows from the long, black clubs. Kira stood back-to-back with the professor. She still had two good legs. Her roundhouse kicks connected time after time, slamming students to the ground.

But they kept coming. They just wouldn't stop. A truncheon came down hard on Kira's bad shoulder. She grimaced in pain as she kicked the attacker away. They were surrounded now, about to be overrun and pounded into the ground.

Doctor Savage grabbed the ATV by the upper frame and lifted it into the air. He threw it into the next assault wave, knocking a dozen students onto their backs.

Kira had her knife out. She slashed the air, daring the closest attackers to move in again. She knew that she was just delaying the inevitable, but she wasn't about to go down without a fight. And at least she wouldn't go down alone.

Suddenly, the air was filled with a tremendous vibration and a stinging blast of wind-blown dirt. The students were blown back, blinded by the swirling cloud. The professor turned toward Kira and pushed her to the ground. Her shoulder bent the wrong way. She grimaced in pain and nearly passed out. What happened next felt like a dream. She felt a strange calm come over her. The deafening noise became a gentle hum. The professor's arms were wrapped around her. She realized that she had never felt safer.

Kira lifted her head and looked into the sky. Directly above, two massive Black Hawk helicopters were blocking the sun. Black-clad men with rifles were dropping out of the doors on ropes. When they hit the ground, they formed a solid cordon around Kira and the professor.

"Face down! Arms out!" a tall officer shouted toward the mass of students. Other commandos spread out through the crowd, kicking weapons away. The officer bent down until his helmet touched the professor's head. Kira could read the insignia on the officer's chest: INTERPOL.

"Sir!" he shouted. "Are you the one who called?"

Kira looked at the professor, stunned.

*"Called??"* she said. "Called from *where*?"

Doc Savage looked stunned, too. The submarine radio hadn't been useless after all.

"Holy shit," he said. "Somebody actually *heard* me!"

# CHAPTER 96

THE HEADMASTER'S DEMEANOR was calm, but his mood was dark. He was angry and disappointed. He had thought that this day would never come. In fact, he had taken extensive steps to prevent it. He believed he had placed people and money where it mattered, but somewhere there was a gap in his coverage, or a failure of loyalty. The defect needed to be corrected. But now he had more urgent things to take care of. Starting with his own survival.

From the window in his office, he could see the helicopters hovering over the firing range. Black-clad commandos were already moving across the main compound.

Kamenev walked to his massive safe and dialed the combination. He pulled the heavy door open and pulled out a thick leather binder, worn with age. It was the school's sacred text. The fundamental principles. The original Doc Savage training methods.

The data and techniques had never been copied or transferred to digital form. Kamenev was too smart for that. Everything was either in the book or in his head. That was all he needed to start over—that and the billions resting in anonymous accounts across the globe.

The headmaster closed the door to his office and walked briskly down the back staircase to the first floor. The whole building was in chaos. Young students and their instructors crowded around windows as another Black Hawk roared overhead at rooftop level. Kamenev ignored it all. This establishment was no longer his concern.

When he reached a room off the middle of the hall, he opened the door and locked it behind him. He drew a shade down over the window in the door. He was standing in a small, utilitarian room with a linoleum floor and bare walls. A worn upright piano sat against one wall. Kamenev opened the piano lid and pressed a lever inside. He stood back. The left side of the piano swung forward two feet, revealing a hatch set neatly into the wall behind it.

Kamenev angled himself behind the piano and pushed the hatch open. Behind it was an opening just wide enough for a grown man. Kamenev dropped to his knees and backed through. His feet found the steps of the staircase inside. He pressed a lever and leaned back as the hatch slid closed. Then he waited for the sound of the piano settling back into place against the wall. He looked down. A row of small amber bulbs lit a winding staircase leading down into a chamber carved out of solid rock.

When he reached the bottom, Kamenev headed down a narrow stone corridor. He was now two stories below the building. In his practice runs, he had never gone beyond the top of the stairs. Waste of time, he'd thought. Now he regretted being so cavalier.

He remembered from the plans that the main corridor

branched off into a maze of passageways, leading to various storerooms and exits. But he couldn't recall which was which. He moved quickly down the main route until he reached an intersection, with tunnels leading off in three directions. Kamenev hesitated. He turned left, then right. Then he froze. There was somebody behind him.

"Looking for a way out, Headmaster?"

# CHAPTER 97

KIRA STEPPED OUT of the shadows and into the dim glow of an overhead light. She could tell that Kamenev was rattled, but he was doing his best to maintain his command presence.

"You're trying hard not to act surprised," she said.

"Meed," said Kamenev, his voice low and calm. "Our master of escapes."

"Meed is not my name," Kira said softly. "But you always knew that."

"It suited you," said Kamenev. He angled his head to get a better look at her. "It still does."

"Do you remember the last time you saw me?" asked Kira.

Kamenev looked past her, down the corridor. Kira shifted her head to block his view.

"There's nobody coming. It's just us," she said, taking a step toward him. "I asked you a question."

Kamenev took one step back, his hand clasped tight around the binder. "Of course," he said. "It was . . ."

"Let me help you," said Kira. "It was fifteen years ago. The day you assigned my final test. *Our* final test. Me and Irina."

Kamenev stiffened his spine and looked Kira straight in the eye.

"It was a necessary mission," he said.

Kira's throat tightened. Her fists clenched at her sides. She wanted nothing more than to choke the life out of this man. But first she needed some answers.

"Why?" she asked. "Why them?"

Kamenev took another step back. The stone wall stopped him. Kira saw his expression curl into a bitter sneer. His old arrogance resurfaced.

"Because my brother was weak," he said.

"Your brother?" asked Kira. "What does your brother...?"

"My brother," said Kamenev firmly. "Your father."

Kira felt the breath go out of her. She struggled to maintain her composure, but she couldn't hide her shock from Kamenev. He knew her too well.

"All your research didn't turn up that fact, did it?" said Kamenev. "From early on, your father and I took very different paths. He was a pacifist. A dreamer. Same with your mother. No concept of how the world really works. When I left and changed my name, I was erased from the family history. I had to make my own way—just like you."

Kira shook her head. Her research had been painstaking. Impeccable. No way she could have missed this.

"My father didn't have a brother," said Kira.

"May 1st, 1955," said Kamenev.

Kira blinked. She recognized the date.

"Our birthday," said Kamenev. "Your father's and mine."

Kira's head was spinning.

"Don't look so shocked," Kamenev went on. "Twins run in the family. But you know that."

The last sentence hit Kira like a club. She blinked and rocked back. Her mind flashed to a small room with a tiny crib, in a time before her conscious memory. But there was something she felt clearly, as if it was happening to her right now. It was the sense that she had her arms wrapped around another body, breaths and heartbeats in perfect sync, like two halves of a whole.

Then the other heartbeat stopped.

Kira felt the blood drain from her cheeks. And in that instant, she knew who she had been missing for her whole life. Kamenev could read it on her face.

"You were better off without her," he said. "*Tantum est fortis superesse*. Only the strong survive."

# CHAPTER 98

KIRA LUNGED AND grabbed Kamenev's jacket with both hands. She winced as the pain from her right shoulder shot down her arm. Kamenev twisted away and turned toward the wall. Kira saw his hand go to his chest. The binder fell to the floor. When he turned back, she saw a flash of metal in his hand. Kamenev fired as he turned, without aiming. The blast echoed through the corridor as the bullet struck the stone arch behind Kira's head. And now, the gun was in her face.

"You froze," said Kamenev. "That night. You couldn't do it. That's what Irina reported. You can imagine how disappointed I was. I thought we'd trained you better than that."

Kamenev brought his fist down hard on Kira's right shoulder. She grimaced in agony and fell to her knees.

"I can sense your weak spots, Meed," said Kamenev. "I have a gift for it."

Kira felt the cold barrel of the gun pressing through her curls onto the crown of her head. She closed her eyes. Then she drew a deep breath and let it out. She had one more question to ask before she died.

"Tell me," she said numbly. "Did you kill her? Was it you? Did you kill my sister?"

Kamenev pressed the barrel harder against her skull.

His voice was almost soothing. "Let's just call it natural selection," he said.

Kira went blind with rage. She reached into her belt and brought her hand up hard. Kamenev rocked back against the wall and slid to the floor, his eyes glazed and still. Kira's knife protruded from his chest, between his third and fourth ribs. The gun dropped from his hand.

Kira knelt on the cold stone floor, breathing hard, cradling her aching arm across her torso. She stared at Kamenev's still body as blood oozed from around the edge of the knife blade. Kira knew it wasn't just his blood. It was *family* blood. The same blood that ran in her. After generations of good and evil, she was now the last of her line.

She had only herself.

Kira rose to her feet, leaned over, and picked up the tattered binder. She tucked it under her right arm. Suddenly, the tunnel was pierced by thin, distant cries. In the eerie echoes created by the tunnels, it sounded like cats howling.

Kira grabbed the pistol and gripped it in her left hand. She walked in the direction of the sound. The corridor curved for about twenty yards until it ended at a stone staircase. The sound was coming from behind a door at the top of the stairs.

Kira raised the pistol. She inched her way up the steps and eyed the door. Above the handle was a clasp sealed with a simple padlock. Kira blasted it apart with one shot. She pressed herself against the frame and pushed the door open. She stepped into the room and swept the pistol from side to side. There were no threats.

The room was huge. Maybe fifty yards long. Both sides were lined with bassinets—filled with crying babies.

# CHAPTER 99

THE HEADMASTER'S BODY was lying on a plastic sheet at the edge of the schoolyard. Kira and I watched as a couple of soldiers loaded him into a body bag. She had told me about the fight in the tunnel, but I knew she wasn't telling me everything. She was quiet and numb, off in her own world.

Another Red Cross helicopter set down in the center of the compound. The first had arrived twenty minutes earlier. Medics and volunteers were already setting up white tents and tables. Nurses in blue scrubs were wheeling bassinets from the underground nursery and carrying wailing infants toward the tents.

In the past half hour, the place had turned into a refugee camp. Kira had finally gotten some medical attention, too. Her right arm was in a sling, but she'd turned down the pain meds. I'd started to ask one of the medics to check the gash in my forehead, but then I realized that it had totally healed. That brought up a question I was dying to get answered. It had been stuck in my head for a long time. Maybe it was a way to get Kira talking.

I looked over at her. "Can I ask you something?"

She nodded.

"What can I *do*?"

She stayed quiet for a moment, then looked at me with an annoyed expression. "What can you *do*?? There's *plenty* to do," she said, looking at the chaos across the compound. "For one thing, we need to figure out where all these babies belong."

She wasn't understanding my question.

"No," I said. "I mean, what can I *do*? What are my powers?"

"Your *powers*?"

"I mean, obviously, I can survive plane crashes. I can learn languages overnight, swim for miles in freezing water, repair my body, lift an ATV with my bare hands. What else??"

"This is really what's on your mind right now?" Kira asked.

"Just curious."

Kira got quiet again and looked away. She was giving me nothing. I'd obviously picked the wrong time. And the wrong topic.

"Never mind," I said. "Forget it."

She let out a slow breath and turned back toward me.

"Okay," she said, "if you really need to know, start with this: your reaction time is three times faster than normal. Your muscle strength and endurance have quadrupled. You can run a quarter mile in under forty seconds. Your vision is 20/10 in both eyes. Your skin is thicker, more resilient..."

"Like Superman??"

She grabbed my arm.

"Look at me," she said. "You're *not* Superman. You're just the best version of yourself. New and improved. We've maxed out your natural potential. That's what the original Doc Savage experiment was all about—seeing how far native ability could be pushed. Not by coming from another planet. Just by starting with what you already have."

"And how did you know what I already had?" I asked.

"I studied your ancestors," she said. "I knew the techniques. I *lived* the techniques. I gambled that you were a diamond in the rough. And I was right."

She went back to staring into the distance. I couldn't leave it alone.

"So could I stop a bullet with my body?" I asked.

"Don't push your luck, Doctor."

# CHAPTER 100

LATER THAT MORNING, another INTERPOL chopper settled down in the main yard and a dozen more commandos poured out. Kira had wandered off. I had no idea where to. I knew I'd pissed her off with my questions about superpowers. Probably good to give her some space, I thought. As the chopper blades wound down, a new squad leader walked up to me, goggles on his face, rifle across his chest. I must have looked like somebody who knew something.

"What the hell *is* this place?" he asked.

"It's a school," I said.

The commando looked around at the crowd of kids sitting on the grass, sullen and quiet. Some of them were picking at the ground or mumbling to themselves.

"So where are the shooters?" he asked.

"You're looking at them," I said.

"Jesus!" the soldier said, lifting his goggles. "They're *kids*!"

"Do yourself a favor," I said. "Don't turn your back."

We'd already sorted through the students from the main attack force, separating them by age. The oldest were about nineteen, and some looked as young as fifteen. They were divided into groups of ten, with one or two commandos watching over each bunch. Other commandos had set up a perimeter outside the compound to snare ATV riders as they returned.

Confiscated weapons were being collected in a huge bin. Rifles and clubs were just the start. A lot of the kids had pistols strapped to their ankles or tucked into their waistbands. Some of the older kids had grenades and stun guns clipped to their belts. They all had knives up their sleeves.

As I walked across the yard looking for Kira, I spotted a slight girl with braids inching backward on the grass at the edge of her group. The next second, she jumped up and started sprinting toward the outside wall. One of the soldiers who'd been minding the group turned and started after her.

"Stay there!" I shouted. "I got her."

The girl was fast. She was almost at the wall when I caught up. When she realized she had no way out, she whipped around to face me. There was a razor blade in her hand. She held the blade across her wrist. I inched closer. Her lips curled into an eerie smile. She slid the blade across her skin, drawing blood.

"Stay back," she said.

"You must've skipped a class," I said, tracing a line up my forearm. "Vertical cuts work much better." She blinked. That's all the time I needed. I snapped my arm forward, grabbed her hand, and squeezed it until the blade dropped into the dirt. Then I scooped her up sideways with my hand wrapped tight around her waist. She started kicking and clawing like a wildcat in a trap. Then she started screaming at the top of her lungs.

"Run, you assholes!" she shouted at her schoolmates. "Fight back! They're going to kill us all!"

I'd had enough. I flipped her right side up and sat her down hard on the dirt. "Knock it off!" I yelled, right into her face. She was so stunned that she quieted down. I did, too. "Nobody's killing anybody," I said softly. "Not anymore. That's done. You're all going home."

She stared back at me, eyes blazing.

"Fuck you, Paul Bunyan!" she said. "This *is* home!"

Two soldiers ran over with a set of zip cuffs and hauled her away.

"Careful," I said. "She's stronger than she looks. And get a medic to check her wrist."

I realized I didn't have any answers for the girl. For *any* of them. They'd never known any life but this. These kids had been raised here since they were babies, the same as Kira. No wonder they were out of their minds. In the last hour, their whole world had exploded.

I saw a group of soldiers heading into the main building and jogged over to join them. The first team through the door stopped to check for booby traps. When they gave us the all clear, we moved in. As we swept through the first floor, we found young kids hiding in closets and under desks. One by one, the commandos dragged them out.

Some of the instructors and security guards tried to make a run for it, but we rounded them up pretty easily. They were all worn down and scared. From the looks on their faces, I think they all expected to be executed, too.

While the soldiers marched the students and teachers outside, I walked up a curved staircase to the second floor by myself. One of the commandos was on his way down, guiding a line of toddlers—*Sesame Street* age. Some of the kids looked terrified. Others just looked stunned.

When I got upstairs, everything was quiet. I walked down the long empty corridor. It was littered with clothes and other belongings. Some of the rooms had been barricaded with chairs and desks. When I got to the end of the hall, I stopped and looked into the last room.

And there she was.

She didn't even look up when I walked in. The room was filled with metal cots arranged in neat rows. There was a sink against one wall. Kira was staring out a window. It was blocked with heavy metal bars. As I got closer, I could see scorch marks on the sill, like old cigarette burns.

"Is this where you slept?" I asked.

"Tried to," she said softly.

She ran her fingers over the windowsill.

"This was my way out," she said. "This is where I jumped. I was eighteen."

I looked at the bars. Not even a skinny teenager could have slipped through. "How?" I asked.

"I burned through the bars and bent them," she said. "These bars are new. Stronger. They made sure nobody else escaped."

"You burned through a set of metal bars?" I asked. "With what?"

"Acid," she said.

Kira pulled up her left sleeve. I bent forward to look. The scars on her forearm matched the scorch marks on the stone. "Nothing was going to stop me," she said. "Nothing."

I could see tears brimming in her eyes. I didn't know how to react, or what to say.

All I knew was that I was sad for her. Angry for her. Angry

for *me*. After all, one of my ancestors had helped build this place. My family. My blood. In a twisted way, I felt partly responsible. I wrapped my hands tight around the bars and ripped them out of the stone one by one.

When I was done, the view was clear all the way to the mountains.

"You're okay now," I said. "It's over."

Kira stared off into the distance.

"I wish," she said softly. "I wish."

# CHAPTER 101

THAT AFTERNOON, I asked the commando in charge to gather all the kids together in the gym. It was bigger than any class I'd ever taught. I stood in front of a massive wooden table and looked out over the crowd. Some of the students looked back at me with cold, dull eyes. But most of them just stared at the floor.

The older kids were in orange jumpsuits and cuffs. A lot of them were still bandaged up from the battle. The younger students were in oversized Red Cross T-shirts, like kids at a sleepaway camp.

A sturdy sergeant stood at my right side, legs apart, rifle at the ready. My personal bodyguard. Kira was standing on the other side. She'd found a microphone and connected it to the gym's PA system. When I brought the mic up to my face, there was a short whistle of feedback. The noise got everybody's attention.

"I want to read you all something," I said. My voice boomed across the gym, loud and clear.

It was a tough audience. Zero interest. Zero expression.

Even the creepy smiles were gone. I unfolded the sheet of paper I'd torn out of my great-grandfather's journal back in the Fortress. I cleared my throat.

"An ancestor of mine wrote this a long time ago," I said. "It was hidden away for almost a hundred years. But I believe somehow he meant for me to find it. It's something I think you should hear. Maybe these words will help you as you move on and start over. Believe me, there is a better world than this place. There is a better life than the one you've all been living."

I realized that my hands were shaking a bit. I looked over at Kira. She gave me a little nod. I started reading what my great-grandfather had written to inspire himself. Doc Savage's personal code.

*Let me strive, every moment of my life, to make myself better and better, to the best of my ability, so that all may profit by it. Let me think of the right, and lend all my assistance to those who need it, with no regard for anything but justice. Let me take what comes with a smile, without loss of courage. Let me be considerate of my country, of my fellow citizens and my associates in everything I say and do. Let me do right to all, and wrong to no man.*

When I finished, the room was silent, except for some awkward coughs. I held the paper over my head. Like Moses with the Ten Commandments.

"Bullshit!" a female voice called out.

I heard a loud crack. A bullet punched a hole in the paper.

Everybody in the audience ducked or scattered, except for one person. A woman in an orange jumpsuit stepped forward from the middle of the crowd. Her dark hair was matted, and her face was swollen on one side. She had a pistol—and it was pointed at Kira.

"My God," Kira gasped. "Irina!"

"Did you think I'd go that easily, Meed?" Irina shouted. "Do you think you're the only one who knows how to survive?? How to come back??"

The sergeant had his rifle up.

"Drop the weapon!" he shouted.

Irina flicked her aim left and shot him through the forehead. He spun backward and landed with a heavy thud, his rifle underneath him. I crouched down, my heart racing. I felt Kira beside me. Irina stepped forward, picking her way through the students hugging the floor. She fired again. The bullet splintered the desk leg right over Kira's head. There was nowhere to go, no way to move.

I glanced to my left. I saw the butt of a Glock in the dead soldier's holster. I reached out and grabbed it. With my other hand, I shoved Kira down behind me. I heard another crack and felt the impact—like I'd been punched in the chest by a prizefighter. I whipped the gun up and squeezed the trigger. Irina flew backward and landed hard on the wood floor. There was a neat purple hole in her chest.

A squad of commandos burst in from outside, rifles raised. Two of them rushed forward to the dead sergeant. One of them stopped and checked for Irina's pulse. I knew he wouldn't find one. He looked up at me and saw the pistol.

"Dead, sir," he said. "Perfect shot."

I dropped the gun onto the floor. I winced and put a hand over my sore chest. Kira reached over and yanked my shirt open. I looked down. There was a circular red welt above my left pec, with a flattened piece of metal in the center. I pried the bullet out of my skin and dropped it onto the floor. Kira didn't say anything. She just held my arm and stared at me. I pushed her away and stood up. I walked past Irina's body and headed for the door.

The crowd parted like the Red Sea.

# CHAPTER 102

I SHOVED THE door open and walked outside, past the huge Black Hawks and all the men with guns. I felt sick. I felt angry. I felt relieved. I felt guilty. What the hell are you supposed to feel when you end somebody's life—even if it's somebody who was trying to end yours?

I walked across the yard to the stone wall that surrounded the compound. I stretched out and leaned both arms against it. I felt burning in my chest, but it wasn't from the bullet. It was from somewhere a lot deeper. I squeezed my eyes shut and felt tears streaming out. Then I felt a hand on my shoulder.

"Thank you," said Kira.

I felt sick to my stomach. I pushed off the wall and turned on her.

*"Thanks??"* I said. "I don't want to be thanked. Do you want me to be proud of that??"

"I'm not asking you to be proud," said Kira. "Would you rather see *me* dead? And you? Because that was the choice. Her or us."

She was right. But it didn't help. I still felt sick and twisted inside.

"I just made a big, noble speech about being human," I said. "Now I'm a killer. And a good one. That's what you made me."

Kira cocked her head. She wasn't joining my pity party. Something about seeing me breaking down made her toughen up. She was right in my face.

"So maybe I should have left you alone," she said. "All by yourself in your one-bedroom apartment with your books and your research papers and your microwave dinners. Maybe I should have let you be nervous and afraid for the rest of your life. Would that have been better for you?"

I looked right at her.

"Everything I've learned over the last six months," I said, "it was for you, not for me."

She knew it was true. I was a tool for saving her life. And I'd done my job. She'd been raised to be a killer, and she'd turned me into one. A miserable piece of role switching. She turned and walked away. But I wasn't done.

"You missed your calling, Kira," I called after her. "You should have been a teacher."

# CHAPTER 103

KIRA SAT AT a long folding table in the Red Cross tent, making the last of her hundred calls for the day. She rubbed her right shoulder. The sling was gone. The pain was not.

After a week of DNA matching and searching missing-children files from all over the world, they'd made progress. The younger children were being sent home to their families or to temporary foster care, the older kids to deprogramming centers. The teachers and security guards had been processed, too. A high percentage had outstanding international warrants, some decades old. A team had been flown in from The Hague to deal with the extradition paperwork.

There were still hundreds of connections to be made, especially for the babies. One whole tent had been set up as a temporary nursery, with the military nurses in charge. From where she sat, Kira could hear squeals and cries all day long.

Something else had changed, too. As she looked out across the compound, Kira saw that the whole dynamic of power in the operation had shifted. Now it was Doctor Savage who was in control. She watched him striding back and forth across the compound like a giant, looming over volunteers, medical staff, and military alike. As he ushered groups of kids onto helicopters, commandos and pilots responded crisply to his orders. Some had even started saluting him.

Kira knew that the only person he wasn't talking to was her. They hadn't exchanged a single word since the day he'd taken a bullet for her. She still wondered if he'd regretted doing it.

One of the newly arrived military staffers dropped a new stack of papers onto Kira's table. He looked out at the powerfully built man in the torn shirt—the one ordering everybody around like a general. He looked bigger than life. Superhuman.

"Who the hell is *that*?" the staffer asked. "Is he from Delta Force?"

"Actually," said Kira, "he's a college professor."

The tent flaps billowed as another loaded chopper lifted off. A minute later, a new Black Hawk settled down in its place. The side door slid open.

Kira saw the professor duck under the spinning blades and yell something up to the pilot. He put one foot on the skid. It looked like his ride had arrived. He paused for a second and looked toward the open tent. It wasn't exactly an invitation, but Kira figured it was the closest she was going to get. Her last chance to say good-bye.

She stood up and walked outside. The chopper was idling now, the propeller in slow rotation, beating a rhythmic pulse. It was still enough to blow back her copper curls as she walked up. Doctor Savage had one hand on the grip inside the chopper door.

"No luggage?" asked Kira.

The professor looked up into the hold of the helicopter, then back at her.

"All I brought was a backpack," he said. "You keep it."

Kira nodded toward the chopper. "This is it?" she said. "You're leaving?"

"You've got all the help you need here," he said. "I'm going home. I'm done. I've got classes to teach."

Kira fought the urge to step closer. *Let it go,* she thought. *Let him go.*

"Okay then," she said. "So long, Doctor."

The professor hesitated, then took his foot off the skid. He took a few steps toward her. "You're allowed to call me Brandt, you know. That's my name."

Kira shook her head. "Nope. Sorry. You never seemed like a Brandt to me."

A commando hustled over and slapped the professor on the shoulder. The chopper engine kicked into gear. "Let's go, Doc!" he said.

Kira smiled. "Doc." That sounded about right.

# CHAPTER 104

*Gaborone, Botswana*

JAMELLE MAINA WAS on her forty-first circuit around the quarter-mile track. Her only competition was a pair of middle-aged joggers. She had lapped them several times.

Jamelle knew that if she ran long enough and hard enough, she could sometimes press the image of her missing daughter to the back of her mind. Otherwise, that was pretty much all she thought about. She slowed for a cool-down lap—as if it was possible to cool down in 91-degree heat.

Jamelle felt the vibration of the phone ringing in her arm strap. She mopped her forehead and put the phone to her ear. The voice on the other end was thin and scratchy. A bad connection. Jamelle could only pick up scraps of what was being said. "Report...match...international..." Her pulse rate was at 150 BPM from the workout. Now it shot up even higher.

"What?? Hello??" Jamelle screamed into the phone.

She spun around on the track, straining for better reception. "What did you say??" It wasn't the PI calling. She hadn't heard from him in months. Besides, this was a woman's voice.

She jogged to the edge of the track and jumped onto a

bench, as if the two feet of elevation would help. Amazingly, it did. The caller's voice was still distant, but a bit clearer.

"Is this Jamelle Maina?" the woman asked.

*"Yes!"* Jamelle shouted into the phone. "Who are you? What do you *want*??"

"My name is Kira," the voice said. "I have some very good news."

# CHAPTER 105

*Eastern Russia*

THE OPEN AREA of the compound was empty now. The relief organizations had finished their work. The huge tents were folded in neat piles on the grass. The students were gone. After intensive interrogations, some of the teachers and staff had been released to restart their lives; others were in custody, awaiting trial on outstanding charges from human trafficking to manslaughter.

Kira was standing next to the INTERPOL commander at the far end of the compound. As they looked toward the complex of buildings, a small squad of commandos ran toward them from that direction.

The squad leader stopped directly in front of the commander.

"Charges set, sir," he reported crisply.

"Copy that," the commander replied.

The commander turned to Kira and handed her a device that looked like a heavy-duty flip phone. "Whenever you're ready, Ms. Sunlight, just press Send."

Kira took a deep breath. She stared at the buildings at the

other side of the huge yard. Administration building. Gym. Classrooms. Eighteen years of her life. And almost a hundred years of pain for the world. Enough.

"Fire in the hole!" the squad leader called out.

Kira placed her thumb lightly on the Send button. She closed her eyes. A Rachmaninoff piano concerto swirled in her head. She pressed down hard.

A series of muffled bangs echoed across the compound. Puffs of white smoke burst from the pillars and windows. One by one, the buildings imploded, walls collapsing inward and downward.

Within seconds, all that remained of the school was metal, stone, and dust.

# CHAPTER 106

*Sir Seretse Khama International Airport, Botswana*

JAMELLE STOOD NEAR the arrival area, bouncing nervously on the balls of her feet. As passengers from Flight 3043 started to emerge, her heart started to pound even harder. Her eyes were wide and her breath came in shallow bursts. She tilted her head back and forth, trying to peer around the passengers as they surged forward to greet friends, relatives, and drivers.

The last traveler to emerge was a tall woman with copper-colored curls. She looked exactly like the picture she'd sent. Her arms were cradled across her chest. She held a small bundle in a baby blanket.

Jamelle ran past the barrier, laughing and crying at the same time, jostling other passengers as she went. When she got closer, she locked eyes with the woman.

"Kira??" she asked. As if there were any doubt.

"Jamelle," said Kira, "it's so good to meet you."

Kira bent forward and slipped the sleeping baby into her mother's arms. Jamelle looked down at her beautiful daughter, then back up at Kira. Tears streamed down her face. Her throat was so tight that she could no longer form words, but Kira understood.

Kira brushed her hand over the baby's plump cheek one last time.

"Keep her safe," she said. "Raise her well."

# CHAPTER 107

*Chicago*
*One Year Later*

DONE.

It was a relief to have the first class of the semester behind me. It felt good to shake the cobwebs off my delivery and get back into the rhythm of a lecture. I'd stayed a few minutes after class to answer the usual assortment of inane student questions. *"Will this material be on the final?"* *"Will you be posting your lecture notes?"* *"Is class attendance required for a grade?"* Christ. Some things never change.

As the lecture hall cleared out, I gathered my notebooks and laptop and tossed my water bottle into the recycling bin. At the last minute, I grabbed the eraser and wiped my name off the whiteboard. Clean slate for the next instructor using the room.

Behind me, a few rows back, I could hear two girls whispering as they headed for their next class. Before my transformation, their conversation would have just blended into the general buzz of the room. Now I could make out every word. My hearing was as sharp as my eyesight. Sometimes it could be a distraction.

"Think this class will be tough?" the first girl asked.

"Who cares?" her friend said, low and confidential. "The professor is really *hot*!"

I felt an odd flush and a flutter in my stomach, and it wasn't from the backhanded compliment. It was something else. I put down the eraser and turned around. The room was empty now, but there was a figure silhouetted in the doorway. I caught a flash of color—and a halo of curls.

Dear God. It was her.

I felt the breath go out of me. I did my best to stay aloof and professorial, even though my heart was just about thumping through my chest. I hadn't seen or heard from Kira since the day I climbed aboard that helicopter in Russia. I didn't think I'd ever see her again. I walked over.

"Am I too late to audit this class?" she asked. Still a wiseass.

I tried not to react. Tried not to reveal all the conflicting feelings running through my head. Tried to play it cool and match her flip attitude.

"Are you enrolled as an undergraduate?" I asked.

"Not really," she said. "I'm a high-school dropout."

"In that case, you're trespassing."

I'd forgotten what it was like to spar with her. I'd forgotten a lot of things. She moved into the room and leaned against the wall.

"Why are you here?" I asked.

"I'm looking to improve myself," she said. "How about you? Anything new in your life? Anybody special?"

"You mean you're not surveilling me?"

"I lost my camera."

"Well," I said, "to quote somebody I used to know—I have only myself."

She smiled. Just a little. "Coffee?" she asked.

There was no way I could say no, and she knew it.

"Okay," I said. "Let's go off campus."

"Agreed," she said. "To be honest, school gives me the creeps."

# CHAPTER 108

THE CHILLY AIR hit us as we exited Cobb Hall. It was only September, but the Chicago wind was already kicking up.

We headed up East 59th. The coffee shop was a few blocks away. The sidewalk was crowded with college folk hurrying to and from campus. We weren't talking. Just walking. I didn't quite know what to say, and I don't think she did either. But it felt good just to be near her again. In the middle of the next block, I slowed down, then stopped. Kira went on for a few steps then turned around. I just stood there. I wondered if she'd remember.

"Why are we stopping?" she asked. "Don't tell me you're out of breath already."

"This is it," I said. "This is the exact spot."

"*What* exact spot?"

"The exact spot where you kidnapped me."

Kira looked around.

"Damn," she said, "you're right. I staked out this street for a solid week."

Suddenly, all the feelings from that day came rushing back.

Confusion. Terror. Panic. Along with my first impressions of Kira—her face, her hair, her voice, her power. That day was the first of many times I thought she was about to kill me. We stood there for a long, awkward moment as pedestrians moved past us.

"Are you sorry it happened?" she said finally. She was dead serious now. "Are you sorry I took you?"

I glanced over at the curb where her van had been parked. I'd asked myself the same questions for a year, every time I'd walked up this block. I'd thought about everything I'd been through, and tried like hell to get past it.

But being with her again, just *seeing* her again, made it all crystal clear. Even after having my whole world ripped apart—I realized that I would do it all again. *All* of it. I'd do it for her. And I couldn't hide it.

"No," I said. "I'm not sorry."

"Good," she replied. "Me neither."

Then she grabbed my arm, pulled me close, and kissed me on the mouth. It was like an electric shock shooting through me. For a second, I was so stunned I couldn't move. Then I wrapped my arms around her and kissed her right back. I couldn't believe it was happening.

It was a serious kiss. When it was over, she leaned her head against my chest and just held it there, syncing her breathing with mine. We stayed like that for a long time, just breathing. Then she spoke up again.

"They're still out there, you know—*thousands* of them. Everywhere."

I knew who she meant. And I knew *what* it meant. I hugged her tighter. And I realized that I didn't want to lose her again. Ever.

"Exactly how many times do I need to save your life?" I asked.

Kira took a small step back and pushed her curls away from her face.

"Probably not as many times as I'll need to save yours," she said.

Suddenly, something shifted. Her eyes widened. Her whole body tensed. She was staring past me, over my shoulder.

"Starting right now," she said.

I turned around and saw the pack heading toward us. Mid-20s. Athletic. Clean-cut. With strange, unnatural smiles.

I turned back toward Kira. I gave her a little smile of my own. We planted our feet and got ready, side by side.

Savage and Sunlight versus the world.

# ABOUT THE AUTHORS

**James Patterson** is the world's bestselling author and most trusted storyteller. He has created many enduring fictional characters and series, including Alex Cross, the Women's Murder Club, Michael Bennett, Maximum Ride, Middle School, and I Funny. Among his notable literary collaborations are *The President Is Missing,* with President Bill Clinton, and the Max Einstein series, produced in partnership with the Albert Einstein Estate. Patterson's writing career is characterized by a single mission: to prove that there is no such thing as a person who "doesn't like to read," only people who haven't found the right book. He's given over three million books to schoolkids and the military, donated more than seventy million dollars to support education, and endowed over five thousand college scholarships for teachers. For his prodigious imagination and championship of literacy in America, Patterson was awarded the National Humanities Medal. The National Book Foundation presented him with the Literarian Award for Outstanding Service to the American Literary Community, and he is also the recipient of an Edgar Award and nine Emmy Awards. He lives in Florida with his family.

\* \* \*

**Brian Sitts** is an award-winning advertising creative director and television writer. He has collaborated with James Patterson on books for adults and children. He and his wife, Jody, live in Peekskill, New York.

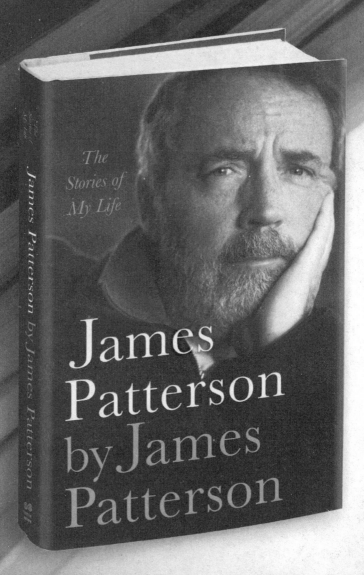

# JAMES
# PATTERSON
## *RECOMMENDS*

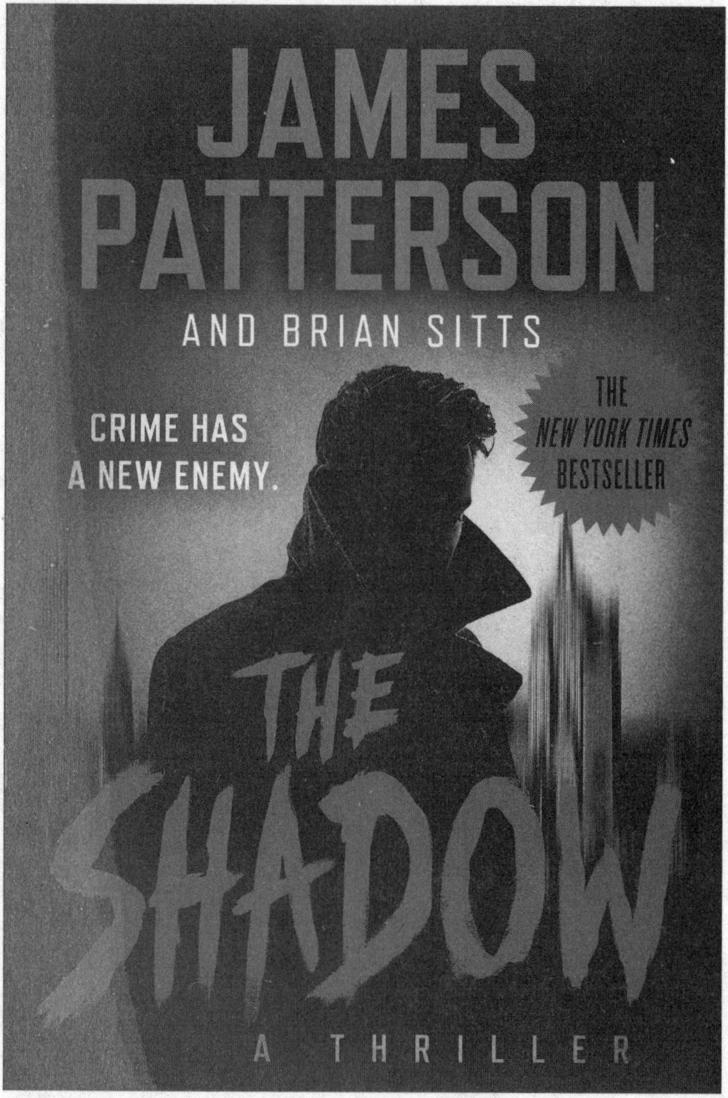
JAMES PATTERSON
AND BRIAN SITTS
CRIME HAS A NEW ENEMY.
THE NEW YORK TIMES BESTSELLER
THE SHADOW
A THRILLER

# THE SHADOW

Only two people know that 1930s society man Lamont Cranston has a secret identity as the Shadow, a crusader for justice. One is his greatest love, Margo Lane, and the other is his fiercest enemy, Shiwan Khan. When Khan ambushes the couple, they must risk everything for the slimmest chance of survival...in the future.

A century and a half later, Lamont awakens in a world both unknown and disturbingly familiar. Most disturbing, Khan's power continues to be felt over the city and its people. No one in this new world understands the dangers of stopping him better than Lamont Cranston. And only the Shadow knows that he's the one person who might succeed before more innocent lives are lost.

JAMES PATTERSON

J.D. BARKER

ONE KISS
AND YOU'RE DEAD

1ST TIME
IN PRINT

DEATH OF THE
BLACK WIDOW

# DEATH OF THE BLACK WIDOW

On his first night with Detroit PD, Officer Walter O'Brien is called to a murder scene. A terrified twenty-year-old has bludgeoned her kidnapper with a skill that shocks even O'Brien's veteran partner. The young woman is also a brilliant escape artist. Her bold flight from police custody makes the case impossible to solve—and for Walter, even more impossible to forget.

By the time Walter's promoted to detective, his fascination with the missing gray-eyed woman is approaching obsession. And when Walter discovers that he's not alone in his search, one truth is certain. This deadly string of secrets didn't begin in his home city—but he's going to make sure it ends there.

# JAMES PATTERSON

## THE BLACK BOOK

### & DAVID ELLIS

# THE BLACK BOOK

I have favorites among the novels I've written. *Kiss the Girls,*
*Invisible, 1st to Die,* and *Honeymoon* are top of the list. With
each, I had a good feeling when the writing was finished. I
believe this book—*The Black Book*—is the best work I've done
in twenty-five years.

Meet Billy Harney. The son of Chicago's chief of detectives,
he was born to be a cop. There's nothing he wouldn't sacri-
fice for his job. Enter Amy Lentini, an assistant state's attorney
hell-bent on making a name for herself—by proving Billy isn't
the cop he claims to be.

A horrifying murder leads investigators to a brothel that
caters to Chicago's most powerful citizens. There's plenty of
evidence on the scene, but what matters most is what's missing: the madam's black book.

THIS BOOK
WILL MAKE YOUR
JAW DROP

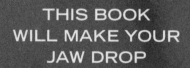

THE WORLD'S #1 BESTSELLING WRITER

JAMES PATTERSON
& DAVID ELLIS

# INVISIBLE

When I started writing *Invisible,* it seemed like every other TV network was telling the same kind of police stories, with the same robberies and crime twists. So I wanted to tell a different kind of suspense story, one that would really make your jaw drop. In the novel, Emmy Dockery is a researcher for the FBI who believes she has stumbled on one of the deadliest serial killers in history. There's only one problem—he's invisible. The mysterious killer leaves no trace. There are no weapons, no evidence, no motive. But when the killer strikes close to home, Emmy must crack an impossible case before anyone else dies. Prepare to be blindsided, because the most terrifying threat is the one you don't see coming—the one that's invisible.